Not Just Friends

T. GEPHART

Published by T Gephart
Copyright 2020 T Gephart
ISBN: 978-0-6487943-2-5

Discover other titles by T Gephart at the retailer of your choice or on Facebook (https://www.facebook.com/pages/T-Gephart/412456528830732), Twitter (https://twitter.com/tinagephart), Goodreads, or tgephart.com.

Cover by Hang Le
Editing by Insight Editing Services
Formatting by Elaine York, Allusion Graphics LLC
www.allusiongraphics.com
Proofread by Rebecca, Fairest Reviews Editing Services

Not Just Friends

To S,

Thanks for not thinking I was crazy or that I was too much work. But most of all, thank you for showing me that strong women are allowed to crumble every now and again too.

Chapter 1

Jared

JARED LEIGHTON—PRESLEY, I screwed up, I'm sorry. You were vulnerable and I was supposed to be the good guy. Last thing I ever wanted to do was betray your trust, or worse, hurt you. I should never have even kissed you, let alone . . . yeah, well we both know how that ended. You're my best friend's sister for Christ's sake, what was I even thinking? Clearly, I wasn't. I'm so mad at myself, I want to break my own legs, save Tibbs the trouble. So yeah, I know this isn't much of an apology, but I needed to make sure you're okay. Let me know things are still cool between us or at least, what I can do to make it up to you. And it's probably for the best if we keep this between just us. I swear on my mother, I'll never touch you again.

Presley Tibbs—Leighton, not sure who you thought you were with last night, but it wasn't some vulnerable little girl who needs protecting. I assumed that was pretty clear when I took you to MY bed. Don't pretend that last night wasn't exactly what we both wanted. We've been flirting with each other for years, and I finally got tired of playing games. As for my brother, he doesn't and will never have a say in who I invite into my life or body—not his business. But if you're scared that's your hang up not mine. So save your apology, and your good intentions, and don't treat me like I'm a woman who didn't know what she was doing. Oh, and tell your mother I said hi.

Christ.

I reread the message thread again for the millionth time before shoving the phone back in my pocket.

It was clear she was pissed.

Never should have sent her that text.

What I should've done was drive to her house, sacked up, and admit to her face what a complete asshole I'd been. But every time I got in the car, hand ready to hit the ignition, I completely lost my nerve.

God, she was gorgeous.

Five-foot-seven with legs for days, her body was insane in every way that mattered. And those eyes of hers were dangerous. Light brown that darkened on a dime, she could say everything she needed without opening those perfect pink lips. Damn, they'd felt good. Both her eyes on me, as I peeled that tight sparkly dress from her body, and those lips on my throat.

Yeah, not helping.

Instead of reminiscing about how fucking beautiful Presley was, I was supposed to be working shit out. And on top of that agenda was making it right between us.

It wasn't going to be an easy fix.

When I'd offered to drive her home from work, all it was supposed to be was a ride. And not the kind that happened in my lap. Jesus, she was not only my best friend's sister but one of the most amazing women I'd ever met. Not to mention she was being terrorized by her shit-for-brains ex-boyfriend, who was going to end up in a ditch somewhere on the Jersey Turnpike if we ever got our hands on him.

Not even going to pretend that I wasn't totally on board with Tibbs on that. She might be *his* sister, but no one messed with one of ours. Of course those feelings had only intensified since we'd stupidly slept together.

What had I been thinking?

Clearly, I hadn't.

All I knew was one minute I was flicking those beautiful brown curls off her shoulder, telling her goodnight, and the next, I had my mouth on hers and my hand touching her in places I shouldn't.

What's worse?

I didn't stop.

Nope, she flashed me a smile, pressed her palm against the rod in my pants and told me to go upstairs with her. And like an idiot who'd clearly lost all his brain cells, I went without a second thought. A complete selfish prick, ignoring the fact I was supposed to be keeping her safe, and instead, I got busy making her come.

And fuck me, did she ever.

"You're quiet." Chief's eyes nailed me from the rearview mirror. "Your afternoon activities wear you out?"

Chief, Tibbs and I were checking out a tip, the three of us looking for the piece of shit Presley used to date

I coughed, wondering if the guilt wasn't written on my face. I sucked at keeping shit from Tibbs and the chief, so it was a wonder I hadn't already 'fessed up. "You want to talk about ladies we're entertaining now, Chief? Because if that's what we're doing, then you should probably start."

Yeah, deflection. Easier than flat-out lying, and would hopefully take off some of the heat.

He flipped me off, obvious that I'd gotten under his skin and launched into a warning about me being respectful. The fucking irony. And while I listened to the man's words, my head was somewhere else. On the sister of the guy sitting to the right of him.

Fuck.

And while we might have been cruising Queens looking for the shithead who clearly didn't deserve Presley, my mind was having a hard time focusing on anything other than her.

Chief leveled me with a stare, my lack of concentration not hearing much other than his woman wasn't a topic of conversation. And if not for the grin Tibbs had on his face, I'd have thought I was in trouble. I laughed, my own smirk making an appearance. "You're such an easy target, Chief. And you know I'm a saint. Wouldn't dream of messing with your woman, even as a joke. But, if Hayden continues to inspire the baking, I'd like to formerly request brownies. Double chocolate."

Chief groaned, pinching the bridge of his nose like he had a headache. "I swear you're worse than preschoolers. How you guys made it through the academy is a mystery."

"It's 'cause we're brilliant, Chief," Tibbs added from the passenger's side, his chin tip to me, making me feel like an even bigger asshole. Not sure he'd feel the same way if he'd known where I'd spent my night.

"Not to mention, fearless warriors." I played along, coughing out the words.

Ironic that I felt anything but.

"And your own biggest fans, too. Let's keep the appreciation society for later, like much later, when I'm not around," Chief offered as he shook his head.

With no visual on Presley's ex, and no idea where the shithead had been hiding, we pulled out of the parking lot of the

Cineplex in Flushing we'd been sitting in. Despite one of the boys in 151 having seen Lewis the night before, there'd been no sign of him or his ugly ass car the entire night. Mack drove around the surrounding area, hitting places lowlifes tended to congregate, but there was nothing. So with no further leads, we called it a night.

"Presley working tonight?" The mention of her name had my head snapping up. Made me wonder if all those internal thoughts hadn't been vocalized, not relaxing until I saw Mack was looking at Tibbs.

"Yep, but she promised she's getting a ride home with one of the girls from the bar. We still don't know if he did it just to mess with her or if he was looking for something. And I definitely don't trust the guy."

That was another thing Tibbs and I agreed on, my hand sliding into my pocket and finding my phone.

Presley and that fucking message.

My head was still reeling, my attempt to apologize not what she wanted to hear. And, fuck me, if I wasn't confused *and* fucking hard at the same time.

Fuck . . .

I *had* to talk to her.

"Speaking of people we can't trust. Either of you two clowns see Melinda?" Mack coughed out, shooting us both a look.

Tibbs glanced at me over his shoulder, tossing me completely under the bus on yet another subject I didn't want to talk about.

Mack's ex-wife, Melinda, was a psychopath. Crazy beautiful with the kind of vibe that would make you want to cup your balls whenever she was around. And, because Presley hadn't been my only lapse in judgment last night, I'd had the fucking displeasure of talking to Melinda at the bar when we'd all been hanging out at *Diablo*. Who knew heading to Presley's club would have turned into such a shitshow. Still, even with the facetime I'd endured with Mack's crazy ex, couldn't say I'd regretted it.

"Spill it. What did she say? And don't try and tell me it was nothing because you're terrible liars."

"So, I saw her at the bar," I admitted, figuring one lie was hard enough to keep. "I swear I didn't say anything, but she walked up all the same and offered to buy me a drink."

"And . . .?" Mack waved his hand, urging me to continue.

I blew out a breath. "And . . . to suck my dick."

See, complete and utter psycho because there wasn't a chance in hell I'd put my dick anywhere near her mouth. Even if I didn't have a hard-on for Presley. Fuck, she'd been looking at me the entire time too. Her eyebrow arched as she smirked, waiting to see how I'd answer. And not that I'd ever admit that to Mack, but it had been kind of hot. Presley, I mean, not Melinda who was clearly a tragedy I wanted no part of.

"Chief, I told her I wasn't interested. And I'd never—like ever—go there. But before she left, she told me to give you a message. And either you call her back and give her what she wanted, or she was going to make your life a living hell."

He shook his head, giving us not much else other than, "I'll take care of it."

"So, what does she want?" I pressed him a little more, curiosity getting the better of me.

"Nothing she can get from me."

Mack wasn't talkative at the best of times and made it clear the topic of Melinda was closed. And considering I had a subject of my own I didn't want to discuss, I had to respect the guy.

Jesus.

What the hell was with Presley anyway? Telling me to take my apology and good intentions and shove them up my ass. And that fucking crack about my mother? I was both angry as hell and irrationally turned on.

I'd been so lost in my crazy internal tug-of-war, I hadn't even noticed when we'd pulled up to the apartment I shared with Tibbs in Hell's Kitchen. Because in addition to him being my best friend, he was also my roommate. Which would make it easier for him to kill me in my sleep when he found out what I'd done with his sister.

Yep.

That would be fun.

Deciding texting her wouldn't be enough, I grunted goodbye to Mack, getting out of his truck and fisting my keys.

"Where are you going?" Mack eyed me suspiciously.

Shit.

"I'm not looking for him, I swear, Chief. Just want to go kill some time or something." I shrugged nonchalantly, not wanting to complicate things. Easier to omit the truth than to out-and-out lie, and I wasn't saying shit until I'd spoken to Presley.

"You going too?" he asked Tibbs, the excuse he couldn't come, ready in my throat

Wasn't the kind of thing I wanted to do with an audience, least of all her brother.

"Nah, I'm going to call it an early night. That six a.m. alarm sucks balls." Tibbs waved goodbye, the sigh of relief coming out fast. "And if you bring anyone home tonight, try and keep it down."

Yeah, there was no danger of that.

I nodded, waving them both goodbye as I got into my car. The Mustang roared to life as I tossed my phone on the passenger seat—the offending message still fucking displayed on the screen—and pulled away.

Presley didn't get off work until two, sometimes three, which meant I knew exactly where to find her. And while she could totally blow me off, I wasn't going to let it slide like I had those choice words she'd texted me.

I'd been a decent guy for fuck's sake, why the hell was she fighting me on this?

Diablo was in Midtown, so it would have been faster to walk there than take my car. But other than the questions it would have raised had I gone for an evening stroll, I liked the idea of having my wheels so I could drive her home. Sure, she'd told her brother she was going to be hitching a ride with someone else, but I had a hunch our conversation wasn't going to be a three-minute chat at the bar. Probably best we had it in private, even if that meant I was going to be tired as fuck for my shift tomorrow. Still, sometimes that shit couldn't be helped.

The employee parking lot was around the back, my Mustang pulling in alongside the cars of Presley's various staff. She didn't own the club, but she might as well have. The owner was some big high roller from Hong Kong who pretty much gave her the keys and told her to have at it. Not that the dude hadn't made back his investment and then some, *Diablo* turning into one of the hottest clubs in the city under Presley's control. And regardless of how beautiful she was, there wasn't a person alive who could deny she was one hell of a businesswoman.

The noise spilling out into the parking lot was minimal, the thick walls containing both the music and whatever else was going on inside the club. And had I not been fairly familiar with *Diablo* and its layout, I might have totally missed the small side entrance the staff used.

My hand yanked on the door, pulling it open to be hit with a wall of sound. The entrance was obscured by a partition, hiding it from the general public and giving me a minute to adjust before being assaulted with the rest of the activity from the club. Not that it mattered, I hadn't even made it two feet before some asshole grabbed me by the shirt.

"Hey, it's me, Leighton." I raised my hands, recognizing it was one of Presley's security goons. They weren't so much as a crew as they were a small army, all of them close to seven foot and made linebackers look like they needed to hit a gym. "I just parked out back."

He brought his face in closer, checking me out before releasing the grip on my shirt. "Should have come in the front. You were ten seconds away from getting put through a wall."

Yeah, no shit.

"Noted. I'll remember for next time." I straightened my shirt, wondering if the guy wouldn't be in a better mood if he laid off the steroids. "Presley around?"

"She is. Wait at the bar." He pointed to it, in case I was blind or stupid and couldn't locate it myself.

"I'll just go to her office." I tipped my head to the opposite direction. Assuming if she wasn't on the floor, she was at her desk. And I'd found my way in there with Tibbs at least a dozen times. Probably for the best if she was there too, the conversation we needed to have, not for public consumption.

He shook his head, taking a step closer and folding his arms across his chest. "I said, you'll wait at the bar."

And as much as I wanted nothing more than to prove to the asshole that I wasn't some dumbass who couldn't handle himself in a fight, I hadn't come to *Diablo* to cause a scene. Not to mention that if one of the staff called in the brawl, I'd have NYPD crawling up my ass and have a lot of explaining to do. Best to avoid that, at least in the short term.

"Sure." I forced a smile, wondering if his hostility was on account his balls had probably shriveled up and he could no longer get hard. "If you could let her know I'm here, that would be good."

Knowing perfectly well being treated like the help would piss him off, I chuckled as I headed to the bar. Besides, chances were Presley had eyes on us already with her fancy surveillance system. And I wasn't leaving until we talked.

Chapter 2

Presley

"**B**OSS," BENNETT RAPPED at my door, "got a minute?"

A minute was exactly what I *didn't* have.

I'd spent more of my evening in my office than I'd have liked, trying to refine my pitch for *Diablo's* expansion. My plans made harder considering my head wasn't a hundred percent in the game. I hated I was distracted; I'd been so good at keeping my personal life out of my head when I walked through the club doors. But tonight . . . well, it had been more than a challenge. And while most people would have been content with managing one of the most successful clubs in the city, I wanted more. I refused to let my plans be derailed by my deadbeat ex or by my possibly—not that I'd felt that way last night—poorly chosen one-night stand.

Sighing, I pushed the button under my desk that unlocked my office door. The security in the club had always been next level, but since Lewis, the ex in question, had recently taken up breaking and entering, I was glad for the extra measures. "You get thirty seconds, and the clock is ticking. Don't make me fire you tonight."

Bennett knew I was kidding, on top of being the head of my security team, we'd also become pretty good friends. And while he stood close to seven foot and weighed more than a compact car, underneath that scary exterior was a mama's boy who had an amazing heart. Lord, the guy even took her to church on Sundays, though he'd probably kill me if I'd ever mentioned it at work.

His big mouth spread into a grin, his eyebrow raising as he walked in and closed the door behind him. "You threaten me every night, Presley. One of these days, you're either going to have to follow through or I'm going to start thinking you ain't got the balls."

"C'mon, B. You know that, despite my appearance, *balls* aren't something I lack." I smirked back. "Which is why I'm going to open up *Diablo* 2.0 in the Meatpacking district, and convince David to let me buy in."

I hadn't breathed a word to anyone other than Bennett about my plans for the expansion or the cash-for-capital strategy I was working on. But while David Cheng—the billionaire who had more money than he could ever use in fifty lifetimes—didn't need my investment, I was done building someone else's empire.

Bennett rolled his eyes. "Stop trying to make the rest of us look bad. Jesus, at twenty-six, all I was thinking about was getting laid and having a good time. I thought only closet nerds and teenage geniuses wanted to be entrepreneurs."

"Who says getting laid, having a good time and being an entrepreneur have to be mutually exclusive?" I laughed. "And considering you had your own security firm at twenty-six, I'd say we aren't all that different."

He shrugged, raising a brow. "You think we should get married and have kids? Settle down?"

"That's the worst proposal I've ever heard. You didn't even get down on one knee," I scoffed, rolling my eyes.

Bennett laughed. "You know that wasn't what I meant."

I loved how uncomplicated things were with him, how we could toggle between business and personal stuff and none of it felt awkward. He knew about Lewis breaking into my apartment, and how a few months earlier he'd pulled a gun on me, which had me finally kicking him out for good. But he didn't coddle me, making sure I knew he was there for whatever I needed, without making me feel like the scared little girl everyone assumed I should be.

"So . . . is that why you interrupted me? To tell me I should have a better work/life balance?" I asked, honestly surprised that he'd come to my office solely for a philosophical chat.

He smirked, the cocky look on his face making me slightly unsettled. "Nope, just wanted to see if you'd pulled a fire alarm. Clearly, you haven't checked the monitors."

Goddamn it.

I *hadn't* checked the monitors, too buried in spreadsheets, cost reports and prospective real estate sites to give them the attention I usually did. But I swear, as much as I loved and appreciated him caring, if the hovering didn't stop, my parents were going to find themselves short a son.

"Tell Tibbs—"

"Not your brother." Bennett cut me off, grinning wider. "It's the *other* one. The one whose tongue hits the floor every time he gets eyes on you. Caught him sneaking in the staff side entrance and was ten seconds from laying him out. Of course, I didn't know if you wanted the pleasure."

Jared. Leighton.

Of course.

Because sending me a text to apologize after we'd had sex was what every woman wanted. Especially when it was from the guy who featured in almost all your teenage fantasies. The same guy you'd harbored deep and dirty thoughts about for longer than was reasonable. And boy, every single one of those dirty thoughts hadn't even come close to how good it had been.

Pity he had no spine and cared too much what anyone else thought. I'd have totally been into cueing up my fantasies and playing them out, one by one.

"You thought *I* might want to lay him out?" I rose slowly, wondering if it was somehow written all over my face that my *ride* home hadn't stopped with the drive. There was no way anyone could have known considering I hadn't told a soul. Unless Leighton had opened his big mouth, and judging by his need to keep it *between us*, I'd say that was highly unlikely.

"Presley, don't pretend like making men piss down their legs isn't a turn on for you." Bennett laughed, my body relaxing as he continued. "You *love* it, so if you want to read him the riot act, I'll let you do the honors. Just make sure he comes through the front from now on. Not like we ever make him or anyone else from your brother's company pay the cover."

That was true, which begged the question why he'd been trying to sneak in. Oh, and I still had no idea why he'd come in the first place, unless it was to humiliate me further by telling me to my face what a mistake last night had been.

"Do me a favor and escort him in. I assume he's alone?" My skin tingled, knowing if he'd been with someone, Bennett would have already mentioned it. Which meant the conversation—or confrontation—was going to happen with just the two of us.

Good.

"Yep, he's without the entourage. I'll send him in." Bennett chuckled, heading toward the door.

My eyes flashed to the monitors I had been ignoring, seeing him at the bar.

Hell.

If I thought sleeping with him was going to stop me from being attracted to him, I was sadly mistaken. I remembered *exactly* how that six-foot-three athletic body had felt against mine, with his gorgeous blue eyes looking down at me. They were so clear, almost translucent, but could fill to an inky black when I screamed out his name. It was like I could still feel his lips against my skin, still see my fingers raking through his sandy blond hair. And as much as I wanted to pretend it hadn't been the best sex of my life, I couldn't deny that it had been even better than my fantasy.

Clearly, the feeling hadn't been mutual, his body language animated while he spoke to Raelle, one of my female bartenders who was never short of male attention. She was beautiful, dressed to maximize her tips, and able to make any cocktail no matter how complicated. It was no wonder he—like anyone else with a penis—wanted her attention. Wonder if he was planning on circling back to the bar after our little chat, picking her up after her shift was over and giving her a little taste of what I'd had the night before. After all, she didn't have the complications I apparently did, so wouldn't get the apology after.

Bennett approached him, Leighton's hand rose in a wave as he said his goodbye—or see you later—to Raelle and followed Bennett back to my office. I didn't move from my desk, watching their progression through the club on the colored screens until there was a brief knock at the door before it opened.

"Thanks, B, that will be all for now." I pretended to be bored, my eyes moving slowly to where they were both standing in front of my desk. It was a big desk too, the wood imposing a five-foot distance between me and anyone I granted an audience. Total mind fuck, which was why I liked it so much, paying the ridiculous price for the custom piece out of my own pocket.

"Presley—"

I held my hand up, not allowing Leighton to say another word until Bennett closed the door behind him. "Well, well, well. Sneaking into *Diablo*, Leighton. Tell me, does your mother know?" My lips twitched into a grin, unable to help myself at landing the little jab.

His face morphed in confusion, probably wondering whether he should be offended or if the fact I was joking about it meant good things. Not that I was entirely sure what I was doing since my feelings for him weren't clear either. It was hard to be angry at him, especially when he was standing in front of me and looking so goddamn delicious.

"I wasn't sneaking in." He tried to move closer, looking down at the desk separating us. If he wanted to close the distance, he was either going to have to vault over it or walk around, and I was curious which way he was going to go. Not going to lie, part of me wanted to see him make the leap, show off the athletic talents he'd so willingly treated me to the night before. "But your brother has friends keeping an eye on the place, and I didn't want to deal with the questions it would invite if someone saw me."

"Then why are you here at all?" I rolled my eyes, huffing out a breath. "If you're concerned about me telling him, you could've saved yourself the trip. I don't kiss and tell, Leighton."

He shook his head, swallowing. "I don't either. But obviously with you . . ."

"But with me, what? You're worried I'm going to run to my brother crying that you fucked me and then left?" I scoffed, the laugh making its way up my throat. "Or maybe you think I'm going to get attached, fawn over you like a love-sick schoolgirl. You think I'm incapable of no-strings, Jared? You're the one making a big deal out of it."

Sure, I'd wanted more, but not in the way he probably thought.

Hell, I'd just gotten *out* of a relationship, there wasn't a chance I was interested in another. But that didn't mean a little fun with a guy I'd thought about naked more times than was probably reasonable, wasn't an option either. And I could have *totally* kept it casual. Not that he'd given me the chance.

"You *know* it was different. Fuck's sake, Presley, there's a fucking lunatic after you for God knows what. Getting into your pants should have been the last thing on my mind. I'm not *that* asshole, Presley. I am not the guy who takes advantage of women, especially women I care about." His hands curled into fists beside him, his muscles tight with agitation.

"Just stop right there!" Anger mixed with embarrassment bubbled in my gut, my skin probably flushing pink. "You want to pretend last night didn't happen, that's fine. But I am not some damsel in distress that didn't know what the hell she was doing, Leighton. *I* invited you up to my apartment. *I* took you to my bed. And *I* was the one who took your cock—"

"Jesus, you trying to kill me here, Presley?" He cut me off, cursing under his breath. I was still mad, but liked how much I'd gotten to him. That his eyes had darkened, that his fists were twitching uncomfortably at his side and that his chest was moving faster.

Good.

"Tell me, are these thoughts of regret because I'm Justin's sister, or Lewis turned out to be a psychopath?"

Not that either scenario would make me feel better, but only one would cease to be an issue. And neither was my fault.

He swallowed, waiting a minute like he was choosing his words. "I just don't want to hurt you."

"Leighton, you *know* me. There's more of a chance of me hurting you than the other way around. Find another excuse."

"You shouldn't . . . I mean, with everything happening. . . you should be—"

I didn't let him finish, not willing to sit there and have him or anyone else tell me how I *should* be feeling. "Let's get one thing straight, Leighton. You can feel however you want about last night. Whether it's a regret or not, is totally up to you. But you don't get to come in here and mansplain to me on how I should be feeling and what I should be doing. Not you, my brother, Lewis, or anyone else gets that. That's my choice. And I'll be damned if I'm going to sit in a corner and cower." *Even if I am scared*, I finished in my head. "So, if that's all you came to say, you can go. I'll find someone else to scratch *that* itch."

That did it.

His eyes widening as his nostrils flared, picking up the edge of the desk and shoving it to the side to clear a path. "Then let me do this instead."

The objects on my desk hadn't even stopped rattling, papers tumbling to the ground as the heavy legs were planted back on the floor. His blue eyes filled with black, his big body filling the small gap he'd created when he hulk-lifted my desk, pulling me out of my chair. And I was in his arms with his lips on mine before I'd fully realized what was happening.

"I don't regret it," he groaned against my lips. "I know I should, but fuck me, I just can't."

I'd wanted to hesitate, to not kiss him back, refusing to give him the upper hand but somewhere in the shock, I'd forgotten to fight him. His hands were on my ass, the heat of his kiss burning up my core while his body pressed against mine. And he wasn't subtle, his tongue exploring the inside of my mouth while his hands got reacquainted with what he apparently wasn't going to touch again.

Famous.

Last.

Words.

The thrill of satisfaction heated my skin as I kissed him back, my fingers traveling down his spectacular torso before pulling him closer.

He was hard. The evidence of exactly *how* he felt teasing me through the fabric of my dress and the fly of his jeans. I loved it, unable to stop the whimper from escaping my lips as I bowed into him, lifting my leg against his hip so I could get better traction. And while I'd promised I'd *never* be that girl, the one who'd have sex in their office like some seedy cliché, I was really questioning how serious my resolve was.

Maybe it didn't have to be sex.

Maybe he could just—

"Boss."

Shit.

If the knock at my door hadn't stopped us, Bennett's loud baritone voice sure as hell would. He knew better than to enter without my permission, but he also didn't interrupt meetings—personal or otherwise—unless it was necessary.

"Give me a minute," I called out, pulling my mouth away from Jared's as I tried to rein in my pulse.

Jared's eyes flashed to mine, panting gently while his hands were still locked on my ass. Not exactly the kind of scene I wanted my staff walking in on, even if Bennett would probably swallow his own tongue before telling anyone my business.

Pretending I hadn't been seconds away from sticking my hands down Jared's pants and possibly letting him do the same to me, my practiced mask fell back into place. I'd never admit how annoyed I'd been at the interruption, a little pissed at myself for being so consumed that I'd momentarily forgotten where the hell I was. And, considering I was at work and making out with a hot fireman—I'd been crushing on forever—wasn't listed in my job description, I had no reason to be so perturbed.

Too bad logic was still competing with my overactive hormones.

Shaking off the tight knot in my gut, I pulled myself together and straightened my dress. My fingers dragged against the edges of my lips, tidying my makeup before wiping the telltale signs of SUE ME Red off Jared's mouth. A quick glance into my mirrored wall confirmed I was presentable, tilting my head to my desk which looked like it had been headbutted by a rhino. "Fix that, won't you," I tossed over my shoulder, not bothering to turn and see if he was going to comply as I headed to the door and unlocked it manually.

Bennett looked bored, a quick survey of the space almost unnoticeable as his eyes slid slowly to Jared who was moving my office furniture, before returning back to me. "VIP, apparently they need an audience. Your presence is required."

His brow lifted indicating he was less than pleased at having to deliver the message, or at least that's what I hoped it meant. He could have equally been giving me the 'I-know-what-you-were-doing' eyebrow lift, but I wasn't ready to deal with that. Instead, I preferred some rock star, model, or social media person had worked his last nerve, exercising their *don't you know who I am?* bullshit and he was done playing interference.

The jury was still out, but either way, that was a discussion we weren't going to be having right now.

"Who?" Jared's voice came from behind us; Bennett's brow getting even higher as he kept his eyes on me and ignored him.

"I'll go back to circling the club. Let me know if you need anything." He didn't wait for my response, turning around and closing the door behind him.

Bennett, of all people, knew names were off limits between the walls of *Diablo,* especially in the VIP section. It was a policy that attracted the A-list clientele, their location only advertised when they checked-in on their socials, and not by me or any of my staff. Hell, I'd only told Mack about his ex-wife's new patronage when he'd been in the club to see it with his own eyes, taking my tightlipped hardline seriously even for friends.

As Bennett left, I spun around to face Jared, the question still on his face even though he hadn't asked again. "First rule of Fight Club . . ." I smiled, gesturing to the door.

"You don't talk about Fight Club." He rolled his eyes. "I get it, but it's just me and you. Besides, who am I going to tell? If I were to bring it up, that would just shine a light on the fact I was somewhere I wasn't supposed to be."

His words stung a little, my expression staying neutral even though it annoyed me. I assumed from his kiss he was done with worrying about other people's opinions, but I'd been mistaken. Not sure why it bothered me so much, it wasn't like I advertised my relationships or took a full-page ad announcing them. But with him . . . it was different. And I needed to work out why.

"Well, we couldn't have that now, could we? Imagine if people knew where you were?" I mock gasped, the sarcasm hiding my conflicting emotions. "So, if there's nothing else . . ." I left my sentence trailing, pointing again to the door.

Jared's brow scrunched in confusion, his eyes flashing between me and the exit I was clearly hinting he take. "I thought maybe we could talk some more." His heated gaze hovered over my lips. And it didn't take a genius to work out talking was the last thing on his mind.

"Well, I don't really have time for a chat. But if you're willing to pull out your wallet and buy a drink or two, I'm sure Raelle will gladly keep you company." I did my best to force a smile.

My terrible suggestion served a dual purpose. One, to see if he'd happily go back to flirting with my attractive bartender, who he may or may not attempt to sleep with. It was a free country and all of that, and she didn't come with complications. And two, to test if the idea would make me jealous.

Technically, it wasn't a fair bet.

Raelle would flirt and talk to anyone—man, woman, hyena—she didn't discriminate. As long as you kept the orders coming and weren't a shitty tipper, you'd have her undivided sexy attention.

But she didn't sleep with customers, something Jared had probably yet to find out.

It was her one rule, refusing to budge even when she *really* wanted to. It was something we both agreed on, refusing to accept the stereotype that the only way we'd succeed was by using what was in-between our legs. Ha, ironic that what was between our ears was so much more dangerous, which meant my suggestion to Jared was more of a set up. Not that I'd ever admit that, tempering my reaction while I waited for his response.

His eyes dipped, following the curves of my body before landing back on my face. "I didn't come here to talk to Raelle."

Ignoring how stupidly pleased it made me to hear those words, my lips pressed into a firm grin. "Then you better go. If you're still wanting that *chat* later, give me a call. If not, I'll see you around."

I tried not to smile, my lips betraying me a little as they lifted at the edges. I was *not* going to lay my cards on the table when I had no idea what was going through Leighton's mind. And considering I should have already been gone, I didn't have the time for it either.

The VIP section, and whatever Big Shot needing my attention, still required my presence, which was why I pushed the memory of that kiss and his hands to the side and nodded to the door. I wasn't going to ask again, my directive that he needed to leave no longer just a suggestion.

I was going to need a minute. If for nothing else to freshen my makeup so I didn't look like I'd been making out like a teenager.

He swallowed whatever words he was thinking of sharing, leaving them unspoken as he headed toward the door. He paused with his hand on the handle, hesitating before turning. "I'll wait around and give you a ride home."

They were the same words he'd said to me only twenty-four hours earlier. But unlike the last time, I was sure how that *ride* would end.

Him.

Me.

Panting against hot skin as we tangled between my sheets.

And even though there was a chance I'd be waking up to an empty bed and another of those *I'm sorry* texts, I still wanted it.

"Thanks, but I've got a ride." I cursed under my breath, depriving myself because clearly I enjoyed torturing us both, and I had some sick need to prove a point. And I'll be honest, when it came to proving a point, I was more stubborn than most. Probably why I stayed with Lewis for so long, putting up with a dead-end relationship when my family had warned me he was a loser with no future.

For a smart woman, I made poor choices when it came to men, hating I got blinded by good looks and an insane attraction to a bad boy. Not that I'd seem to realize that at the start, my stupid hormones running the show instead of my head. I'd hated that they'd been right about him, but more so, that I'd waited so long to kick him to the curb.

Poor impulse control was definitely a family trait.

"Do you really have a ride?" Leighton asked, tilting his head like he didn't believe me. Or maybe he could read my mind, more perceptive than I gave him credit for, not leaving like I asked.

"Yes, I do." Without explaining who, I yanked his arm toward the door.

It would have been more satisfying to turn on my heel and leave him watching me walk away. I had that perfect hip sway locked down. But unfortunately for me—and my hip sway—I didn't leave anyone—even people I trusted—in my office unattended. It was one part of the club where video surveillance only activated after we closed. David had drummed that into me from the start, and there was too much in those filing cabinet drawers I didn't want public. Namely my plans for expansion and the investment I intended to make.

So drama would have to wait, Jared taking the hint and following me outside as I locked my office once we'd reached the other side of the door.

"Presley, I—"

"Leighton," I cut him off, "I need to go."

And with the problem of leaving him in my office no longer a concern, I was able to be as dramatic as I wanted. Which is exactly what I did as I flipped my hair over my shoulders and walked away.

You're move, Leighton. Let's see if you're the man I assumed you were.

Chapter 3

Presley

THE CLUB WAS busy as usual, the bodies parting as I made my way through. It was either from my reputation as a hard-ass manager who didn't take any shit. Or my terminal resting bitch face which I seemed to wear during business hours. It wasn't intentional, my smile missing in action when I was on duty, too busy making sure everyone else was having a good time and we stayed in the green. Seemed more of an important concern rather than making sure my disposition was cheery. Besides, no one ever asked a man to smile and look pretty, and while I never stepped foot onto the floor looking less than perfect, I'll be damned if I was going to plaster a fake grin on my face for someone else's benefit.

"Took you a while." Bennett chuckled from behind me, his ability to enter and leave a situation silently more impressive than my lack of smile.

I rolled my eyes, ignoring him as I crossed the floor to the roped-off section which was mostly shielded from the public.

"Boss." Thomas, the security guard who took care of the VIP

team, nodded as I walked past, only taking his eyes off the crowd for a minute to acknowledge me.

"Thanks, Thomas. How's the wife?"

"Hasn't filed for a divorce yet, guess there's a positive," he deadpanned, hiding his grin. "Back left. Scott Collins. Actor. Famous Dad. From L.A." He gave me his concise report which was as valued as his eagle eyes. "And Jared Leighton is still at the bar."

Damn it.

I inhaled, putting those yoga breathing exercises to good use even though there wasn't a chance I'd be finding my zen.

What the hell was he doing at the bar, and why hadn't he left like I'd asked? Still not the problem that needed my immediate attention which meant I'd forget about him, his sexy body and his hotter-than-hell kiss, and be the professional everyone expected. Not an easy thing to do when what I really wanted was to head right to the bar and find out if he'd had a change in heart about Raelle or if he had some other agenda.

"Lucky him," I breathed, moving away from the entrance and into *Diablo's* club within a club.

It had its own bar, its own bathrooms—totally autonomous, and stocked with so much top-shelf liquor, the inventory alone was worth more than a brand-new car. It was our star attraction, and even if most people didn't get to see the inside, it made me proud I was in charge of all of it.

Even if Thomas hadn't pointed him out, I'd have seen Scott Collins the minute I'd walked in. Hollywood blond hair that looked too perfect to be real, his flashy white smile had probably paid for his dentist's new yacht. He was classically handsome, his well-toned body covered in designer down to his Ferragamo loafers, with his face and name attached to the latest blockbuster I hadn't had time to see.

I might have been impressed, except his kind weren't so rare. Before Scott, there was a Brad, or Keanu, or Chris—multiple of them actually—who'd have sat in a chair exactly like the one he was in. And in a few years, those two busty women who were hanging on his every word would be trying to impress someone else. But that was really the point though wasn't it, and why *Diablo* was open seven nights a week. Someone had to give their "kind" a safe haven, and I was more than happy to provide it.

Besides, for as good looking as Scott was—and trust me, he was hot—every time he opened his mouth, it was like listening to a licensing agreement for a new iPhone. No personality. None. Boring as a tax audit but with less excitement. Hell, if it wasn't for his dad, he'd probably be promoting leisure wear for someone like Tommy Hilfiger, at least then he could just look pretty and not talk.

"Mr. Collins, welcome to *Diablo*." I approached his posse, giving him the smile I rationed out when I was at work. "Hope you're enjoying your time with us."

"Presley!" He peeled off his sunglasses, his pricey shoes hitting the plush carpet as he rose to meet me. "I've heard a lot about you. Wanted to see for myself if all the rumors were true."

From his grin, I wasn't exactly sure what *rumors* he was talking about. I'd heard things from time to time, where people assumed my rise had been courtesy of talents on a mattress. I understood it, I was a twenty-six-year-old business manager who was running one of the hottest clubs in the city. And since my daddy wasn't bankrolling the operation, it stood to reason my talents were sucking dick.

Couldn't have been the four years of college and the five years of bar experience. Or even the five years before that, when I'd worked either as a waitress or hostess in some form of hospitality venue since I was sixteen.

Nope.

Had to be my tits.

"Well Mr. Collins, I don't waste my time listening to rumors. You of all people would know, they rarely get it right." My lips edged wider.

It was a talent, telling someone to go fuck themselves while sounding like I was wishing them a good day. And trust me, it was the one time when I was at work where the smile was *not* completely manufactured. Hell, part of me loved they underestimated me. Made my success even sweeter, reveling in their slack-jawed expressions like a demon would lost souls.

"Of course. I mean, you should read what they say about me." He laughed, clearly enjoying the press coverage, however inaccurate. "And call me Scott. Mr. Collins is my dad." He held out his hand, waiting for me to take it.

"Scott." I returned his shake, ignoring how his eyes were lingering over my cleavage. "Well, if there's anything else we can do for you, be sure to let one of my staff know."

"Wait, you're going? I thought we might spend some time together. Not every day I get to meet such a powerhouse. Well, to be honest, I *do* get to meet powerhouses most days, but none are as pretty as you."

Snore.

Really, Scott? That was the best you could do?

I really hoped he had a huuuuge penis, because if his dates were looking for stimulating conversation this evening, they were going to be shit out of luck. "And now we've met, so—"

"C'mon, Presley. You going to make me beg?" He leaned in, keeping his voice low so no one else could hear him. "I can see charm isn't going to do me any good here, so I'll be straight with you. I have a business proposition. You hear me out, and I *promise*, you're going to be interested. And if not, I'll sit down and run up my bar tab and enjoy my female company. Either way, you can't lose."

And as much as I hated to admit it, he definitely had my attention. I was used to guys asking me out, trying to slip a hand here or there, and even *propositions* of a different kind. Rarely did men want to talk business, especially on the floor of my club.

My eyes glanced to his *dates*, their lips pouting with disappointment that he was no longer sandwiched between them. And because I didn't intentionally embarrass my guests, and knew how to be discreet, I leaned in too. "Scott, let me be clear about one thing. Outside these doors, you might be a big deal. I'm positive you have more money than you could ever spend in a lifetime and are used to people telling you exactly what you want to hear. But this is *my* house, and in my house, there's only one God. And you're looking at her. So if you have business to discuss, you'll have to set up an appointment like everyone else. I'm sure you have a person who can help you with that?" I moved back, lifting my brow and maintaining my smile.

"Yeah, I can do that." His grin widened. If he was offended, he sure as hell wasn't showing it. "By the way, you're exactly how they described. You have a card?"

"I'll make sure you get one before you leave. Have a good night." I tipped my head to the waitstaff, letting them know his next round was on me.

It was why I was so good at what I did, able to balance diplomacy without being anyone's doormat. Pity it didn't always extend to my personal life. Which was why I usually ended up with a relationship that was a dumpster fire and a boyfriend who I should have avoided.

Of course, my night of meaningless sex with a nice guy hadn't worked out so well either.

Soooooooooooooo.

"Shot him down, huh?" Bennett chuckled, sidling up beside me as I wandered out to the main part of the club. "You want to take a guess as to how long it's been for him? I bet he's still reeling from the shock."

"Well, someone has to keep them humble. Think of it as a calling. Some people do missionary work, and I—"

"Annihilate egos," he laughed. "Guess that's why *Ladder 49* is licking his wounds at the bar. Raelle lets them down easy."

I didn't want to look, ignoring the impulse to glance—just somewhere in the general direction—and see.

Casually.

Completely from a business point of view.

Leighton was still a guest, not to mention my brother's best friend. And I wanted him to have a good time. Right? Right.

Given permission, my eyes briefly darted to the bar, and I was met by his icy blues aimed right back.

Like he'd been waiting.

But he wasn't smiling like he usually was, his mouth occupied as he slowly knocked back a beer. He didn't even pretend he wasn't staring, watching me as his Adam's apple bobbed with his slow seductive swallow.

"Do me a favor, Bennett." My eyes stayed on Jared while addressing my head of security. "Tell Raelle I need to see her in my office when she has a minute."

"And 9-1-1?"

"You *know* his name."

"Doesn't mean I have to use it." He didn't even try to hide how pleased he was.

I shook my head, not bothering to argue. Waste of time and breath, and I had bigger issues to deal with. "It's a free country, unless he's stepping out of line, no reason why he can't stay."

Bennett cleared his throat, making it obvious he wasn't convinced. "Fine. We'll let him stay. Can I toss out the mouthy blond at least? She's been looking at my dick like she thinks she has a chance. Has to be high."

"Melinda is harmless. Ignore her." I shook my head, not sure why she had suddenly become a regular or why she was propositioning men. She'd flat out offered to blow Jared the night before. The look of disgust and shock was enough to make me laugh. There was a snowball's chance in hell that would ever happen, and Jared was far from an altar boy. "I'm not sure what her angle is, but I'm assuming she's looking for her ex-husband's attention. Mack won't make that mistake twice, so let her spend her money. Just keep an eye on her, and keep me posted."

If there was a need, I'd escort her out myself, but other than being a pain in the ass and having zero class, she didn't have any major infractions. And if I threw out *every* tacky annoying bitch, I'd have a half-empty club.

"Got it. I'll let Raelle know." Bennett gave me a two-fingered salute before disappearing into the crowd.

Against my better judgment, I glanced back over at Jared. His eyes hadn't shifted, raking up and down my body like his hands had done last night. But he didn't move, seeming to be recommitted to his vow of no-touchies.

Ugh.

Such a shame.

Because if he followed me back into my office, I wasn't sure I'd stop him.

Sighing, because thinking about him and his hands got me hotter than I should be when I was on the clock, I walked back to my office and closed the door. My desk stood in testimony; the scattered papers strewn across its lofty surface reminding me exactly what I'd been doing before I left.

I'd barely sat down when there was a knock at the door, Raelle, clearing her throat on the other side. "You need me?"

The lock disengaged with a click, my finger still on the button by my desk as she yanked open the door and came inside. She didn't wait for the invitation, taking a seat opposite me once the lock had reengaged.

"Let me guess," she settled into the chair, her bright pink lips edging wide, "you need a ride home tonight?"

I rolled my eyes, slightly annoyed I'd promised my stupid brother I wouldn't go home alone even though I'd done it a million times before. "I don't *need* the ride. I'm happy to call a cab or an Uber. But I'm positive Tibbs has someone watching to make sure I don't leave alone."

"He's only doing it because he cares. Not saying I wouldn't accept some of that *concern* if he were throwing it my way." Her brows arched, hinting the concern she'd like was a little less platonic.

She did that a lot. Pretended she had deep, dark sexual fantasies about my brother to annoy me. But I knew who she *really* wanted was Bennett. So, instead of coming clean, admitting she had a thing for the guy we worked with, she went through an intricate charade where she told me she wanted to sleep with my brother, Justin.

"You know, Rae, I think you should go for it. I mean, if he's busy with you, he can't really be concerned with me, can he?" I called her bluff, my mood off. Between the pent-up sexual frustration from Jared's kiss and annoyance from Scott, I wasn't up to the usual game we played.

Raelle coughed, surprised she'd been given the green light. "What?"

"You and Justin," I leaned back into my large leather chair. It was wrong that I got joy out of it, but given the status of my evening, I was going to have to take my satisfaction where I could get it. "I bet you guys would make such a cute couple. You want me to call him, set it up? Orrrrrr maybe I'll give him your number? Then you can tell him all those naughty things you want to do to him."

"Okay, stop. You win. And I'll drive you home, just don't give him my number. I don't want to give your brother the wrong idea, and to be honest, I can only deal with one Tibbs at a time." She held up her hand, conceding quicker than I'd expected.

"Fine, be that way. We could have been sisters, Rae. So it's totally your loss." I sighed, pretending to be disappointed. "Oh, well. Guess we'll have to go back to the original reason I called you in here."

"Hey, if this is about Leighton, we can skip that too. I wasn't flirting, and he couldn't have been less interested if he tried. So let's go back to me pretending like I didn't notice the two of you leave together last night and that his hands were waaaaaay too close to your ass. Besides, you know he's not my type. Anyone who walks through those doors and hands over cash or a credit card is automatically out of the running. And as much as I hate to admit it, cute firefighters with smoking hot bodies aren't exempt."

It shouldn't have made me happy to hear that, but it did. Because I had issues, and it gave me a warped sense of satisfaction to know he hadn't even tried. Which was stupid because clearly what we'd done had been a one-time deal.

Looked like neither of us were going to be getting laid.

"Actually, it wasn't about Leighton, but thanks." And since I wasn't exactly sure what my feelings were, there was no need to talk about them. Nor did I have the patience of the pretense. The one where I acted like I didn't give a shit, and Raelle had mis-seen what she had.

Please, she was too smart for that.

"It's about Scott Collins."

Rae shook her head, grinning. "Don't even bother, boo. I hear he's a terrible lay. Such a shame because he looks like *that*." She waved her hands animatedly like she was conjuring up his spirit. "But I heard it's all just window dressing. Two pump, chump. No stamina, and doesn't even go down on a girl. Says he doesn't like the taste." She rolled her eyes. "And yes, I saw him and his *friends* slide on past to the VIP room. But trust me, not worth your time or your birth control."

Raelle wasn't only the best bartender in my crew, but also one of my best friends. We weren't looking to join a book club, or share lipstick as we giggled in the bathroom, but when shit went down, Rae was the one woman I could count on. There was no bullshit with her, and even if she hadn't proven again and again how awesome she was, it was a flat-out tie between her and Bennett as to who was my most invaluable employee. Only reason she didn't know about the expansion yet, was because she—like most bartenders—liked to talk. And I didn't need information shared before the time was right. But she didn't just have a big mouth, her ability to listen an even bigger commodity. Hell, I was positive Rae had heard more confessionals than a Catholic Cardinal, and unlike the Padre, she wasn't bound by the constraints of the cloth.

"The warning is unnecessary. I don't sleep with guests or movie stars. And I've made enough bad decisions for a while." She probably assumed I was talking about Lewis and I wasn't going to correct her. "But apparently he has business to discuss, and as much as I think it could be a line, I don't think he's smart enough."

Rae laughed, tipping her head back and letting her mess of red curls go wild. "Business? Presley, I've had vibrators with higher IQs, only business he's capable of is screwing up an orgasm."

"Still, I've invited him to set up a meeting, and I don't want to go in blind. Do your thing and let me know what you find out. A man like that isn't able to keep his mouth shut. I'm sure it won't be too hard to find out what he wants."

The smirk on Rae's lips was instantaneous, her excitement for my random assignments almost more than the love of her job. And she'd never let me down. Because if you needed to know something, a bartender could usually find out. Hell, I was sure they had some secret society or something. A skull-and-bones underground establishment with better networking than the Freemasons. And when they gathered, Boston shakers and jiggers in hand, they traded the secrets no one else knew.

"I'll call my guy in L.A. at *Tight* and see if he knows anything. Scott likes to hang out there."

I leaned forward, no doubt the information would be landing in my lap faster than any P.I. I could hire. "Good. Do your thing and let me know if you need anything. I'm not expecting a freebie."

"Girrrrrl, you know I've got this." She waved her hand, shrugging like it was all good. "Besides, Blaze has a crush on Scott, so will be only too happy to spill. I keep telling him the man is pretty but incredibly straight, not that Blaze will listen. Who do you think told me about his inability to give a woman an O? He's freaking tickled about it, convinced since Scott needs an orienteering map to find the G-Spot he is probably better suited to the D."

The laugh bubbled up my throat. "Good, then I'll see you later on the floor. We can discuss it further on the ride home."

Rae flipped her hair over her shoulder, eyeing me suspiciously. "You *sure* you don't want to ask Leighton for that ride? He's probably still at the bar. I can send him back here if you want. You know, to make sure *things* are all good."

There was no need to clarify the subtext, I was positive I knew what things Rae was referring to. And unlike Scott, Jared did *not* need a map.

"Thanks, but no thanks. I've got a mountain of work to get through." I motioned to my desk, the papers still in disarray.

"Okay, girlfriend. Enjoy. I'll see you on the battlefield." She mock saluted, turning around and then sashaying her lithe body out the door.

My eyes went to the monitors, Jared putting his bottle on the bar, looking toward the back of the club where my office was.

He was considering it.
And then he turned and walked toward the exit.
Damn it.

Chapter 4

Jared

AS FAR AS making shit right, I hadn't.

Nope, instead I was laying in my bed, staring at the ceiling with a hard-on for a woman whose brother was occupying the next room.

But Jesus Christ, that mouth.

It was easier for me to remind myself I was going to be hands-off when she wasn't standing in front of me. But one look at her, that body and that smartass mouth, and I was making bad decisions all over again.

Hadn't intended to kiss her, but fuck me, if I could stop myself.

"Fuuuuuuck," I groaned, squeezing my eyes shut and trying to ignore the pain in my balls. I had to be up in a few hours and wasn't liking my chances of getting any decent sleep.

Who knew what would've happened if that big bastard hadn't interrupted us, and not sure if I was grateful or pissed.

Probably pissed.

My dick definitely was, the ache reminding me I'd yet to jerk off.

Jesus, Presley, my hand reached down as I gave myself a tug, the need for release crawling up my spine.

Last thing I wanted to do was lay in bed with my cock in my hand and think about a woman who was supposed to be a no-go zone. It was stupid, counterproductive, and solved nothing. What I should have been doing was imagining *anyone* else, getting off, and then moving on.

Hell, if I was really serious, I'd be finding a pair of willing lips to take over from my hand and put it to bed. *Literally*. Because there was no way I could keep my mind on one woman if I was with someone else, right? Pity, I couldn't think of anyone else, nor work up the motivation to even scroll through my contacts.

My mind tried to help me out, flashing an image of the sexy redheaded bartender with a great pair of tits. Raelle was *hot*. Tattooed and toned, her shirt so tight even in the dark you could see both nipples were pierced. Wonder what they'd feel like in my mouth, flicking those babies with my tongue.

"The fuck?" I glanced down at my cock, noticing I was no longer hard. I was literally thinking about tonguing a beautiful woman's tits and somehow had lost an erection. That wasn't how it was supposed to work, staring at my dick in my hand and wondering when was the last time I couldn't get hard.

It had been years, and I'd been drunk. Tibbs and I had been out, finding women at a bar and bringing them home. He'd gone to his room, I'd gone to mine, and the poor girl whose name I barely remembered, got a cramp in her jaw trying to get some wood.

Nothing.

Completely limp.

So I did what any self-respecting man would do, flipped her on her back and made her come with my mouth.

And then never saw her again.

"Fuck it." I kicked off my covers, deciding it was a lost cause. Might as well find a better use of my time, and considering I had a twenty-four-hour shift to get through, I needed to get my mind right.

I threw on some sweatpants and a sweatshirt, pulling on my Nike's and grabbing the keys on the way out. I didn't usually run on the street, preferring to get my cardio on a treadmill or rower, and then put some reps in at the gym. But desperate times called for desperate measures and I either hit the sidewalk and got in some miles or went into work early and got three million questions. And trust me, there was enough going on in that stationhouse. Between Mack's new romance, North's wife about to have a baby, and Tibbs worried about his sister, they didn't need my surly mood.

The crisp morning air hit my lungs like a ton of bricks. February wasn't as brutal as January but was still on the frosty side of the temperature gauge, my breath coming out like a huff of smoke. It was tempting to turn around and go back inside, get a warm shower and kill some time doing something that wouldn't freeze my balls off. But as I looked down the street, the streetlights still on because the sun hadn't come up, the cold turned into calm and I decided I'd come this far.

Living in Hell's Kitchen had its advantages, but it also made it difficult to get away from the noise. Didn't matter what time of the day or night you ventured out, there was always some action happening on the streets. It was one of the things I loved—losing myself in the bustle, being a part of the mayhem—and in a weird kind of way drowning out my own thoughts until all I could hear was my breathing as I ran.

It felt good, the muscles in my legs warming as I crisscrossed with no real plan, picking up speed as I jogged through the familiar streets. I cruised past the stationhouse, giving the closed bay doors a nod as I continued. Then I found myself in front of *Diablo*, the distance covered faster than usual since I wasn't dodging foot traffic and had kept a decent pace.

Without realizing I'd stopped, my feet kept moving while staying in the same place. My eyes surveyed the big black doors to the club, the queen to the empire not currently in residence. And to think I'd gone on the run to get her *off* my mind and that was where I ended up.

Should have tried harder to jerk off.

And how did a woman I've known for nine years have my head so messed up? It wasn't like I'd just met her, or suddenly realized she was fucking hot. My eyes almost popped out of my head when Tibbs had introduced me to his sixteen-year-old sister. But even without his repeated warnings, I wouldn't have been stupid enough to try something. She was so young.

Or so I thought.

Nope, and given what I knew now, not sure my eighteen-year-old self would've stayed away.

Because Tibbs' little sister was not only crazy beautiful, smart, and funny.

She was *insane* between the sheets.

In. Sane.

Shaking off the memory, I got my feet moving again and headed back to my apartment. The run hadn't been as successful as I'd hoped—my head not any clearer—but it had killed some time.

I tried not to think, concentrating on my breathing and the sounds of the city as I sprinted back home.

"You went for a run?" Tibbs yawned, a cup of coffee in one hand, his phone in the other. It seemed I wasn't the only one who had issues sleeping.

My head nodded, trying to catch my breath. "Yeah, thought I'd get a workout in before we needed to head in. What are you doing up?"

"Actually, I'm glad we are both awake. Something we need to discuss." He gave me a pointed look.

Hmmmm, that didn't sound good.

In fact, it sounded the opposite of good.

Trying to not get ahead of myself, I tried to act cool, calm and collected, willing to hear my buddy out. It probably had nothing to do with Presley, and I was rocking way too much paranoia.

"Oh? What about?" I asked, genuinely concerned and selfishly hoping whatever his crisis was, it had nothing to do with me.

"C'mon, man, what do you think?" His eyes didn't drop. "Presley."

FUCK.

Although my concern for my own ass only lasted a second, the phone in his hand giving me a whole other set of possibilities—none of which I liked—to fixate on. "She okay? Please tell me the bastard didn't try anything."

I knew I should've driven her home.

Should've stopped thinking with my goddamn dick.

Waited outside and insisted I see her safely to her apartment. Could've kept my hands to myself like I'd done a million times before, not touched or kissed her no matter how much I wanted to, and made fucking sure she was okay.

Jesus, I was a coward.

And was so pissed at myself I couldn't see straight.

"Tibbs, is Presley okay?" I asked again, every muscle in my body so tight, shit was starting to hurt.

Tibbs swore, shaking his head. "Shit, sorry, I'm a dick. Yeah, yeah, she's fine. I keep forgetting you care about her as much as I do." He laughed, tossing his phone onto the coffee table. "I know she's like a sister to you too."

Yeah . . . not so much.

My body relaxed a little knowing she wasn't in danger. "So what's up then?"

The hesitation was unavoidable because I literally had no idea what he was going to say. It wasn't a good thing either, usually able to read my best friend like a book.

"Did you happen to go past *Diablo* last night? After you left here?"

Annnnnnd there we were.

Fuck.

They might have been questions coming out of his mouth, but his eyes told me he already knew. And while he was still living in the delusion that I thought of Presley as a sister, he probably had fucking questions. Like why the hell I hadn't told him. To be honest, I was surprised it had taken him that long, and not jacked me up the minute I'd walked in the door when I got home. It had been late, or early depending on how you wanted to look at it, and he was already passed out. Of course, that was what I assumed since his bedroom door was shut and the lights were off. Little did I know he was probably biding his time.

"Yeah I did."

I'd been tempted to lie, pretend like I had no idea what he was talking about, but it just wasn't in me. We'd been through some hairy situations at work, and I respected the man too much.

"Thank fuck." He visibly relaxed. "Mitch said he saw your car around. I hoped you stopped by, maybe gave her a ride home."

"Tibbs, I stopped by, but I didn't drive her home. I tried," *and wasn't that the fucking truth*, "but she said she was going to get a ride home with someone else. I waited around hoping she'd change her mind but. . ."

"Yeah, no need to tell me. When Presley gets an idea into her head, no one is going to change it. Goddamn it, she's stubborn. Thanks for trying, and for looking out for her. I know you have my back, and there isn't a man out there I trust more than you."

I was such an asshole.

I'd been ready to come clean and accept the consequences.

Fuck. It.

But then he had to go on and tell me what a good guy I was, and how he trusted me. And yeah . . . I just couldn't do it.

"How was she?" he asked, making me realize I hadn't said anything else.

Hot.

Beautiful.

And so fucking edible I could barely stand it.

I shrugged, careful to say the words my mouth wanted to say instead of what I was thinking. "Moody," I settled on, figuring if nothing else, it had been accurate.

He rolled his eyes, probably imagining a different *mood* than I'd experienced. "Sounds like her."

Yeah, yeah it sure fucking does.

"So, what's with the phone?" My head tipped to the phone that had been in his hands, chilling on the coffee table. "And why are you up when I'm usually pulling your ass out of bed five minutes before we have to leave?"

Knowing Tibbs was going against his own M.O., a grin crept across his face. "Spoke to one of our old buddies. Detective Shapiro. You know that guy could never read a fucking watch. Finally got around to returning my message, and to be honest, I wasn't dumb enough to tell him five a.m. wasn't a good time to chat."

Ain't that the truth. There weren't a lot of guys I was scared of, but he was definitely in my top five. The chief—when he was angry—still had the number one position, and number two as well.

Assuming Tibbs had more to share, I parked my ass into a La-Z-Boy and watched as he did the same, taking the other. We still had a good hour before things got critical, meant I had time to find out about the early morning phone call and not be at risk of the chief's wrath.

"Didn't Shapiro retire last year? And I thought you and Presley already spoke to the NYPD."

She'd made a report about the cocksucker ex-boyfriend breaking in and rummaging through her place, and even mentioned he'd pulled a gun on her too. Not that they'd be able to do anything yet, the dick still MIA.

Tibbs nodded, confirming what I already knew. "Yes, and yes. But you know as much as I do that the detective had a tendency to do things," he waved his hand as his brow rose, "less by the book and more result based."

Shapiro was old school. A hard ass, who drank and smoked, and had at least three ex-wives. But he was a damn good cop and wasn't afraid to bend the rules if it meant getting criminals off the street. The brass didn't agree, making him retire before Internal Affairs got involved.

"What did he say?"

"That he was bored, and was happy to have a new hobby. Honestly, if he can't find Lewis, then he's skipped town for sure. Shapiro might not be on the force, but he has the city fucking wired. Hell, I didn't even have to tell him about Presley, he already knew. Asked me why I'd waited so long to call him."

Knowing Lewis was out on the loose and Presley was unprotected made me angrier than I'd ever felt. Tibbs had tried to talk Presley into staying with their parents, or a friend, or hell, even with us—that would have been interesting—but she'd shot him down. Flat out refused, saying she wasn't going to live her life afraid. And I got it. All that shit about taking back the power and reclaiming whatever—perfectly fine. But it didn't mean I had to like it, or think she was being slightly unreasonable considering it had been less than a few days.

So hearing Shapiro was on the case—albeit unofficially—made me feel better about the situation. Well, *that* situation at least. I still had another fucking issue that was gnawing at my gut.

"I'm glad, dude. And it goes without saying. If you need anything from me, you know I'm there."

Meant every single word of that too. Tibbs was the brother I never had—my two older sisters not really the same—and all he ever had to do was ask. Even if it hadn't been for Presley, but knowing it was for her sure as hell upped the ante.

A look floated between us with the unspoken gratitude on his face. "Well, actually, there is something you can do."

"Name it." I didn't hesitate, knowing whatever it was, was a done deal.

"I need you to talk to Presley."

Ah.

Fuck.

He took a breath, deciding to continue. "Look, I know she can be a ball buster and the last thing you want to do on your time off is chase after my sister." *Really? I was positive somewhere up in heaven those guardian angels my mother always raved about were laughing their asses off.* "But dude, she trusts you. And she's about a minute away from filing a restraining order on *me*. You can get closer to her. Make sure she's not taking any chances, and keep an eye on her. Meanwhile, I'll work the backend and make sure we nail this cocksucker."

My mouth opened but words failed to fall out. Because really, what could I fucking say? *Sure, Tibbs, as much as I'd love to follow your sister around and keep her safe, I'm worried I might sleep with her again?* Like that was even a possibility. And hell, even if she did press every button I had, stripped naked and begged, I could still say no. Not that it would be easy—or enjoyable—but I'm positive I could. But je-sus, if his *favor* didn't come with a buttload of complications.

"Man, you know I would do anything for Presley. And keeping an eye on her is the absolute least I can do." *Ain't that the truth.* "But you think she is going to be down with a babysitter?"

That the babysitter was me, well, that was going to be another bone of contention.

Tibbs laughed, punching me in the arm like he couldn't see the problem. "Use that charm of yours, brother. Hell, you talked Quinn into taking those photos for your mom when her and North were broken up. Seen you sweet-talk the chief when he was about to blow a fuse. And it was *you* who managed to convince Presley to let you drive her home the other night when she told me to fuck off. Flash those baby-blues, give her that charismatic grin, and say whatever you need to say. We've got to do what we have to do. I take full responsibility, and if she gets mad, I'll take the heat. Only fair since it was my idea."

There was so much in there, I didn't even know where to start. And if Tibbs only knew the half of what we'd done, he wouldn't be volunteering to take the heat.

The way I saw it, I had two choices. Sack up, tell him his sister and I had crossed a line and give him the option to change his assessment. Or shut my fucking mouth, be a man and do what I needed to do so she was safe, and her brother didn't blow a gasket.

"I'll talk to her later today. But Tibbs, if I'm going to be busy with Presley." *Such a baaaaaad choice of words.* I swallowed, trying to recover. "I mean, keeping an eye on her, then you need to clue me in on the shithead. I want to be there when it goes down."

Tibbs held out his hand, giving me a grunt of approval. "Easy. Done. Couldn't think of anyone else I'd want there more. Besides, I'm going to need someone to run interference with the chief. Mack will be so far up my ass, I'm going to need some Preparation H."

"You should thank your lucky stars he's got Hayden to distract him." The chief's new woman not only gave the man something to smile about, but would take most of his attention.

"Right?" Tibbs laughed. "Quinn getting him that dating profile for his birthday was a strike of pure genius. If North hadn't already married and knocked her up, I'd totally have made a play."

I rolled my eyes, knowing he wouldn't have gotten very far. "Sure you would've. And I'd be visiting you at Mount Sinai where you sucked your dinner through a straw."

"I can take North. He's a big bastard, but I'm quick." He nodded, convincing himself—because he didn't have a hope in swaying me—that he'd have won that fight.

"Go make us coffee, moron." I lifted myself out of the La-Z-Boy, needing a shower before heading to work. "And make it extra strong."

"Don't use all the hot water," he yelled, hopefully heading to the kitchen as I disappeared into the bathroom.

Yeah, because me using all the hot water was the biggest problem we had.

I was going to have to talk to Presley.

Shit.

Chapter 5

Presley

CLUB HOURS WEREN'T conducive to regular sleep patterns. I went to bed between four and five, and slept till about noon. Which meant mornings were not my friend.

So when my phone went off sometime before lunchtime—me, the idiot, believing turning it to silent was for suckers—I knew it couldn't mean anything good. Groaning, my hand reached out blindly, grabbing it off my nightstand and bringing it to my ear. I couldn't face opening my eyes, keeping them scrunched tight as I coughed out, "Presley Tibbs, this better be an emergency."

"Presley, it's Scott Collins. How are you doing?"

Oh Lord, give me strength.

I peeled one eye open, checking my phone display for the time and saw it was only eleven. Cursing him and his movie star dad—and anyone else who had anything to do with him—I shuffled up the bed.

I'd assumed I'd be hearing from him today, Hank giving him my card before he left. But he couldn't have waited an extra hour? The missed sleep mourned as I tried to be pleasant.

"Scott, hi. I assumed you'd have an assistant call me."

"Yeah, and miss out on a chance to talk to you? No way. So tell me, Presley, you been thinking about me as much as I've been thinking about you?"

Apparently, I hadn't made myself clear last night, the inference that I wasn't interested in flirting or whatever the hell he was attempting to do, I thought pretty fucking obvious. But it seemed Scott needed a refresher, and since I hadn't had my required eight hours sleep, I was positive it wasn't going to be pretty.

"Scott, Scott, Scott," *you poor beautiful, boring, and soon-to-be dead man,* "I know you probably don't hear this a lot, but I'm really not interested. I assumed when you said you wanted to discuss business with me, you meant *actual* business. Not sure what kind of business that would be, but I was willing to give you the benefit of the doubt. I do that, Scott, not because I have a kind heart, but because that's what businesspeople do. We listen to people who talk shit because there might be something in it for us. But trust me when I say that you aren't the first—and will not be the last—guy I blackball from the club for wasting my time and misappropriating my phone number. And, it won't just be *my* club. You'll suddenly find yourself persona non grata to a long list."

At *Diablo* I made an effort to be diplomatic. I wanted return patronage and to keep my ledger healthy. But in my own time—not so much.

"Wait. I promise I'm legit. Just hear me out."

It gave me a warped sense of pleasure to hear a man beg. I liked it, especially when I knew the man would rather swallow glass than submit. Which was the only reason why I hadn't hung up.

"Tick, tock, Scott. What have you got for me?"

"It's about a club. Here in L.A. I mean, *there* in L.A. I want to talk to you about a partnership." He stammered through most of it, the cool Hollywood heartthrob he was in interviews, sidelined with the flirting.

"Elaborate," I breathed into the phone, not convinced I still wanted to listen.

"Can we do this in person? Set up a meeting?"

"Not until I know this is going to be worth my time. What club in L.A. and what does it have to do with me?"

It had been a while since I'd visited the west coast, and I was okay with that. I wasn't fond of palm trees, and all that sunshine wasn't good for my skin. So how I fit into the equation was still a mystery.

"I want to buy a club, okay, and I need someone to run it. I want it to be you."

And silence.

On both sides of the phone. Because I still wasn't sure he wasn't deploying a new tactic. *"Hey baby, come run my club,"* meaning something entirely different. And he probably was preparing for me to tell him to go fuck himself.

Which I would.

Once I worked out what he was saying.

The measured breath slipped silently from my lips as I kept my tone unemotional. "Thursday, one in the afternoon, at *Diablo*."

"Huh?"

"Your meeting. Be prepared, Scott. And don't ever call me before noon again." I hung up the phone, not waiting for his reply.

He was either going to turn up at the appointed time or not. And while I had an itching curiosity to know what Scott had to offer, I wasn't going to advertise that to him. Nope. I never showed my cards. It was the quickest way to get taken advantage of. And if I wanted a long and successful career, I could not be making stupid mistakes. Ones that would probably be forgiven if I didn't have a uterus, but have me vilified for the same reason.

It was unfair, but that's the way it was. And I wasn't going to cry about it. So instead of thinking about what I couldn't control, I turned my attention to what I could.

Diablo.

The new site for expansion.

And Jared.

Okay, so two out of three I could control.

It had been hard to tear my mind away from him when he left, my body still feeling the aftereffects, but I didn't have time to dwell. Of course, time was no longer an issue since I was awake earlier than I wanted to be and didn't have a chance at getting back to sleep.

My hand scrolled on my phone, my social media apps left unopened as I hovered over my contact list. I wasn't tempted to call him, knowing nothing good could come from it when I was annoyed and sexually frustrated and he was at work. And as moody as I was, he really did have an important job. The heroic aspect and that uniform somehow made him more attractive. And I'd seen my brother in the exact same outfit a million times and never batted an eye, which confirmed what I already knew.

Jared Leighton was hot.

Sigh, if only that was where all his virtues lay, then it wouldn't be so hard to resist him. But he was sweet, and kind, and thoughtful, with such a great smile it made my insides squirm. And I didn't squirm for anyone, which just made it more perplexing. He was smart too, and ridiculously loyal, the kind of guy you could depend on even if the world turned to shit. Which was why when he drove me home, his concerned look telling me he would follow me inside to make sure I was safe, I couldn't help myself.

I kissed him.

Kissed him like I'd wanted to and had no regrets.

And wow, what a kiss it was.

"This is so not helping, Presley." I shook my head, annoyed I was daydreaming about a guy who I couldn't have when there was a city overflowing with available men right outside my doorstep. All I had to do was walk out there, find someone suitable, and lose myself with a guy who might be just as wonderful.

Like Lewis? my subconscious asked, my last mistake lingering like a bad smell.

He hadn't always been bad, especially not at the start. He was impulsive, wild and creative, and seemed to love me for who I was. That right there should've been the tip off it was all an act, his support and adoration for my demanding high-powered job tossed to the wayside when I didn't help launch his career. Not that he knew how hard I'd tried. Calling in a favor or two, and asking a producer to give him a shot. All because I loved him and wanted him to succeed. But he just didn't have what it took, his talent highly exaggerated, and in the end, I wasn't willing to put my name on the line. Not when he wasn't even *trying* to find a gig, too comfortable living rent free in my apartment and mooching off my goodwill. And in the end, the gloves came off and I knew all I'd been was a meal ticket.

Hurt like absolute hell—not that I'd ever let him see it— hiding my feelings and embarrassment and kicking him out. I didn't even know he *had* a gun, let alone think he'd ever pull one on me. The shock when he did excruciatingly real.

So yeah, maybe finding a guy wasn't such a good idea.

Which left . . .

My finger had hit the call button before I gave it another thought, leaving lingering doubts and mixed feelings exactly where they belonged. In the past.

"What?" Raelle groaned into the phone. "I thought we had a deal, no conversations before noon."

Her response made me smile, a little too glad I wasn't the only one who'd been subjected to a rude awakening. "*We* did, but Scott Collins had other ideas. I just got off the phone with him."

"Why are all the cute ones so dumb? You know if he just shut his mouth and didn't say anything, I'd totally do him." She was lying of course, but I didn't care enough to point it out.

"You sleep with whoever you want, Rae, but I was hoping you might meet me for lunch."

And unlike Scott, Raelle wasn't stupid enough to think my lunch invitation was anything other than business. She sighed knowing better than to say no. "Fine, and I'll have what you asked for by then too."

As predicted, she didn't need a reminder on why we were meeting. "Good, I'll see you then. I'll make reservations at that new Japanese place near *Diablo*. I've heard great things."

"Send me the details. I'm going to go back to sleep. Bye." Unlike me, Raelle could fall asleep on a park bench. All she needed to do was close her eyes and she was gone. So I had no doubt that once I'd heard that click she'd probably waited maybe four seconds before she was blissfully back in dreamland. Definitely a skill I envied.

With my plans made and no hope of crawling back in between the sheets, I decided I'd get in the shower instead. It was worth the rent I paid on my midtown apartment for the bathroom and closet space alone. The loft was mostly open plan, the interior not wasted with barriers and doors. It allowed the light to flood the apartment and make it feel bigger. Didn't give you a lot of privacy if you had company, but considering I'd been living alone for the last few months, it was no longer an issue.

But the only exception was my huge bathroom. It was tucked away from the main living area behind a frosted glass wall. The only "room" with a door and lock, it was a hidden eutopia of white tile, mirrored surfaces, and silver fixtures.

My eyes closed as I tipped my head under the warm cascading water. The waterproof Bluetooth speaker provided the soundtrack, competing with the spray of the shower as I washed my hair and body.

It was the one place in my apartment where I refused to be stressed, the powerful jets pounding my muscles as I allowed my mind to wander. As the steam fogged up the room, I let out a slow, extended exhale.

I'd never once had sex in my bathroom despite the room being sexy as hell. Sure, Lewis had suggested it, jerking off in front of me and trying to entice me to bend. But I'd always refused, not wanting my sanctuary tainted. Guess I knew even back then that eventually our relationship would end, and I didn't want the peace and tranquility of my shower taken from me for a cheap orgasm I could've given myself.

Which had me thinking . . .

I'd barely slipped my fingers between my legs when I heard my phone ringing. I hadn't brought it into the bathroom with me—no business or stress allowed—my ringtone overriding the music on my speaker.

"Fuck," I cursed, annoyed that for the second time that morning I'd been disappointed. It was turning into one-of-those days, and I hadn't even had my coffee yet.

Grabbing a towel, still dripping water I sprinted to my phone which was sitting just outside the door. In a perfect world I would have ignored it, but I was still waiting to hear from the police about Lewis. And while I was fine to do the bravery thing while I was in public, I allowed myself a small amount of grace in my private space. It was the bathroom, it definitely brought out my vulnerability. And since I had no idea what he wanted when he broke into my apartment, I was hoping the NYPD might have some answers for me.

I didn't have time to check the call ID, answering the phone before it kicked over to voicemail. "Presley Tibbs."

"Presley, it's Lorena. How are you this morning?"

Oh fuck, I groaned internally, knowing the call didn't mean good things.

"Hi Lorena, I'm fine," I lied. "How are you?"

Lorena was David Cheng's personal assistant, which sounded much less important than it was. But the owner of *Diablo* didn't do regular. He was progressive and aggressive in business, not subscribing to the traditional rules which had seen his father almost run the company into the ground. Instead he went against his conservative upbringing and culture, conducting meetings and dealings with zero fear. And he expected the best from his team, which is why his personal assistant not only had a Harvard law degree but could speak five languages.

"Fine, busy day. I'd continue with the small talk but it bores me, and I know you don't have time for it." She was also incredibly direct, with no soft edges at all. Like none.

"Of course, Lorena," I agreed, not wanting to continue the charade either. "I'm assuming you're calling about my request to meet with David."

Before my ex-boyfriend was trashing my apartment, and I was making questionable—though I'd never regret Leighton—decisions about who shared my bed, I'd called wanting to set a date to pitch my expansion idea. I was even prepared to fly to Hong Kong, my passport anxious to have its first international stamp.

"Yes, both David and I are intrigued. I assume all is going well at *Diablo*, yes?"

She was cocky, knowing that when it came to our boss, she was higher up the pecking order. And while I appreciated we were all trying to prove our worth, I wasn't going to submit either, Harvard Law degree or not.

"Lorena, I know you see our figures on the central portal. You know exactly how *well* we're doing. I've exceeded the projections for the quarter, and we still have two months to go. Not an easy thing to accomplish in a city which has more than twenty thousand establishments just like mine." I didn't even pretend I hadn't meant the last part. It might not be my name on *Diablo's* title, but it didn't make it any less mine. It was my turn to be cocky.

She laughed, knowing we could go toe-to-toe for hours if that's what it took. But there was a twelve-hour time difference between Hong Kong and New York, which meant she was looking forward to ending her day rather than starting it.

"Yes, I've noticed. Which is why David wanted me to call. I'm assuming the topic of discussion was going to be a request for a pay increase, yes? Well, we thought we'd save you the trouble, I've already sent the authorization to payroll. An extra fifteen percent which can be further negotiated in twelve months. David sends his best."

"Lorena, I want my meeting." While I was thrilled to have been given the pay increase I rightfully deserved, I'd hoped to use it as leverage. Being dismissed with more cash hadn't been the plan, and I wasn't giving anyone other than David my pitch.

"Presley, come on. You know that fifteen percent is more than fair. Like I said, you can renegotiate in twelve months. You keep doing what you're doing, and I have no doubt you'll walk away a very rich woman. It's a wonderful thing to be self-sufficient, to have that security a full bank account can give you. But don't confuse greed and ambition, that would be a mistake."

She didn't need to spell it out, knowing that he'd taken a chance on me and loyalty was valued above all else. "It's not about the money. There was something else I wanted to discuss."

"Really?" Lorena's usual impenetrable exterior showed a crack, the surprise evident. "Is everything okay?"

"Yes, of course," I lied for the second time.

The pause on the phone had me guessing Lorena knew it as well, but surprisingly she didn't call me on it. "Fine, David is flying out to New York in a week. I'll set up a meeting while he's in town."

"That will work, let me know the time. I know he's not interested in seeing *Diablo*, so tell him if he wants to meet elsewhere, I won't be offended," I answered, wondering if he was coming into town, why he wouldn't just stop by. But if given the choice, I was going to be pleased he trusted me so much instead of disappointed he didn't see the club as a priority.

I heard the smile in Lorena's voice, "You don't think he'd want to inspect a business he's sunk a few million into?"

"We both know I could level it into a parking garage and he wouldn't care if I'm giving him the profit margin I am now." I rolled my eyes, amused she thought I'd be so needy.

"He did always like you, Presley. I'm positive if you went and got an MBA, you'd be managing a lot more than a little club in New York."

It wasn't the first time I'd heard it, David himself hinting that if I was agreeable to more school and some serious mentoring, that I'd have a place higher up in the corporation. And if I hadn't been so in love with the city and my job, it might have been appealing. But I'd already made my decision, and I was going another route. Let's just hope he was as equally excited. "It's not a *little* club, Lorena. Next time you visit, you should come see for yourself."

"Maybe I will." She chuckled. "Have a nice day, Presley."

"Goodnight, Lorena."

Still mostly wet, not managing to wrap the towel around me, I headed back to the bathroom to dry off. There was no point attempting anything else, my earlier thoughts of releasing some tension via an orgasm, left for another time. Instead I got dressed, put on my makeup and blew out my hair. No point wasting the head start, and if I was meeting with David next week, I was going to need every spare moment I had.

Chapter 6

Jared

"SO WHAT HAPPENS with North when he has the baby?" Evans asked, looking up from his broom as he swept the bays.

Tibbs laughed, shaking his head as he checked the hose on the ladder. "Didn't you have Sex Ed in high school, Rookie? Looks like Uncle Tibbs is gonna have to take you aside and tell you how that shit works."

Evans rolled his eyes, looking to me for a bail out as I shrugged. "Dude, you walked into that one."

"You *know* I mean, Quinn." He flipped off Tibbs before turning his conversation back to me. "I meant is he going to be gone awhile? They going to replace him?"

Even with everything on my mind—Presley and my new extracurricular activities—I had a hunch where the conversation was heading. "Jesus, between Tibbs taking his deodorant and you gunning for his job, poor North doesn't stand a chance. Steady on, Rookie, you'll get your place at the table."

"I've been here for over twelve months, guys. When are you going to stop calling me Rookie?"

"When we get a new one." Tibbs offered honestly, chuckling with no apology. "And you technically aren't out of your probie period, so I wouldn't be making suggestions about replacing North."

Evans was a good trainee, and as far as progress went, he'd made some massive strides. But you can't just replace a guy like Riley North, and sure as hell not with a kid who was only recently been allowed to buy his own beer.

"Dude, seriously? I ain't looking to replace him, I just want to show Cap, I can do more than what I'm doing. Maybe I'll go chat with the chief, see if I can't get him on my side."

Honestly, I had to admire the guy. He had some balls because Mack usually intimidated the fuck out of the new kids. Not intentionally, but there was only so much intensity the man could dial down. "Maybe aim lower, and mention it to Cap first? Chief baked us cookies the other day and I'm hoping he might continue the trend. Last thing we need is you pissing him off and us missing out on that goodness."

"Leighton's right. Don't fuck it up for all of us. Those cookies were almost as good as Rev's wife's." Tibbs pointed a finger in warning at Evans.

Evans shoved the broom to the end of the bay. "Yeah, okay. I'll go catch up with him now."

Deciding it was none of my business, I let the kid go do whatever it was he was going to do. If my head wasn't so clouded, I might have suggested he cooled it and let natural progression happen. Initiative was always encouraged, but the brass liked to see it rather than hear about it. Still, it wasn't my funeral.

"I think you should call Presley."

If I hadn't already been thinking about her, the mention of her name would be enough.

"Tibbs, it's not even noon. You know her rule. If it's not life or limb, that's a hard pass." I tried to shrug it off casually like I wouldn't fucking leap at the excuse. Couldn't even pretend that I wasn't thrilled I had a reason to call her and that hopefully she'd be forced to talk to me. Not that I could admit that without raising some serious eyebrows, which was why I attempted to play it cool.

Tibbs looked at his watch, our day having started a lot earlier than hers. "Just don't forget. And try and make it sound like it's your idea. She'll be more receptive if she thinks it's coming from you."

Yeah, on that we disagree, buddy.

"I'm not lying to your sister, Tibbs. If she asks whose idea this was, your ass is totally going under the bus." I didn't even apologize, only willing to bend so much.

Between the two of them, I was between a rock and a hard place and that didn't even take into consideration what was happening in my fucking pants. So I had no interest in being the moron-in-the-middle of their sibling fight, and the only reason I agreed was because I didn't totally disagree with Tibbs. She needed protection, especially until Lewis was wearing metal bracelets gifted to him courtesy of the city.

"Don't lie, just . . ." he paused, trying to choose his words, "be creative."

Oh, I was going to have to get creative, just not in a way he was going to like.

"I'll call her, stop riding my ass." I pointed to the doors. "Go make sure the rookie didn't mess shit up with the chief."

His eyes cut to the main part of the stationhouse, "On it," leaving me in the bays by myself.

I was going to call her for sure, but I was going to have to find a way to keep it all business. And that was exactly where I was going to have to be creative.

Apartment fire.

Two engines responded to an apartment building not far from where we lived in Hell's Kitchen. Some asshole had tried to cook burgers inside because he was cold, dragging in a grill that had no business being in the shoebox he was paying rent for. So many code violations and stupidity I couldn't even understand it, thankful we were there just to put out the fire and not deal with the insurance claim.

"Tibbs, Leighton. Everyone out?" Cap called as he returned back to the truck. It was only four floors, with most of the residents having cleared out when they saw the smoke. But a "maybe" wasn't good enough. The two of us were sent in to go door to door while the lines tackled the flames, making sure everyone who should be out was chilling at the front, catching the spectacle on their phones like the rest of the neighborhood.

"All clear, Cap." I nodded, pulling off my mask and sucking in regular air.

Tibbs shivered, also losing the O2 assist from the SCBA. "Man, it was getting toasty in there. Lucky it was the top floor, gave everyone a chance to get out."

Not sure how "lucky" anyone felt as the black smoke continued to pour out. Considering the dude responsible for the fire hadn't bothered to see a problem with *literally* lighting a fire inside his home, we couldn't be sure he didn't have some other surprises lurking in there. Last thing we needed was a store of rubbing alcohol or worse, gasoline, being discovered by the flames.

Man, I hated stupid people.

North and Rev were on a line nearby, trying to contain it from one side, while Evans and Brown were on it from the front. And other than a few watery eyes and some anxiety, no one was going to need a ride to the hospital.

It was as good an outcome as we could hope for, able to save most of the structure and finally put the fire out. The water damage was going to be intense though, which meant everyone was going to be finding somewhere else to call home for a while.

"Tibbs, Leighton," Rockefeller—the detective, not the famous kind—approached us. "You wrapped this one up nice and quickly." He looked to the building which was black but no longer on fire.

"That's what we do, Detective. We get tasked a job, we get it taken care of." The edge in Tibbs' voice unmistakable.

Rockefeller didn't flinch, barely raising an eyebrow. "Tibbs, you of all people know I can't and will not discuss ongoing investigations with a civilian. Not everything goes by your timeline. Having said that, is Presley okay? You want one of the guys to check in on her?"

I guess twenty some odd years on the force gave you the skills to handle a guy, the hostility from Tibbs easing out. "She's fine. Maybe if someone can circle around during the time she's at the club?"

"Consider it done. Now, I'm going to find Cap, see you guys later." Rockefeller left, leaving us to finish packing up the engine and getting ready to leave.

"Speak of the devil. Hey, Tibbs, isn't that your sister?" Evan's tipped his head to the road, the woman in question striding up the street in possibly the sexiest skirt and jacket combo I'd ever seen.

I couldn't even blink, my eyes wide-open absorbing every inch of her like it had been a month since I'd last gotten the chance. And what I was seeing, I was definitely liking. Dressed more conservative than she usually did for the club, she was all business, her sexy dark brown curls tamed into a ponytail that swung a little with each of her stilettoed steps.

"Yeah," he checked his watch, noticing it was almost two. "Guess she must have a meeting out here."

Not really able to miss two engines and a congregation of firemen in the middle of her path, it was no surprise when she stopped. "Guess it's only fair I visit you at your work since you visit me at mine." Her beautiful pink lips edged into a smile. "Everyone get out okay?"

I didn't even care who she was addressing, convinced that smile had been for me. "Yep, everyone is fine." Which was mostly true, unless you counted the weird tempo my pulse was keeping. "We're just heading back."

"Just think, if I'd gotten here any earlier, I'd have been able to see you all in action. North, how many women tried to hit on you while you were evacuating, be honest?" She turned to North who didn't even have the decency to blush.

"Presley, you know I wouldn't have even noticed if they'd tried," the bastard laughed. "But I was on a line with Rev, your brother and Leighton were handling the door-to-door."

Her eyes swung back to me, then moved to her brother who'd yet to speak. "Well then, guess the answer would be none."

Tibbs—my friend and not the woman I'd slept with—rolled his eyes and flipped her off. "You live in that delusion, Pres. I can't go one block without attention. Don't be jealous that I'm the one in the family who got the looks."

"Dude, have you even *seen* your sister," Evans unwisely scoffed, saying what every single one of us was thinking but no one dared vocalize. "If there's anyone with your last name that can't go a block, it's her. You're gorgeous." His eyes left no mistake about what he was thinking.

Oh, Rookie.

And to think he'd gone to all that trouble to talk to Chief this morning about his upcoming future. Pity all that promise was about to be undone by that big fucking mouth.

Before I could either punch the asshole for looking at Presley in a way I didn't like, or yell at him for being disrespectful, she laughed. Her bright eyes lit up, enjoying the trouble a statement like that was going to cause, as she gently—seriously, could it get any worse—touched his arm. "Evans, you're adorable."

"He's going to be dead in a minute," Tibbs straightened, the glare he was throwing crystal clear. "Don't get any ideas, Rookie."

North slapped Tibbs on the back, getting his attention. "Relax, Tibbs. Evans was merely making an observation that Presley, is in fact, the better-looking Tibbs. Now as a married man, you know I have no skin in the game. But I have to say, I do agree with him." He tipped his head to Presley and grinned. "Evans was correct, you're gorgeous. And since that's on record, he doesn't need to say it anymore, do you, Champ?" The hand that had slapped Tibbs moved to Evans, his heavy palm landing hard on the rookie's shoulder.

"Really?" Presley narrowed her eyes at North before moving to Tibbs. She didn't spare me a sideways glance either, waiting to see if I had something to say. "Well, it's been fun. I'll leave you alone to grunt and slap each other around like Neanderthals. Bye."

She turned, giving us a wave as she continued to wherever the hell she'd been heading in the first place. Tibbs elbowed me, trying to telepathically communicate whatever was pissing him off at that moment.

It should have been me instead of North setting Evans straight?

We need to beat him up anyway for even thinking it, let alone saying it?

Presley isn't gorgeous?

Little Timmy was trapped in a well?

"What?" I coughed out, hoping his dodgy telepathy only went one way, and he couldn't read my thoughts.

"Go tell her you're calling her later. This is the perfect opening," he huffed under his breath, making absolutely zero sense.

"She's going somewhere," I pointed, trying not to notice how amazing her ass looked in that skirt as her hips swayed with each step.

"Yeah, and so are you. Go tell her and then let's get back to the station. Go. I'll deal with Evans." He pointed at his sister who was stopped at a crosswalk, waiting for the light.

"Fuck you, Tibbs." I shook my head, jogging up the street attempting to catch her before she got the green. I wasn't even sure why I was pissed, wanting to get her alone ever since—well, since I woke up staring at my ceiling and unable to jerk off. So why I felt heat up my neck, I wasn't entirely sure.

"Presley," I called out, stopping her from joining the rest of the pedestrians on the other side. "Wait."

"Wait for what?" She crossed her arms, her beautiful brown eyes moving to where her brother, North, and Evans were before letting them settle where I wanted them. "You draw the short straw? Come to tell me not to encourage Evans?"

"Fuck Evans." It came out a little harder than I would have liked.

Her brow rose, as her lips twitched. "Maybe I will. He's a little young, but they're easier to train that way."

I wasn't positive it was a joke, the idea she'd even consider—

"Oh, Leighton." She laughed. "Jesus, I was kidding. He's what, twenty-one? He's a child."

Well, at least *I* wasn't killing Evans, no way of knowing which way Tibbs was going to go.

"Look, can we talk later? I need to get back, shower, and then maybe when I get a minute I can call." I hated I honestly didn't know if she'd say yes. A woman, who in the past, I'd spent more time on the phone with than my own sisters, and I couldn't be sure she'd pick up.

"You realize, he's looking, right? So you should probably just pretend you said whatever it is you were made to say and go back." Her arms unwrapped, one hand falling to her hip where it anchored.

Man, her curves were insane. I needed to stop looking.

Forcing my eyes back where they belonged, I ignored the audience who were thankfully out of earshot. "Tibbs wants me to keep an eye on you for the next few days. And I think it's a good idea."

"My brother said what?" She was throwing off so much aggression I actually took a step back. And damn if it didn't turn me on all at the same time. Thank God I was wearing turnouts because a visible hard-on right now would be bad on so many levels.

"I know, I know." I put my hands up, showing her that I wasn't going to throw her over my shoulder. Though given a choice, I'd like nothing more than to do that exact thing. "You don't need him, or me, or anyone else hovering. If it were me, I'd feel the exact same way."

She calmed, caught off guard by me agreeing with her. "It's ridiculous, and more to the point offensive. I'm not going to be handled like some little kid. I'm a grown woman, and I know what's best for me."

"You're right. It is offensive, and for whatever role I've played in that, I'm sorry. You're a grown woman who knows her own mind."

Every single word of that was true, and I didn't doubt for a second I would have reacted the exact same way if Tibbs, North, or even the chief were trying to muscle me. Hell, even I had weighed in, assuming I knew how she felt or how she should feel. Not my fucking finest hour and not something I wanted to repeat. But seeing her in front of me, I just couldn't contribute to that. Not anymore.

Her eyes darkened, probably trying to guess if my one-eighty wasn't more of the handling we'd spoken about. She couldn't be sure, and I didn't blame her. "Right. So then that's settled."

"If that's what you want, Presley, then it's settled. I'll go back and tell Tibbs to lay the fuck off and make sure he does. But," I moved closer, closing the distance between us. "If you wanted me to just . . . I don't know, be around a little, just to be sure, I can do that. Your rules. You say back off and I'll leave. No bullshit, Presley. It will be totally your call."

It wouldn't be easy, and if anything happened to her, I'd probably never forgive myself. But I wasn't willing to burn down the whole fucking bridge, we were still friends, right? Us sleeping together had done damage, no doubt about it, but I wasn't willing to put any more cracks in those foundations.

"You'd back off?"

"If that's what you want, yeah." I nodded, praying to God that wasn't what she asked for.

"And if I agreed—and I'm not saying I am—to this—" She waved her hand around. "Keeping an eye on me. Then what? You're going to follow me around like a puppy." Most of the anger was gone, a small, hesitant smile that she was fighting pulled at her lips.

"Presley, is this where you ask me to sit and beg?" It was my turn to grin. "Part of me thinks you'd love it. Ordering me around, testing how far you can push me."

And, fuck me, if she wasn't the only one who was curious. I wasn't even sure the idea was still a good one, the dirty part of my brain rationalizing if she *asked* me to get naked that I'd be duty-bound to comply. So much gray area, and yet, there I was, willing to sign on the dotted line.

Her lips pressed into a line, the urge to smile wider, a battle she was losing. "Well, maybe it's something we could try. Like for a day. And only if you promise on your mother that you will do exactly what I say."

"Firstly, you're never going to let me forget that, are you? I said it, one fucking time and I was trying to get my point across.

So, you need to leave her out of it," I warned, seeing the humor in it while not needing the visual of my mom's disproving face. Best she kept thinking her baby boy was a saint, living in denial that my place on the wall of saints and angels was deserved. I sure as hell wasn't going to tell her any different and break the woman's heart. "And secondly, within reason. You want to use me as your own personal science experiment, we're going to have issues. But, other than that, I'll agree."

It was a bad deal.

I knew it, she knew it, even the fucking dumbass lawyer who'd handled my oldest sister's divorce and fucked it up—she was still paying her ex-husband's tax bill—would agree it was a huuuuuuge mistake.

But regardless of all that knowledge, the risk, and the chance of epic fallout, I wasn't saying no.

I put out my hand, the shake the only acceptable physical contact I was able to offer with her brother watching and my turnouts covered in ash and soot. Which was probably for the best anyway, because I was sure the kind of physical contact I *wanted to offer* wasn't fit for a public street.

"What do you say, Presley? Trial run?"

The hand that was so deliciously resting on her hip moved and gripped mine, the pressure when she closed it making my balls ache. "Okay, but you can't get weird on me."

"Weird how?" I asked, dropping her hand and wondering what she meant. Like when I kissed her in the club the other night, or the night before that when I took her to bed.

"Like sending me messages the next day, pretending you didn't sleep with me. We're adults, I'm not going to get amnesia and forget we slept together. Which I might add, was a problem for you and not for me."

Oh, she had no idea.

None.

"Well, isn't it lucky we're going to have all this time to work it out then? And if you thought for a second I'd forget that, then you're even dumber than your brother." I leaned forward almost whispering in her ear. "I haven't forgotten shit. Not about you, and not about that night. And especially not how good my name sounded when you moaned it." I pulled back, watching as her pupils dilated. I wondered if she was thinking about what we did, about how good I'd made her feel. And if it made her as hot as it did me. "Now, if I don't get my ass on the engine and get back to the station, I'm going to hear about it for the next week. And I'm sure you have somewhere you need to be too. So I'll call you later, and we'll work out how this will go down. I'm off for the next forty-eight, I'll come by your place after I finish shift tomorrow. Take care."

Giving her a quick wave, I turned around before I did something stupid.

Like kiss her.

And considering she hadn't even asked me to do that, that transgression would've been all on me.

Wasn't sure it wasn't worth the risk.

"Wait?" She grabbed my arm, her hand stopping me from leaving. "Tomorrow morning? You guys finish at like what? Seven, eight? I'm not going to be coherent that early. I'm going to be at *Diablo* tonight until three." Her head shook, thinking something as minor as a locked door was going to be a roadblock.

Not. Likely.

Especially not if I had permission.

"Your brother has a spare key, I'll let myself in. You won't even know I'm there," I offered, thinking it was less invasive than just breaking the door down.

Her hand didn't let go, keeping me from moving. Little did she know, I was in no hurry to go. "Yeah, because that doesn't sound creepy at all. You're going to just let yourself into my apartment and wait until I wake up? You going to watch me while I sleep too?"

"Is that what you want?" I asked, having no problem with that scenario. I'd probably enjoy it a lot more than she'd think too. "I tell you what, have a think about it and leave me a note. It will be a test on how good I am at following instructions. And I know how much you love giving them."

"Leighton, we've got to go," North yelled from down the road. We'd already loitered longer than we needed to and if we didn't get back soon there'd be all kinds of questions.

"See you in the morning, Presley. Don't forget that list." My head tilted to where her hand was, her grasp relaxing.

Her nod lacked her usual confidence, a mumbled, "bye" tossed my way before catching the light which had changed again.

And with her heading on her way, I had no reason not to be on mine, turning back to where North, Evans, Rev, and Tibbs were all assembled, waiting for me.

"Leighton, the other engine already left." Rev shook his head. "What were you doing?"

Tibbs eyes cut to mine, the expectation all over his face. "She cool?"

"All good, brother." I clapped him on the shoulder, trying to convince myself as well. "I'll explain everything when we get back to the station, but she's agreed. Oh, and another thing, I'm going to need her spare key."

He didn't even ask why, a relieved smile breaking out across his face. "I owe you. Now let's get back before Cap and Chief both blow a gasket. We'll just tell him the rookie needed to take a piss."

"Hey!" Evans objected, the evil look spelling out he wasn't taking the fall. "Cap saw Leighton walk off, you guys aren't pinning it on me."

I rolled my eyes, popping open the door to the engine and jumping in. "Let's just get back. It's probably going to be a long shift."

Chapter 7

Presley

YOU'D THINK SUNDAY nights would be easy, but not in Manhattan. It was just another night, the club packed to capacity, the hours just as long. Add to that the information Raelle had so helpfully dug up, and it was an interesting night.

Scott Collins had decided to spend more of his daddy's money. He and a few of his—beautiful but not all that bright— friends had conspired to buy a club in L.A. and turn it into the biggest celebrity haunt on the west coast.

Morons.

The lot of them.

Firstly, none of them—and I'm talking about seven successful actors, some who had a few awards on the mantel—had any kind of industry experience. Unless you counted frequenting clubs and bars, they were all completely oblivious. And if that weren't enough of a deterrent into dropping a whole bunch of cash into an investment that had a high chance of failure, none of them had any business experience either.

Nothing.

Not even a fundraising campaign when they were all freshman at Beverly High.

Zip.

Instead, they were a crew of young, sexy, and privileged white guys whose good looks and connections—and sure they had *some* talent—got them onto our screens. And when they weren't on their daytime drama/recurring series/B Grade movie/streaming service original/token hot guy in the blockbuster, they traveled in packs, drinking and partying. Posting pictures on their social media and living their best lives. Guys would give their right arm to trade places, while hordes of women wanted to fuck them. And for someone like me, they were an easy mark.

They only bought top shelf or exclusive, not even bothering to check the amount on their tab before closing it out with a thick black Amex. Their tags and check-ins provided advertising that money couldn't buy, and for the most part they were harmless. Sure, there was the sex in the bathrooms, but they kept it to the VIP area so other than their "own kind" no one else had a clue. And there was the occasional drug use that needed to be dealt with as well. We had a zero-tolerance rule on the floor, not willing to lose my liquor license because some asshole needed to get high. Which meant they were kindly—making a scene didn't serve a purpose for any of us—asked to leave and not return.

But other than that, it was all good.

We each had our part and we both did it so well. You made them feel special, stroked their ego and it was easy money in the cash drawer.

So why they wanted to screw with the system and get their hands dirty was beyond me. But apparently that was exactly what they had planned, Scott spearheading the movement which was probably why he was all dick-in-his-hand at *Diablo* the other night propositioning me. I had a hunch I knew what he wanted; the lack of experience, savvy, or even just knowledge, a clue as to why someone like me was needed.

I groaned as I entered my apartment, tossing my keys onto my sideboard and locking the door behind me. Raelle had given me a ride again, but she didn't come up, me convincing her it was all good. It still sent a shiver down my spine when I opened the door and checked everything was as I left it. But surely Lewis wouldn't be stupid enough to come back after he knew the police had been called.

Thankfully, the apartment was empty. Nothing out of place, the soft smell of lemon floor cleaner still lingering in the air from my aggressive mopping before I'd left. I'd been excessively cleaning, hoping to cleanse the feeling of his invasion. But other than a super clean apartment, it hadn't really helped.

The tension in my shoulders relaxed, the air in my lungs coming out a little slower as I took a moment to stand in my entrance way and assure myself I was fine. I was home, safe, and I was going to be horizontal and asleep very soon.

Before I could settle into my soft sheets and hopefully peaceful dreams, I needed to shower. The smell of the club got into your skin and hair and there was nothing more therapeutic than washing it all off after a long day. I undressed in my bathroom, dropping my clothes to the floor while the hot water kicked in, the room filling with steam shortly after. My hand instinctively reached out, testing the water and adjusting the faucets before I got in, an audible groan of relief pushing past my lips as the water cascaded down.

It was quick, my nightly/early morning ritual so ingrained that I did it with my eyes mostly shut. And then when I was clean, my body and hair smelling fresh and floral, I shut off the water and stepped out. I didn't even bother getting into my pjs, towel drying my hair as best I could and then slipping into my bed, naked.

I wasn't sure if the exhaustion of my mind or body was responsible, sleep coming quickly as I shut my eyes. I didn't even think, my brain hitting a flatline the minute my head hit the pillow.

It had to be hours later before I moved for the first time, my body stretching out in my king-sized bed as I rolled onto my side, my eyes slightly opening as I repositioned.

My apartment was kept dark. Given my nocturnal hours weren't conventional, I didn't need a cheerful sunrise ruining what should be my nighttime. Which was why I had blackout drapes, the heavy folds of fabric so thick they'd probably withstand a nuclear blast.

The only exception was a small essential oil diffuser, the soft glow of blue light piercing the darkness as the water gently bubbled. Which was how I knew it was still early, my hand hitting the timer for five hours, set just before crawling into my bed at four. And that dim blue glow was just enough for me to see the dark shadowy figure, slumped on my couch.

My body held in a breath, my pulse kicking up speed as I willed my eyes to focus. I wouldn't panic just yet, giving my mind a chance to assess the situation before I totally freaked out. My phone was right beside me, and the figure wasn't moving, so if nothing else, I had options. The open plan didn't give me a lot of places to hide, the thing I loved most about my apartment also the most dangerous.

Oh.

Hell.

I hadn't even fully debated whether I should go lock myself in my bathroom and call 9-1-1 when I remembered exactly who that figure was. And had yesterday not been such a shitshow between Scott's early morning wake-up, Lorena's follow-up and then an intense night at *Diablo*, I'd have remembered I was expecting a house guest. Might have reminded myself to put on pajamas as well.

Jared. Leighton.

My body flushed hot without even saying it out loud, the idea that the only thing between us was a couple of feet, making my pulse race again.

I'll admit, the thought of sliding out from my covers and confronting him naked, was appealing. Wondering if he'd push aside that duty/honor bullshit and cave like he did the other night in his car. Or if he'd think it was some tragic and desperate attempt at attention.

And he probably wouldn't be wrong.

No.

No, I wasn't tragic or desperate, and there was nothing wrong with having a healthy sexual desire. No one made my brother feel like a freak when he couldn't keep a steady girlfriend, or when he was dry humping random women in the corner of *Diablo.*

Deciding to compromise—rejection when you were naked would sting like no other—I slithered silently from my sheets and grabbed the nightie I hadn't put on after my shower. It was still hanging off a chair where I'd left it, the pale pink satin more like a slip than sleepwear, pulled over my head and smoothed down my body.

Underwear was an issue, my collection of panties sitting in a dresser drawer I didn't open as I crept on my toes out to the living area. Sneaking around in my own apartment was ridiculous, and yet, there I was, doing my best not to make any noise so I maintained the element of surprise. It reminded me of being sixteen again, cracking the door open early in the morning when he'd sleep over, his big, sexy passed out figure sprawled over the spare mattress in my brother's room. I fantasized about crawling under those covers more than just a few times, my brother being less than two feet away in his own bed stopping me every single time I wanted to be brave.

My feet hadn't even made it all the way to the couch when his eyes cracked open, and then went wide.

"Fuck," he coughed out shifting himself back up the couch.

His long legs had hung over the edges, my generous three-seater comfortable, but still not big enough for his large frame.

"You look pathetic on that couch." My hand anchored on my hip as I switched on a small table lamp. "You should make it a point not to piss off your future wife, I'm almost positive you wouldn't be able to afford the back care." I pointed to his hand which was rubbing the back of his neck.

His legs shifted, two socked feet landing on the floor and accepting his weight as he stood. "Yeah, well, I'll be sure to remember that when I get married, thanks for the tip. I must have dozed off. And isn't it early for you to be up?"

From his vantage point he could see straight down the top of my nightie. I wasn't wearing a bra, the tiny ribbon straps doing their best to keep everything contained. And if the heat from his gaze was anything to go by, they'd have burned my nightie right off, his eyes roaming across my body like they didn't know where to look.

"Yeah it is, but I forgot you were coming, and I was three seconds away from calling the cops." I tried to ignore there was literally a slither of satin between me being naked, acting like his eyes all over me wasn't turning me on.

His Adam's apple bobbed, the swallowing looking like it was causing him actual pain. "I checked on you."

"Did you?" He was clearly better at sneaking around than I was because I hadn't heard a peep. "I'm surprised you were able to see anything, it's so dark in here."

He moved closer, his hands curling into balls at his sides. "Yeah, I was able to see enough to know you weren't wearing *that* a few hours ago."

"You want me to take it off?"

"Yes."

I wasn't even sure I'd heard him correctly, my mouth stopped from asking him to repeat it by his on mine. His arms pulled me close, fingers sliding down my back and gripping my ass as he deepened the kiss.

"Jesus, Presley." His hand touched my bare ass, hauling me off my feet. "You're killing me."

It hadn't been my plan.

Or maybe it had, my hands gripping his T-shirt and pulling him closer. "Kiss me again."

Just like he promised, he did exactly what I asked, my legs wrapping around his waist as he took my mouth. His hungry lips demanded more, a whimper escaping from my throat as I let him dominate.

I loved the way it felt, so intense and passionate. Less like he was kissing me and more like it was his calling. He moved slowly, pressing me hard against his body as he carried me through the space. He smelled of soap and shampoo, my fingers running through his hair as I kissed his neck.

"You need to sleep," he whispered between kisses, laying me down on the mattress and pressing his body down on me. "I'm not going to be held responsible when you're cranky later."

I groaned, wanting more as I rubbed myself against him. "I thought we agreed you weren't going to tell me what to do. You should take your shirt off, you're wearing too much."

His hands left me for a second, reached around to his back and pulled off his T-shirt. He was perfection, the toned muscles of his abs flexing as the shirt got tossed to the side.

"Your pants too," I panted, pointing to the jeans that were still very much in the way. Since he'd already stopped kissing and touching me, it made sense to capitalize on it. And I'd already decided that I wanted them off.

He hesitated, taking a second or two before unbuttoning his jeans and lowering the zipper. He kicked them off, stripping his socks from his feet but leaving his boxer briefs.

I was stopped from arguing by his mouth back on mine, kissing me as he positioned me on the bed, his body slipping into the gap between my legs. "I'm not fucking you tonight, Presley." Teeth grazed against my shoulder, making my skin tingle.

"What?" I gasped between kisses, not wanting to stop for proper clarification.

Fingers traveled up my leg, following the curve of muscles until they rested on my hip. "You heard me."

My mind was swimming, too turned on to think straight and confused that if sex wasn't our end game, what the hell were we doing? I didn't imagine the hard-on brushing against my core. Or the way he panted with desperation at my mouth. So unless this was a really vivid dream and I hadn't woken up, his words were at total odds with his actions.

"You need to . . . do . . . what I say." I tried forming sentences while continuing to kiss him. And it wasn't one-sided either, his lips just as busy as mine. "You promised."

"I said within reason, gorgeous. And *reason* has nothing to do with what we're doing now."

Irritation crawled up my skin, wondering if it was payback for kissing him in my office. But unlike then, we hadn't been interrupted or stopped, continuing to tease each other as we struggled to breathe. I pulled back, angling my mouth out of the way so I could look him in the eye with the limited light I had. "Are you just going to turn me on and then go take a cold shower? You know *that* isn't going away by itself." My eyes tipped to the cock straining against the cotton of his boxer briefs.

He shook his head, a smile edging across his lips. "You let me worry about *that*. And I said I wasn't going to fuck you; I didn't say I wasn't going to make you come."

With his intentions clear, he pressed his hard length against me. I was wet, already turned on from everything that came before, the friction as he rubbed making me even hotter.

It felt amazing, the gentle roll of his hips teasing me so much I could barely stand it. My head lolled back as my eyes shut, my knees widening to give him better access. "Oooohhhhh mmyyyyy Goddd," I stuttered out, feeling a finger move to where his cock had been.

My slip had ridden up, exposing my naked lower body while the straps had fallen off my shoulders, no longer containing my breasts. The fabric was completely redundant, but he didn't stop to take it off, lowering his mouth to lick and suck my nipples as they fought to break free.

He pressed his cock against me again, a wet patch forming on the cotton as he thrust against me. He didn't stop, his mouth moving to the other breast while his finger circled my clit.

Okay, maybe it was a decent compromise, the disappointment of no sex disappearing as he continued his assault with his lips and hands. "That feels so—"

"Good," he finished, pushing a finger inside me as his hard-on took over on my clit.

I wanted to touch him and make him feel as good as he was making me. My hand reached out, trying to wedge between us but he shook his head. "And what would you be trying to do? You enjoy trying to make me cave way too much, Presley," he chuckled.

"Let me touch you," I moaned, my hand not making any progress. "I thought I was the one who was supposed to be in control."

"You are, say stop and see what happens." I felt his grin against my skin.

It was frustrating, the feeling in my body building while I tried to remember what I wanted to do. That's right, I wanted to touch his cock, to stroke it and get him harder, to drive him as crazy as he was me. But I was definitely not saying stop, not wanting it to end.

It was the best *no sex* I'd ever had, tingles spreading across my limbs as I fought the urge to close my eyes and give into it.

And when he plunged in another finger, I lost the ability to make the choice.

"Jared, don't stop," I warned, bucking against his hand and totally ignoring what we were doing was completely one sided. "Oh my God, just like that."

The pressure of his cock was gone, his fingers getting in deep without the obstruction as his thumb rubbed tight circles against my clit. "Fuck, I love watching you like this." His voice was raw, rough around the edges, straining with control.

There was no way he was loving it more than me, my back arching off the mattress as he brought his mouth back to my nipple and sucked.

BOOM.

Like an explosion, my body splintered into a million pieces. My muscles contracted and then released in tiny waves as I collapsed against the bed and whispered his name over and over again.

"Yes," he mumbled against my skin, thrusting his fingers inside of me and teasing out my orgasm. "Just like that, baby."

My skin was hot and then cold, goosebumps breaking against the surface as I tried to slow my breathing. "Kiss me."

There was no hesitation as he moved his mouth back to mine, my feeling of euphoria still echoing through my body as I relaxed onto my pillow. He was still hard, the new position enabling me to feel the steel rod in his boxer briefs as he continued to drive me out of my mind. It had to be painful, the need for release gnawing at him like it had been at me moments ago. But as I lowered my hand, he grabbed it, stopping me from getting any farther south and raising it back above my head.

I was sooooooo *not* in control.

"What are you doing, Presley?" He grabbed the other hand, caging me in and using his body for leverage. "Because I already told you, we're not having sex."

My hips lifted, rocking against him but not getting very far. He was not only taller and heavier but stronger too, and if he wanted to keep me still, there wasn't a lot I could do. "Well that is incredibly dumb, Jared. You know it's you who is going to suffer."

He laughed, lowering his lips to my forehead and feathering a kiss. "Yeah, I know. And I don't care. Now go back to sleep. I already told you I'm not taking responsibility for your mood later, and if I'm going to come hang out at *Diablo*, I'm going to need a nap too."

I stilled, a little surprised he was taking the idea so seriously. Sure, I expected he'd show up, hang around a little and maybe drive me to work. He had a point to prove, and to be honest, I wasn't disappointed for the company. We still hadn't really talked about that night—and I was going to have to add this one to that conversation as well—so in a way I was glad. But at *Diablo*, well, there was no need. Bennett more than had it covered, and the walls were like a fortress, reinforced steel, lead lined—it was going to take a rocket launcher or a tank to break in.

"Jared, you don't need to *hang* with me at work. I won't have time to babysit and you'll probably get bored. Besides, it's your day off. I'm sure you have heaps to catch up on after spending the day with me."

Laundry, groceries, the gym—both he and my brother had their little daily routine, and I didn't want to get in the middle of it.

"Who said I needed babysitting," he scoffed, rolling his eyes. "I'm more than capable of entertaining myself. You will barely even notice me. And when you're done, I'll drive you home."

He withdrew his fingers from my body, rolling to his side as he settled on the bed. "You going to let me stay?" His eyes tipped to the mattress. "Or you going to make me sleep on the couch like my pissed off future wife?"

"I should," I warned, because despite the blistering orgasm, I was slightly pissed off. "But I'll take pity on you and let you stay."

"Good. And you might want to rethink that thing you're wearing. Might as well have been naked." He yawned into a grin.

"You're right. Can you go turn off the lamp?" I pointed to the end table beside the couch throwing off more light than I'd like.

He grunted his agreement, readjusting himself before standing up and doing as I asked. Unfortunately, I didn't get a chance to enjoy the view, whipping my tangled nightie off my body and slipping between the sheets. After all, he'd mentioned he'd wanted it off earlier and we never got to that. And I didn't have to be argumentative all the time.

His feet froze as he neared the bed, the crumpled pink satin on the floor hindering his path. I rolled onto my side, hiding my grin. "Night, Leighton."

"Night, Presley." The exhale long and hard as he tossed open the covers from his side and slid in. "Thank fuck this is a huge bed."

Chapter 8

Jared

CLEARLY, I'D HAD a messy breakup with sleep.

Not sure if she'd dumped my ass or it had been the other way around, but for the last few nights I'd spent more time contemplating the crown molding than catching the Zs I needed. Still, hard to close your eyes when the smoking-hot woman, you just made come, was laying naked beside you.

And I knew she was baiting me, tossing the scrap of fabric on the floor because she knew it would drive me crazy. Not that it covered much when it had been on her body, so not sure which way was better.

Seeing her sleeping naked when I'd walked in early that morning had been a kick in the balls. I'd gone home, showered, changed and picked up the key from Tibbs. He'd given me a pat on the back, the appreciation he was feeling thankfully left unspoken, so I didn't feel like a complete jerk. He had no idea what he was doing and the kind of runaway train that was about to leave the station.

Don't get me wrong, I'd made a silent commitment to both of us—him and me—that I wasn't going to fuck his sister. Well,

83

not at least in the immediate future. And not because I didn't want to. But he was right to be worried about her, and I was too, wanting to do anything to make sure she was happy and whole. Best way to do that was to keep my dick in my pants and not complicate things. Or, more to the point, make them more complicated. So, sex with Presley—as much as I hated to admit it—was off the table.

But a naked Presley would test the resolve of a saint. And, fuck knows, I knew most of them. My mom had their framed pictures mounted on the wall, their smiling faces and judgmental eyes following you around the room like some Catholic parlor trick. But if Saint Michael had seen that dark-haired beauty, her dangerous curves barely contained by her covers, the man would have caved for sure.

She'd tried—or did she?—to cover up, throwing on some silky thing that did nothing to hide what was underneath. Instead it showcased it, curling around her hot body and just made things worse.

So . . . I compromised. My dick stayed in my pants as promised, but I also couldn't ignore what was truly a gift. And given the opportunity to make Presley come, that was a chance I was not passing up.

Not.

A.

Chance.

And how was I rewarded for my good behavior? Condemned to sleep beside her with the silky torture device sitting on the floor while she lay naked. Oh, and I still had her voice ringing in my ear, my name repeated in a breathy moan as I'd made her come.

I needed to go to church.

Or confession.

Or, at the very least, gargle some fucking holy water because it was going to take a miracle for me to lose the hard-on. And hopefully at some point I would regain the feeling in my legs.

But sleep.

Not happening.

A soft and feminine moan notched up my misery, Presley not sharing the same predicament. Sated and sleepy, it hadn't taken too long till her breathing evened out and she was asleep like she'd been when I'd walked in. But it had been a few hours, and a casual look at my phone had clued me in that it was getting closer to afternoon, the rest of the morning slipping away.

"Did you sleep?" I felt her turn, my eyes still glued to the ceiling as she shuffled closer to me.

"A little." Which wasn't a lie if you counted the time I got on the couch before she'd noticed me. That was before my plan went to shit, and sleeping was still a possibility.

My eyes dipped down, treated to the skin on display and I was grateful she was taking it easy on me. The parts that had started most of the trouble were kept under wraps, her body encased in a fluffy white cocoon.

"You want some coffee?" I asked, deciding I needed to get out of the bed before I made a decision I wasn't sure would be a bad one. "I can go get us some breakfast if you want?"

"Coffee sounds amazing," she groaned, unintentionally—or not, who knew anymore—making shit worse. "No breakfast though, I'm more of a lunch girl but feel free to help yourself."

Oh, I wanted to help myself, just not to the contents of her pantry.

"Yep, coffee. Anything else?" I hesitated, because I was a masochist and clearly hated having functioning balls.

And that's where I underestimated myself, my eyes connecting with hers and I knew whatever I'd been trying to avoid was happening. I didn't even give her a chance to respond, pressing my mouth to hers in what was supposed to be a gentle good morning. Instead it turned into a dirty how-are-ya that was going to undo all the good work I'd done by not sleeping with her.

"I'm so glad you didn't get weird again," she mumbled against my lips. "I didn't want to have to go ahead and call your mot—"

"Don't you dare say it," I warned, chuckling. "We agreed."

She nodded silently, moving her mouth to mine. It was slower this time, the kiss less urgent probably on account she'd been the one controlling the tempo.

"Look, we can both agree that when it comes to you, I'm incredibly bad at saying no." I blew out a breath. "And while I'm still not convinced this is the right thing to do, I'm not sure I want to stop."

She deserved my honesty, to know what the fuck was going on in my mind. And while it probably would've been better if we could go back to not touching each other, I wasn't sure I was capable.

"It doesn't have to stop," she breathed into my mouth, the heat of her lips driving me fucking crazy. "If this is what we both want, what's the harm?"

Ironic I'd asked myself that exact question a million times.

We were two consenting adults and if we wanted to fuck each other's brains out, then who the hell cared? Except with Presley it wasn't just sex, the fallout monumental if it all went bad.

"The harm is, I don't want to fuck this up. You trust me, Pres, and I trust you. We're friends. You throw sex into the mix, shit gets complicated. This isn't even about Tibbs anymore. It's about you. I don't want to be another jerk in your history."

There'd been more than a few, her taste in men just as bad as her brother's taste in women. And while it was completely her prerogative to be with men who let her down, I wasn't going to be adding my name to that list.

She'd obviously been expecting something else, the reason I'd been keeping my distance taking her by surprise. "You'd never be another jerk. I trust you, Jared. You've always been such a good guy. I still remember when you beat up that guy because he tried to grab my ass at Burger King when I was seventeen."

"He shouldn't have touched you. No one gets to touch you without permission." The memory of that piece of shit with his hands on her all those years ago, still making me angry.

She smiled, not seeming to share the same dark feelings of that night. "Right, which is why you'd never hurt me. So what if we had some ground rules? Some guidelines so we don't have to worry about it?"

"Yeah, because we did so well with those *guidelines* before." I laughed, knowing it was asking for trouble.

Her gorgeous brown eyes narrowed, the trouble no longer hypothetical. "So what's your solution then?"

Christ, if she was looking to me for answers, I knew we were in trouble. "I need to be your friend first. Anything happens to jeopardize that, I'll never forgive myself. I'm serious, Presley. A choice between sleeping with you or having you in my life, and there's only one answer."

"Okay," she sighed. "When you put it that way, I guess it makes sense."

I laughed, "I'm glad it does to someone."

She leaned forward, her finger tracing my bicep. "You're a really good guy, Leighton. Like *really* good. And I'm positive we're going to work this out."

Wasn't sure I could agree on either of those statements but wasn't going to argue either.

"I'll go get that coffee," I offered knowing it was only a matter of time before I volunteered to give her something else.

With one last kiss, I moved off the bed and into the kitchen area. The lack of walls meant my vision was not impeded, her hot sexy and very naked body revealed when she pulled off the covers. She knew what she was doing too, taking extra time to complete the task and stretching for effect. Yeah, that evil grin didn't help either, the slow walk to her bathroom showcasing her ass before she disappeared behind the opaque glass wall.

I even contemplated following her into the room, the idea of her wet, slippery body making me groan under my breath. Yeah, I was definitely going to have to get a handle on things if my resolve not to sleep with her was going to stick. And yes, I knew technically I'd blurred the line, but the technicality was all I was holding onto at the moment.

I purposely didn't look when I heard the bathroom door open, keeping my eyes focused on my phone. I'd gotten dressed while she'd been in there, thinking about jerking off but decided against it. Last thing I needed was for her to walk out and see me with my cock in my hand. So instead, settled on scrolling through stupid memes Tibbs had sent me. He'd asked how things were and I was grateful to answer honestly that his sister was in the shower and I was chilling on her couch. Might have been a different response if that text had come a little earlier.

"I have to go to a meeting." She appeared before me, transformed from the hot but disheveled brunette who'd been lounging around in her bed to a sex bomb ready to serve you up your balls.

My eyes widened, taking in the plain dark green dress that fit like it had been molded to her skin, the fact none of it was really showing not stopping the hot visual I had going on. Not sure who her meeting was with, but I was sure they had no idea who they were going up against. I rose to my feet, taking in the view as I grabbed my keys. "Cool, I'll drive you. Where are we heading?"

"It's at *Diablo*, Bennett is meeting me there and it's the middle of the day. You don't need to come." Her brown eyes were focused, connecting with mine in a way I couldn't read. Not sure if it was some kind of test, or she was trying to throw me off, but I thought we'd established I was going to be her shadow.

"You're right, I don't need to come. But I'm here, have a car, and I want to. Never seen *Diablo* during the day. Plus, it will give me a chance to say hi to Bennett. I didn't the opportunity the other night."

She laughed, her eyes lighting up her face as she flicked back her hair. "You know he's not really your biggest fan, right? Trying to sneak in didn't win you any popularity contests. But if you are offering a ride, then I might just take you up on it. It will save me calling for one."

If it made her feel better to think of me as her chauffeur, then I could live with that. Mack had apparently offered to do a similar thing with his woman. And if the mood he was in the day after was anything to go by, it had worked out for him. Not that it was the same thing, but when it came to being a decent guy, someone dependable who people turned to, he was pretty much the pinnacle. Shit, I probably respected the chief more than my own dad—and I loved the hell out of my pops—so that was saying something.

"Then it's settled. Got everything you need?" I asked, waiting to see if she was ready to go.

She nodded, grabbing her handbag and phone. "Yep, all good."

I followed her out the door, standing beside her as she locked up and then we continued down to the lobby. I'd expected her to take the elevator, but she walked the six flights of stairs in heels without breaking a sweat. Not that I was questioning her stamina, I'd seen firsthand just how in shape she was.

My Mustang was waiting downstairs where I'd left it a few hours earlier. I'd been lucky to find some off-street parking which was one of the benefits in finishing a shift early in the morning. Was fairly sure I wouldn't be so fortunate when we got back, but that wasn't stopping me from leaving the prized space.

"Don't you think it would be more fuel efficient to drive something else?" She settled into the passenger seat and buckled up while watching me do the same. "Might be worth considering trading *this* in for a hybrid."

If it had been anyone else, I'd have assumed she was serious. After all, I worked and lived within a few blocks, and other than visiting my family out on Long Island, I didn't get the opportunity to stretch her legs very often. But I'd wanted a silver Mustang since watching *Jolie* and *Cage* trying to boost Elenore in *Gone in 60 Seconds*. Lusted over that car before I'd even discovered girls, that '67 Shelby Cobra was my first real crush. And while my income didn't allow me to have that baby, I went ahead and got the next best thing. A brand-new silver Shelby GT350—Elenore's sexy, lower maintenance, younger sister, Elena.

"I'd sooner pimp my ass on a street corner for gas money than get rid of my car." I hit the ignition, giving the dash a little rub. And considering what the repayments were, it wasn't such a stretch. But there'd be a cold day in hell before I'd be driving a hybrid.

She laughed, knowing exactly how much I loved my car. "Just make sure you get a good price, don't go under valuing your ass."

"Thanks, I'll be sure to call you in for the consult." I smirked, the stupid comment about me prostituting myself making me irrationally turned on.

I was one sick puppy, that much was clear.

Without asking, she hit one of the presets on the stereo, changing the station. The inside of the car filled up with the smell of her perfume, my eyes finding their way to her side of the car more times than was necessary. She was oblivious of course, her head down scanning emails on her phone, while I tried to make sure I didn't end up hitting a sidewalk or someone's bumper.

Fuck, she was beautiful.

And even though I'd wanted her for a goddamn long time, now that I'd had her, that compulsion was getting harder to fight.

Like déjà vu, I pulled into the staff parking lot of her club and cut the engine. I had just undone my seat belt, ready to pop my door when her hand landed on my chest. "Look, I know you said you wanted to hang around, but I'm going to be fine inside. How about we compromise? You can watch me walk in, see I'm safe and sound and then you can go do whatever it is you need to do. I'll be a couple of hours. Then if you still feel like you need to play bodyguard, you can pick me up later and we'll have an early dinner. I assume you're going to be our guest tonight?" Her beautiful pink lips spread into a smile.

Fuck, she was sexy.

She'd always been beautiful, even at sixteen when my dick had no business taking an interest. But somehow she'd gotten even hotter.

So goddamn gorgeous it was slowly driving me insane.

I couldn't even be angry, knowing that being sexy for Presley was like breathing—she couldn't help it. "Yeah, I'd like that." I reached over and brushed a brown curl off her shoulder. "Text me when you're ready and I'll come pick you up."

She leaned forward, her hand still on my chest as her lips brushed mine. "Kissing you is probably a bad idea."

"The worst," I groaned, not stopping her as she pressed a little harder.

It was going to take practice, needing to find our new normal being around each other. I couldn't forget I knew what she tasted like, how she felt when I was inside of her. And if I was going to attempt—who the fuck knew if I'd succeed—to keep things platonic, we were going to have to work it out as we went along.

And I wasn't sure what I'd miss more. Kissing her or hearing her say my name when I made her come hard.

"Okay, I'll call you." She pulled away, the irritated look from the last few days gone, and in its place, a smile.

It really made me feel good knowing I had a hand in putting it there. "Good, be safe, and call me if you need anything."

She laughed, sliding out of her seat and holding the door open. "I might get used to this. I like having you as my driver. Play your cards right, Leighton, this could be a side hustle. And you know I'd pay you really well."

I shook my head, raising a brow. "You couldn't afford me. Especially not since you dissed my car. You should go inside before you make it any worse."

The door closing muffled her giggle as she strolled to the staff entrance of the club, the hip sway from earlier in the morning making a reappearance.

I was definitely going to have to jerk off.

And unlike earlier, I wasn't going to pretend I wasn't thinking about her.

Chapter 9

Presley

JARED LEIGHTON HAD two different sides.

Leighton was the fun, loveable, dependable guy I'd known forever who happened to be my brother's best friend. While Jared was the good-looking guy with an insane body that made me so hot I could barely stand it.

And I liked them both.

I'd had dinner with Leighton.

He was funny and sweet, picking me up at *Diablo* and taking me to a small bistro not far from where I lived. It wasn't awkward, the weirdness I was worried about never showing up as we ate pasta and laughed like it was just another Monday night. And when we were done, he took me back home so I could get ready for work at the club.

Leighton sat on the couch, flicking through the sports channels while I was in the bathroom. And as much as I'd said that I didn't need anyone around "watching" me like a five-year-old, knowing he was in the other room made me feel calmer.

It was just nice.

Not having to be hyper alert, able to let down my guard for a while as I slipped into my dress and put on my makeup like it was just a regular day before the break in.

Had to admit, it hadn't been a totally terrible idea.

My good mood was still riding high when I walked out of the bathroom. I was wearing one of my favorite things in the world, a strapless gold embroidered *Monique Lhuillier* that had cost me almost two months' rent. It had been a present to myself when I got my first bonus check, the short, sexy cocktail dress making me feel like a million dollars.

"Fuuuuck, that dress. You look amazing."

Leighton was gone, Jared having taken his place.

He smoldered, his icy blue eyes raking over me with an undeniable hunger as his tongue darted across his lips. He was hot, the same fitted black Tee and dark blue jeans he'd been wearing suddenly looking different as he stalked closer with purpose.

His hands moved up and down my arms gently, a wave of goosebumps following in their wake as my pulse quickened. "You trying to make me insane, Presley? Because you in that dress would pretty much do it."

"That wasn't the plan, I just like the dress," I answered honestly, the look in his eyes, lethal. "But if this is too much for you, I can just get a cab."

"You're not getting a cab." The argument over before it was started, his gaze searing me.

So much for it not being weird.

"Well then, we should go."

Neither of us moved, our bodies inches away from each other as the sexual tension hung in the air.

"Leighton?"

I hoped calling him that would help but it didn't. He was Jared, and Jared was looking at me like he wanted to eat me with a spoon.

He sucked in a breath, nodding his head with an unspoken resolve. "Yeah, we should go."

At least that's what his mouth said, but his eyes were saying something different.

We took the elevator, the enclosed space making it worse. There were still no ground rules for what we were doing, so for all I knew pushing him up against the wall and kissing the hell out of him would be perfectly okay. As long as we stayed friends, right?

"Uh hm," I cleared my throat, feeling hot despite wearing a dress that didn't cover much. I was going to freeze outside for sure, but I welcomed that feeling over the inferno currently radiating in my core.

The elevator pinged, the doors flying open as we reached the bottom. Jared's arm-braced the door, holding it open as I went ahead. I could feel the weight of his stare. His eyes on me as I walked slightly ahead, his strides only taking a step or two before he was right beside me.

"The car is parked a street away, why don't you wait here, and I'll pull up in front." His voice was rough around the edges, as he stopped in front of the glass door.

It should've been a question but it wasn't, his feet rooted in place as he turned to face me. "It's cold out."

He wasn't telling me something I didn't already know. I'd meant to grab a jacket or coat on my way out but stumbled on the Jekyll/Hyde transformation in my living room. There was only so much I could recover before leaving, and insuring I didn't freeze to death had rated low. Probably since I was running so hot, I was actually looking forward to it. Clearly I had issues and didn't want to advertise that.

"I'm fine, I'll warm up in the car," I responded with hopefully enough sass he'd assume I was being difficult. I had a habit of not liking being told what to do so it fit the narrative, and I'd rather him believe *that* than know I had issues.

He looked like he wanted to argue, not opening the door despite his hand on the handle. His eyes flicked down to my dress giving it a final inspection before pushing open the glass and allowing me to walk through.

I could feel the tension in his body, evident his muscles were tight even underneath the Tee. He hadn't worn a jacket either, his toned arms flexing as they pressed against the door.

It gave me a twisted kind of pleasure to know I wasn't the only one suffering, wondering if that was going to be the theme for the night. At least once we got to *Diablo* I'd be too busy to notice, industry night Mondays almost as crazy as my Saturday nights.

My heels hit the sidewalk, clicking on the concrete as he directed us to where he was parked. It wasn't close, the air hitting my skin like a slap and making me shiver as I walked.

He glanced over, his mouth opening like he was going to comment and then thought better of it. Good, talking would show my teeth chattering, and I didn't want to confirm he was right—that I'd be cold—even if I was freezing.

Doing my best not to shiver the entire way, we made it to his silver Mustang before frostbite set in. Just as well too, because losing a toe or an arm would have totally ruined the esthetic of the dress. He hit the fob, the locks clicking open and I had to literally stop myself from throwing my body into the car. He shook his head as he walked around to the driver's side, pretending not to notice as I huffed into my hands and tried to warm up. Hey, he could judge all he wanted, I said I didn't need a coat, and I'd made it without complaining, hadn't I?

Being inside the car definitely took care of one issue. He had the ignition on and the heat blasting simulating a tropical day in Hawaii before we'd even pulled away from the curb. Although since I was no longer preoccupied with regulating my temperature it brought a whole other set of problems. Namely being in a confined space with Jared.

Wow, he was hot.

Unlike mine, his arms weren't covered in goosebumps. Instead I was treated to the subtle flexing of his muscles as he steered and changed gears. Those strong, toned legs were working the clutch and the gas, my eyes having a hard time knowing where to focus. How had I ridden in a car with him so many times before and not climbed into his lap? And more to the point, how was I going to stop myself from doing it now?

Look somewhere else, I begged, forcing my head to turn and stare out the side window. Better. I mean, I could still smell that intoxicating mix of shampoo, soap and deodorant that made my hormones go haywire for no apparent reason, but at least if I wasn't looking at him directly, I had a chance of controlling myself.

"Are you too hot?" I heard his voice rumble from the other side of the car, not bothering to turn. That would've been a bad move, we didn't have that much farther to go and I could definitely hold out a little longer.

"I'm fine," I deadpanned, studying the sidewalk we were whizzing past like there was going to be a test on it later.

It wasn't until he cleared his throat that I noticed my hand fanning myself. My intention to keep my steamy thoughts to myself manifesting themselves in what could only be described as sabotage courtesy of my body.

Knotting my hands in my lap so they could no longer continue their mutiny, we finally pulled into the staff parking lot at *Diablo*. It was one of the amazing benefits of the site, the large area backing onto shrubbery, giving my staff plenty of space to put their cars and trucks and not have to fight for prime real estate on the street.

He cut the engine, his intention to sit in the club all night fairly clear. And while it was something he'd done a million times before, it was feeling a whole lot different this time around.

The door beside me opened, his exit from the car taking place while I was strategizing how I could keep my distance from him and not look like a freak. I had a job to do which should have made it easier, and it would've been perfect if I didn't like to spend the majority of the time on the floor. The last few nights I'd been holed up in my office and I needed to be seen, so I guess I was going to have to get creative in ways to circle the club and not get distracted by his sexy body.

I smiled, because that's what I'd have done for Leighton if *he'd* opened the door, and stepped out into the mostly empty parking lot. Other than Bennett and possibly Hank, it was too early for the others, the idea that I might have to entertain him until we opened making me nauseous.

"You still cold?" He eyed me carefully, mistaking my self-administrated upper body hug as having something to do with the temperature. I mean, he was half right, it was cold. But I was more concerned about my nipples cutting through the fabric of my pretty gold dress because I was so turned on.

It didn't make sense.

Leighton, I reminded myself, just think of him as *Leighton*.

"A little," I answered honestly, figuring I had the whole night to lie. "I'll be fine once we get inside."

He nodded, thankfully not asking questions as he followed me into the club. I shuffled a few steps ahead, using the cold as the excuse for my hustle when really I could use the extra distraction of people. Bennett would definitely have something to say, his big mouth not only predictable but would probably earn him a raise if it helped break the sexual tension.

"Boss." Right on cue, Bennett showed almost no reaction to the man accessory a few steps behind. Just a slightly raised brow and the thinnest of smirks, he was saving his twenty questions for when we were in private. Yet another reason to give the man a raise.

"Hey, B, Leighton," *good, keep calling him that,* "gave me a ride and is going to hang out. Can you make sure Hank takes care of him and then come see me in my office?" I threw the words out casually as I strolled through the space. It wasn't unusual for me to talk to Bennett on the run, especially when I first arrived. I liked to get to my desk and attack my to-do list so I had time to have staff meetings with each section. Bennett and I always met first, so to the outside observer it would look like business as usual.

"Right on it, Boss." The voice came from behind me as I left, not bothering to stay to see what was said next.

It was when I was in the privacy of my office that I finally let out a breath. Getting a handle on things was my first priority, then I'd move to other things like not kissing or touching Jared. I had the whole night to psych myself up for that car ride home, not to mention staying over was probably not going to happen because A, we were trying to not sleep with each other and B, he didn't bring a change of clothes. So unless he had an overnight bag tucked away in the trunk of his sexy Mustang, he was going to say goodnight and go home.

I should have felt gratitude, swimming in the relief we wouldn't have to do the dance of pretending to be friends when there were no referees to keep us honest. But it was disappointment that I felt, understanding his reasoning for keeping it platonic but wanting to eat my cake too.

My door had been left ajar, Bennett's fist giving it a cursory knock before pushing it open. "NYFD providing a driver's service these days?" He didn't even try to hide his grin as he closed the door. "Sounds like an overuse of city resources if you ask me. You know if you want a ride, all you have to do is ask."

"I'm pacifying my brother." I flicked my hand casually as I sunk in my chair. "It's easier to let Leighton tag along than the tracking bracelet Justin would have me wear. My parents are just as bad, so this is an easy fix."

That was all true. Tibbs—aka my brother when he was being a pain in my ass—had convinced my parents I needed a twenty-four-seven security detail and to be sequestered to the Tower of London. I'd tried to make them see how ridiculous it was, but it was hard to argue with concerned parents who just wanted you to be safe. So I compromised and ended up in my teenage fantasy.

"Fine, but if you need me or one of the guys to shadow you for a few days, let me know. I'm assuming *Backdraft* is going to have to go back to work eventually." He eyed me hard, his displeasure evident that an outsider was dealing with something he believed should be handled in house.

"Thanks, I'm all good. And I want you to know that Leighton's here just as a guest tonight. He's not going to try and get in the way or make things harder for you or your team. He is just my ride."

While necessary, the words felt bitter in my mouth. Leighton was a friend, not an employee, and was sure as hell sacrificing a lot more than I was. Other than our friendship and a loyalty to my brother, he had no reason to give up the precious free time he had when he wasn't working. And the fact I'd been so bratty about it didn't sit well.

"Okay, Boss. I want to check the exterior cameras and then I'll meet with the team. Anything else you want to discuss for this evening?" He folded his arms across his broad chest, settling into his boots.

"Nope, there's nothing else. I'll be on the floor most of the night. I think the pitch is as good as it's going to be."

Bennett laughed, the first real smile of the night exploding across his face. "You're gonna rock that meeting, Presley. We both know it. But I think it's cute you are pretending to be so nervous."

"I'm not pretending, nothing is a sure thing." And wasn't that the truth, in either the expansion or anything else.

"I'd still take that bet." He unfurled his arms, tipping his head to the door as the grin crept back on his face. "Now, if we're done padding your ego, I've got actual work to do."

I rolled my eyes and pointed to the exit. "Just go already. And for the record, you suck at making me feel good. Let's just leave that job to Raelle."

"Ha, you're going to need new friends. I'll see you later, Boss."

As he left, my eyes moved to the monitors. Jared was at the bar talking to Hank and a few other staff members had started to arrive.

"So, are we keeping him? What's the deal?" Raelle appeared in the doorway, Bennet having left it conveniently open.

She wandered in, falling heavily into the chair opposite me as she waited for my response. "He's not a pet, Rae, he's just hanging around."

"Oh, oh, is *that* what he's doing?" She feigned shock. "Please, we both know you're both counting down the hours until you can get out of here and get busy. I'm surprised he isn't in here, under your desk with his face in your lap. Have to admit, it's kind of hot."

Well, she wasn't wrong. The idea of Jared going down on me at my desk was kind of hot. "That isn't happening. We're being friends instead." I tried to keep the disappointment from my voice, not willing to advertise it hadn't been as mutual as I was leading her to believe.

"Really?" She laughed, tossing her head back, unconvinced. "Well, O-kay then."

"What's that mean?" I bit back not liking the unspoken subtext.

Raelle shrugged, polishing her fingernails on her tight Tee. "Nothing, I'm agreeing with you. Isn't that what you wanted?"

I narrowed my eyes, not trusting her for a second. "Rae, you don't just blindly agree with me for anything whether it's as your boss or your friend. What are you up to?"

She kicked up her legs, landing them onto the floor before leaping out of the chair with more theatrics than necessary. "Nothing, Boss. Better go help Hank prep the bar. I'll see you later. Let me know if you need a ride home." The stream of words following her out the door before I had a chance to question.

Great.

Not only did I have to try to act normally around a guy who was too perfect for words, but I had to wonder what my best friend was up to. And because I knew better I'd guess the two weren't going to be mutually exclusive.

Ignoring what would no doubt give me a headache, I finished the paperwork I needed to do and then headed into the main section of the club. There, I worked each area, meeting with my supervisors and staff members, going through the expectations for the night and listening to any feedback they had. It was important for me to have my finger on the pulse, not willing to leave to be a figure head who sat in her office all night and barked out orders. I think they liked it too, having an avenue to voice their opinions or concerns without the red tape of a chain of command.

Since the club was still empty and I had a direct line of sight to Jared, it was also a welcomed distraction that I was incredibly grateful for. It would be easier when guests arrived, the temptation to go over and talk to him gnawing at me like an itch.

"Hey, Presley, there's a delivery from our liquor supplier." Hank caught me as I finished up with the VIP team. "They're around back in the truck, want me to help them get it into the storeroom?"

"A delivery this late?" I checked my phone, our usual driver making his rounds much earlier in the day. "You sure he said it was alcohol?"

Hank shrugged, his face pulling into a grimace. "Yeah, Lenard is sick so some other guy picked up his route and is running behind. He's sorry, but he couldn't get here any earlier. He still has one more drop off after us."

Late night deliveries were not only an inconvenience but created a safety issue too. Even with external security lighting there was a chance of tripping or falling. Or if you watched too many late-night movies, a gang of good looking but devious villains performing a heist.

"Okay, I'll walk out with you," I offered, wanting to make sure nothing shady was going on. "Marcus, you want to join us?"

I wasn't stupid, not only was I limited in the help I'd be—my gold Lhuillier not practical for manual labor—but I wasn't an idiot either. If anything unsavory was going down, I wanted Bennett's second in command with us. The guy was not only ex-Special Forces but just like Bennett, could stare a guy into submission.

Marcus nodded, signaling to Bennett we were leaving as we walked out the staff entrance. There, we found everything as it should be, the large white truck with a tired looking delivery driver already loading up his delivery trolley.

"Sorry, Ms. Tibbs, I know I should have been here hours ago but I'm doing double the work. It was either come now or push it back to Thursday." He wiped the sweat from his brow with a dirty rag.

"It's fine," I nodded, looking over the invoice and checking off the items as Marcus and Hank helped move the inventory. "Thanks for fitting us in and I hope Lenard gets better soon."

"You and me both, I'm dying here." His eyes crinkled as he tried to smile.

Satisfied the guys had it handled, I left them to load into our storeroom which was accessible from the parking lot as well as inside the club. It had been my idea, the addition added to the existing structure so not to disrupt the club. It was times like these I was thankful not having to walk a delivery driver into *Diablo* when we were moments away from opening.

"Anything I should know about?" Bennett asked, flanking me as I strolled back to the bar.

I shook my head, doing a quick survey of the area before my eyes landed on Jared. "Nope, Marcus and Hank have it handled."

Regardless of my plan to keep my distance, I didn't want to be rude either. At least that was what I was calling it, my feet taking me to where he was standing. "I've set you up on my tab at the bar. You can order anything you want."

"Driving," he smiled. "And even on my salary with my crazy car payments, I can cover my own beer."

Lewis would have never turned down a free drink.

Never.

He could have hundred-dollar bills falling out of his pocket and still taken the freebie. And when he was with me, he not only took it, but expected it. Which of course, just made me feel like an even bigger idiot for not getting rid of him sooner.

"Are you sure you want to hang around, Leighton? I'll text you when I'm ready to leave if you really want to drive me home."

It just seemed. . . well, silly. He was literally going to sit solo, not drinking, watching me work. It had to not only be the least interesting way to spend a night, but a complete waste of one too. I'd already taken up so much of his time, surely he wanted to go do something else.

"Just go work, Presley. I'll find a way to entertain myself." His brow lifted and I wasn't sure what that meant. Was he going to play on his phone? Take a random survey? Join the sweaty masses on the dance floor when the DJ started playing?

Shit.

It suddenly occurred to me how a man—as good looking as Jared—might entertain himself in one of the hottest nightclubs in the city. Wasn't like in an hour or so it wasn't going to be a swarming with beautiful and available women, ready to keep him occupied.

I'd seen him with girls before, perching themselves on his lap and gazing dreamily into his beautiful blue eyes. Not with the same level of frequency as my brother, but he'd definitely had his fair share.

And what could I say? No, he shouldn't be with some other girl because I wanted him for myself? Or be jealous about a guy who wasn't even mine in the first place. I was conflicted, knowing that even if nothing happened with another woman tonight, it would eventually.

Ignoring what was rational and reasonable, I forced a smile and left to continue my rounds. People were starting to file in, and Marcus and Hank weren't back yet.

Raelle was behind the bar with Chase and Bridgit, the three of them waiting for the first wave of orders. Rae was already shaking something, testing it with a straw before sharing it with the others. She didn't even look up, completely involved in whatever new drink she was probably inventing.

Within an hour, the landscape had completely changed. Laughing, talking and music had shattered the silence, the space filling with bodies as more people started to come in. It was good, the organized chaos making me feel more settled than when I'd walked in.

Arms grabbed me around the waist, and I wasn't sure I was glad or disappointed when I saw Raelle's distinctive tattoos decorating them. I mean, of course it was Raelle, who else would it be?

"So, you wanna give me a raise?" She almost levitated, her blue eyes shining with mischief.

"Why do I think I'm probably *not* going to give you a raise but also not like whatever it is you've done?" My eyes narrowed, studying her like it might give me a clue. "What is it Rae? I'm not feeling very patient tonight."

She laughed, completely amused at my expense. "Probably sexual frustration. Which is why I'm helping. You're welcome, and enjoy your night."

A chill ran up my spine. I had no idea what she'd done, but I was almost positive it wasn't going to help.

And one look to where Leighton was sitting confirmed it.

Chapter 10

Jared

"HEY MAN! HOW are you doing?" Tibbs grinned, taking a seat beside me. "I was bored when Raelle called and told me you were looking pathetic by yourself. Figured might as well come and save you." He slapped me on the back, taking a swig from the beer I'd been nursing. "Seriously though, you'd be less conspicuous with a girl or two as company. You look like a cop."

Tibbs was the last person I was expecting to see. And had I been prepared for it, I might've been able to form words. Instead, my mouth stayed shut as I glanced over to where Presley was, oblivious that her brother had just walked in. "You know you're going to piss her off," I coughed out, the *her* in question not needing to be named. "I thought the plan was you find out what was happening with Shapiro and I was keeping an eye on Presley?"

Sure, he had as much right as anyone else to visit *Diablo*—it was still a public place and everything—maybe more so since his sister was running it. But I'd spent the better part of the day and evening trying to disguise my hard-on and pretend the woman who shared a bed with me last night wasn't the hottest thing I'd ever seen.

And yes, I'd said all that bullshit about us being friends while trying my best to keep my hands off her. What I didn't need when I was already fighting that battle was Tibbs looking over my shoulder, noticing shit that would pretty much confirm I was terrible at that game.

It had been what? A day? Twelve hours? I was still in deep with the DTs and had to pretend like it was all good.

Tibbs looked out to the dance floor, smiling in appreciation at the gyrating bodies. "Shapiro is on it, but investigations take time. He's not just going to dig up something in an hour if the PD haven't found anything. Besides, I'm climbing the walls. North and Quinn have gone to Hayden's house for dinner with the chief, and I didn't feel like dealing with the rookie."

"North AND Quinn went to dinner with Chief and Hayden? Jesus, did Mack lose his mind?" I shook my head, wondering what was stranger. The chief having a girlfriend or that he was letting North's beautiful but slightly crazy wife be involved in a date. Things were obviously going well for them if they'd moved to that stage. Still, I could understand why Tibbs didn't want to sit home alone.

"Hi boys." Two girls we'd met once before slithered into the two vacant seats. "We were hoping we'd see you."

They meant Tibbs, the pair of them hooking up with him not so long ago. While the brunette had originally showed interest in me, she quickly changed her target when she wasn't getting the attention she wanted. Tibbs didn't seem to mind, happily picking up my slack and entertaining them both.

"Ladies." Tibbs raised his eyebrows, widening his arms. "So glad you could join us. What an amazing strike of good fortune."

Not sure any of it was good fortune, especially since my night had taken a dramatic turn. It had gone from working out how I was going to drive Presley home and not fucking kiss her, to watching my best friend tag-team two women. Which should have helped the situation in a way, the sideshow he was providing enough to get my mind off his sister. Except that Presley had suddenly diverted her attention to us and not only saw her brother, but the ladies he'd attracted, one of which who was trying to sit in my lap.

"Oops, we've been spotted." Tibbs laughed, waving to Presley who was shooting such a murderous vibe I was surprised we weren't laying in pools of our own blood. "And she doesn't look happy."

No, asshole, she doesn't. And while I was sure she didn't enjoy watching Tibbs get down and dirty in her classy establishment, she was saving an extra special death glare for me.

Fucking.

Awesome.

"Yeah, not going to happen, Babe." I shook my head, making it clear that my lap and everything in it wasn't on offer. "But thanks."

Even if I didn't have the woman I wanted glaring at me a few feet away, like hell I wanted to go where Tibbs had been not even a week before. We were close, but not *that* close. And one thing we never shared was women.

And while I was dealing with Ursula the sea witch and her many arms, Presley had made her way over to get a better view.

"Tibbs." Her voice was ice cold, using the name we all did especially when she was pissed off. "Wasn't expecting you tonight." She smiled at the two ladies, both more handsy than was probably needed.

"Better I spend my money in your club than anyone else's, right?" He winked at his sister, trying to smooth it over.

She rolled her eyes, not seeing a drink in front of him other than my half-consumed beer. "Well, then enjoy. And stay out of trouble."

Her eyes glanced over to me, but she didn't say anything, forcing a smile before walking off. It wasn't even an angry walk, her measured steps taking her hot fucking legs away.

There was no need for an explanation. We weren't dating and as far as sleeping together, well that was supposed to be stopping too. But whether or not she deserved one, didn't matter. I wanted to give her one. To let her know that even if we weren't a thing—which we weren't—that I wasn't some guy who went between women like a dog. Sure, I'd had my share of casual hook ups in the past, but nothing like Tibbs. I preferred if there was a connection, with nameless random sex making me feel weird. Maybe it was my upbringing, or maybe I just needed more than the physical release. And while I never really cared what people thought, with Presley, yeah, I fucking cared.

"Listen, it's not going to happen." I did my best not to shove the brunette out of my lap. "Tibbs, I'll be back."

Not bothering to give him any more than that, I stalked after Presley. She might have been wearing killer heels, but she could really move in them when she wanted to. My path was obscured by bodies, all of them in no hurry to get out of my way as I watched her brown curls disappear from sight.

"Looking for someone?" Raelle appeared, her hands landing on her hips.

The look on her face was enough to know she knew there was *something* between me and Presley. And considering she'd been the one to call Tibbs, she was partly responsible. "I'm not fucking around, Raelle. Why did you call Tibbs?"

"Because you two seem hell-bent on keeping away from each other. So, there you go." She pointed in the direction I'd left Tibbs and his female friends. "But you can't have it both ways. You want her, then go get her. You don't, let her find someone else. She's been dicked around plenty, she doesn't need that from you."

Raelle was maybe five-three, and would've been lucky to weigh one fifteen. But what she lacked in physicality she made up for in attitude, her intention to protect her friend, clear.

"I'm not dicking her around, we're friends," I answered, annoyed I had to justify myself to her.

She laughed, flipping me off. "Then go back to your posse, Leighton. Presley's busy."

Not giving me a chance to respond she left, heading back to the bar like the conversation hadn't even taken place. Meanwhile, I was left in the middle of the floor surrounded by people I didn't know and/or like.

Annoyed and determined to find Presley, I moved back where I knew her office was. There was a better-than-average chance that Bennett was going to stop me, but that was the risk I was willing to take.

Surprisingly, it was someone else.

Marcus.

He didn't even speak, tipping his head and waiting for me to explain.

"I need to see Presley."

"Does she want to see you?" he asked, drilling a hole in my head.

"Yes, she does."

My voice had been calm but underneath I was itching to move the guy out of the way and get to her. I hated I had to do the song and dance every time, and that she was already neck deep in assumptions.

Marcus turned, knocking on Presley's door. "Boss, you have a visitor."

She didn't respond, the click of the lock popping open as Marcus twisted the knob and held it ajar. He nodded to the door, waiting until I'd stepped through before closing it again.

I'd expected her to be seated, the huge desk of hers in the way, but she wasn't. Her beautiful body was leaning against the wood, her long legs crossed at the ankle as her hands kept her steady. She looked fucking beautiful, her long hair covering her soft bare shoulders, and I was all out of steam. "Leighton, I'm not sure why you came in here, but it was unnecessary. You're a big boy and you can do what you want. I'll still drive home with you if that's what you want, unless of course your plans have changed and then I'll get a ride with Rae."

Her voice didn't crack, no anger or sign of jealousy, lacking the venom that I was sort of expecting. And, fuck me, if I wasn't a little disappointed.

"I lied to you." I shook my head, annoyed more at myself than anyone else.

Her eyes narrowed, the calm exterior showing its first sign of a crack. "What did you lie about?"

I moved closer, not even hesitating as I touched her chin. "That I'd be able to be this close and not touch you. I know you need a good guy right now, but I just can't be him."

My mouth went to hers, kissing her liked I'd wanted to when she first walked out in that dress, my hands yanking her from her perch on the desk and into my arms. She didn't hesitate, kissing me right back as her fingers threaded through my hair.

It was primal, the urge to rip off our clothes and go at it right on the floor edging up my spine. I needed to touch her everywhere, to show her exactly how much I wanted her and how much my original idea sucked. "Fuck me," I groaned, her body positioning against my hard-on as she settled between my legs.

The pressure was delicious, her hips rocking as she found exactly where she wanted me, a satisfied moan mumbled against my lips.

"You're a good guy, Jared. But I want to fuck you too."

Her usual control was missing, her hands locked around my T-shirt as she tried and failed to rip it off. I was positive having sex with her in that office was not a good idea but since we'd already established I was done trying to be the good guy, I couldn't work up the energy to care.

Maneuvering us to her desk, I lowered her back on the edge. She kept rocking, trying to recover the friction she'd lost as I continued to fuck her mouth with everything I had.

"Yeah, right here?" I asked, my fingers moving between us and hiking up her dress. Her white satin panties were pressed against my crotch, her leg lifting on my hip to give me better access.

I took that as a yes, lifting my body from hers just long enough so I could push those panties down. I didn't even bother taking them all the way off, letting them fall to the floor so they pooled around her ankles.

Her eyes widened as my fingers went right in for the kill, no hesitation as they circled her entrance and then plunged all the way in. She was hot and wet, clamping around me as her body shuttered, jutting her hips forward so I could get in deeper.

"Yes." Her head tilted back as she arched, her breathy moans getting more desperate. "Please, yes."

Trying to use the hand not buried inside her, my uncoordinated attempt to undo my belt and button was taking too long. "Give me a minute." I kissed her, pulling out my fingers and undoing my pants.

Her eyes widened seeing my already hard cock as I yanked down my jeans and boxer briefs. I didn't even bother getting them all the way down, pushing them below my hips and reaching for the condom in my back pocket.

Yeah, I might have intended not to fuck her, but I wasn't completely delusional either. And on the chance I wasn't as honorable as I was trying to be, I needed to be prepared. Present me was currently giving past me a massive high-five.

"Jared," her hands went to my dick, jerking me off while I was trying to get on the condom, "fuck me already."

"Jesus, Presley." I was going to come in her hand if she didn't stop. I'd been turned on for hours and now that I had the opportunity, I wasn't sure how much longer I could hold on. "Let me get this on."

I ripped her fingers from around my shaft, sheathing myself as quick as I could, my eyes unable to stop looking at her.

She was beautiful, so fucking hot and ready for me, and if I thought for a second I'd be able to give all of that up, I was insane.

It was too effort to take off the rest of our clothes, positioning myself at her entrance as she rocked her hips. It was impossible to hold back, pushing into her in one swift thrust as I felt her tighten around me.

Man, it felt good. Tight and hot, and so fucking perfect I needed a second to just absorb it before I started moving again.

Greedy, needy moans escaped her lips, making my pulse spike, and suddenly not moving was no longer an option. "I want you, Presley. I want you so fucking much."

My hips pistoned, chasing the high as my balls rose up tight. Her brown eyes flashed to mine, one hand planted on my chest while the other was at her side helping her balance.

I wasn't gentle, dragging my length in and out of her, harder and faster with each swing. "You know how hard it was to see you in this dress and not touch you," I grunted, unleashing the pent-up frustration I'd kept a lid on since she walked out wearing it. "Pure torture, Presley. Sweet, sexy, motherfucking torture."

"It wasn't supposed to be torture." She arched into me. "I just like the dress."

Whatever her reasoning was, I no longer cared, the dress the least of my concerns as her breathing got faster.

She was close. Hanging off the edge, needing the tiniest of pushes and I was more than happy to give it to her. I reached down between us, not a lot of space for my hand, and pressed my thumb against her clit. It was swollen and needy like the rest of her, her body reacting almost instantly on contact.

"Oh, Jared," she breathed out, her hand against my chest fisting my T-shirt in desperation. "Yes, yes."

My thumb circled, keeping the pressure tight against her as I continued to thrust.

She was right there, right *there*, her beautiful brown eyes opening wide as she let out a scream. She smacked her palm against her mouth, deadening the sound as I felt the tight squeeze followed by the gentle pulses down my shaft.

That was all it took, knowing she'd found her high giving me permission to find mine as I detonated into her. I couldn't even stop, needing to tease every last drop of ecstasy from both of us as my dick continued to throb.

"I've never had sex in my office," it came out in a pant, her eyes still wide, "but I couldn't wait."

"Baby, you think I could?" My lips brushed against hers, needing to kiss her some more. "I already told you I've been dying since we left your apartment. It took everything I had not to take you in my fucking car."

She smiled, the thought of defiling my prized Stang, pleasing her. Or maybe it was because I'd finally come to my senses. Because just being her *friend* was no longer a choice.

My forehead pressed against hers, kissing her some more. "I want you. I want you tonight and tomorrow, and every night after that. You think we can make that happen?"

Her hand reached up tracing my jaw. "Yes. But is this going to be a friends-with-benefits kind of deal? Because I'm not ready to lose Leighton."

"What are you talking about? I'm right here." I laughed, slightly confused.

"No, you're Jared. The sexy firefighter who makes me wet. Leighton is the sweet thoughtful guy who is my friend. And I kinda like both of them."

"Presley, you're making it sound like I have a split personality. I'm the same fucking person, and you're not going to have to choose. You get it all, Baby." I landed a playful bite on her bare shoulder, amused by her logic.

Guess I'd kind of done the same thing, seeing her as the sweet innocent sister of my best friend as well as the hot sex bomb who made me irrationally hard.

Giving her one last kiss, I slowly pulled out, holding my dick at the base. I discarded the condom, cleaned up and got myself back into my jeans while she did the same and fished her panties from the floor.

"You should probably go back out there. Tibbs is going to wonder where you've been." Her panties dangled from her fingers, making no attempt to slip them back on.

Oh.

Fuck.

It wasn't like I'd forgotten about Tibbs, or his lack of knowledge, but it was hard to think of anything other than Presley when she was standing in front of me. Probably how I was able to literally leave him at the table and then go fuck his sister. Still, while I was positive he wasn't going to like it—the danger of a physical confrontation very real—I wasn't going to run from it either.

"You want me to tell him? Because Presley, I will. I'll go right out there and let him know."

"Are you crazy?" She laughed, her eyes widening once she saw I was serious. "You *know* he's going to be a complete asshole about it and cause a scene. I don't want that at the club, especially not when I have a crowd. We should tell him, but we need to find the right moment. In the meantime, my life and who I'm sleeping with aren't any of his business."

Yeah, she had a point there. Tibbs wasn't exactly known for being level-headed and reasonable, the audience not enough of a deterrent to stop the explosion.

"So we wait. I'm sure once everything cools down with Lewis and everything else, it won't be so bad." It was wishful thinking but there was no point losing any sleep over it in the meantime. Tibbs would have to get over it, and he had to know the last person on earth who'd disrespect Presley would be me.

"Agreed. You should probably go back to your little party." Her brow rose, waiting for my response.

"You think that's what I'm going to do? Leave you and then go off with one of them? You know that isn't happening. If Tibbs wasn't sitting beside me, they wouldn't have even bothered. Everything had been going just fine until he showed up."

Presley closed her eyes, shaking her head as she cursed under her breath. "Right, everything was fine until Raelle called Tibbs. I swear, I'm going to kill her."

Not that I didn't disagree that the need to call her brother was unnecessary—didn't need my hand held—but how that warranted Raelle's death didn't add up. "Why? Because she made the call?"

"No." Presley huffed out a breath. "Because she knows he's basically a whore and there'd be women too. She knew about us, and this was her way of forcing our hand. She played us both."

"So you were jealous?" The smile edged at my lips.

She rolled her eyes. "Maybe a little."

It was cute, that she thought she'd be so easily replaced by a cheap knock off. "Or maybe she was just showing me what I didn't want. Let's not kill her just yet."

"True, and to be honest trying to replace her mid shift would be such a pain. I'll at least wait until I find another bartender." She shrugged, like she was actually giving it some thought.

"Now that we have that sorted," I kissed her, finding it hard to stop, "I better go deal with Tibbs. And in case there's any confusion, I'll be driving you home."

"You don't think he's going to ask any questions?"

"Just leave that up to me."

Chapter 11

Jared

TIBBS WAS A simple man. You put a woman in front of him and the room could be on fire and he'd only notice after he started to choke on the smoke. With two, the poor bastard would burn alive in that room. Which was why when I walked back to the table, my buzz still riding high after sex with Presley, I wasn't surprised to see him making out with both of the girls. He didn't even ask where I'd gone, thankful that when I'd returned I'd brought beer with me.

As an added bonus, the two ladies weren't just interested in dry-humping and making out, the suggestion they leave and find somewhere more private happening sooner than later. Tibbs was conflicted for about three seconds, fisting his keys and waving me goodbye the minute I'd reassured him I'd drive Presley home.

Couldn't have gone better if I'd planned it myself, thankful for Raelle and her evil genius plan, even if I didn't like being a pawn in anyone's game.

So while I spent the rest of the night solo, I was far from bored. My eyes followed Presley around the room like a stalker, content to sit there like a loser, yet knowing I was going home with her.

It was late by the time we finally got to Presley's apartment. And even though both of us were dead tired, a tangle of arms and legs impatiently reached for each other the minute we'd shut the door. I only had one more day before I was back on rotation, and I was going to spend every last minute of it with her.

We had sex more times than I could count, fast and hard, and slow and soft, the need to take her only more amped up now that I'd given myself permission.

Her body was insanely hot, and she knew what to do with it, every inch of her perfection as I covered all of it with my mouth, hands and cock.

And when we were finally exhausted, I slept beside her in her bed. I loved the feeling of her warm body up against mine, my hands being able to touch her, teasing out those soft, breathy moans as I explored.

It was late afternoon before either of us moved off the bed. We'd skipped both breakfast and lunch, keeping our hands off each other long enough to order pizza and then eat it naked on her couch. It was going to be tough leaving, Presley, absolutely my newest addiction.

"I'm just going to take a shower," her hand reached down and stroked my cock. "I know you have to go home soon and get some sleep."

Just hearing those words made me antsy, knowing whether I wanted to or not, I was going to have to walk out the door in an hour or two. "Maybe I can nap here," I groaned as she jerked me off. It wasn't just me who was having trouble keeping my hands to myself, Presley, just as guilty. "And I can head back after I drop you off at work."

It was a good plan, or at least the best one I could think of when her hand was wrapped around my dick. Although the way she was looking at me, she could've suggested I call in sick and I'd have agreed.

She shook her head, sliding down to her knees before circling the head of my cock with her tongue. "I need sleep too, and I won't get any if you're here. You're too tempting."

"Presley, telling me to leave when you're doing that isn't exactly convincing. Not that I'm complaining." My eyes squeezed shut, her mouth taking my length. "Fuck, that feels so good."

Yeah, leaving was going to suuuuuuck.

She pulled my cock out with a pop, kissing the tip before slithering back up to her feet, my eyes flashing open. "Then I'll stop." The grin spread across her lips.

Evil.

She was pure evil.

"You're just going to stop?" My straining dick in as much disbelief as I was. "Whatever point you're trying to prove, I've got it."

"My point is for you to go home, sleep and then come back here after your shift. I assume you still have my spare key. I really like having you in my bed, Jared, and like waking up with you even more."

On that we could agree.

My arms wrapped around her body, pulling her close as I kissed her. "And there's no place I'd rather be. You going to be okay tonight by yourself?"

I hated even asking the question, worried it implied that I thought she wasn't strong enough to deal. She was plenty strong, and she sure didn't need me or anyone else. But even I would want backup if I had a crazy ex breaking into my apartment and whose intentions hadn't been ascertained.

"I'll be fine. Rae can give me a ride home and I'll give Bennett a call to drive me in. I promised I wouldn't take any unnecessary risks, and I mean it."

Hearing her say that gave me a relief I didn't know I needed. Not to say I was pleased that another guy was going to be involved. I still had no idea where *Bennett* fit into her life, and I wasn't going to ruin what we had by asking.

"So now that we've gotten that taken care of." I kissed her lightly on the lips, my dick still hard. "How about we go take a shower together, save time and water, and it means I can make you come one last time before I have to leave."

Her body stiffened. Not a lot but enough for me to notice. And even though she was wearing a smile, I knew I'd crossed some invisible line. "Not sure much showering would go on, maybe some other time. You wanna go first?"

It was an offer I wasn't excited about accepting, not wanting to push an issue I didn't really understand. So instead of just asking her, putting whatever crazy ideas out of my head, I shrugged and told her she should go, and I'd get one at my place.

Tibbs had already messaged three times looking for me and I hadn't responded. And if I hadn't occasionally been known to spend the night with a girl and not check in, he might have been worried. So while he hadn't put a trace on my phone just yet, looking to locate me, I had a hunch there would be questions when I eventually got in.

"Baby, I'm going to head home." I grabbed my clothes and tossed them on, the redress not taking long since I was no longer distracted. "Text me if you need anything, and I'll be back Thursday morning."

Her head popped out from her bathroom door, the frosted glass hiding her beautiful body. "Okay, be careful out there and I give you permission to wake me with sex when you get in. Seriously, Jared, if you're not going down on me when I open my eyes, I'll be disappointed."

"Not a difficult promise to make, Presley." I swallowed hard, wanting to take her up on the offer right the hell then. I was still hard from the abandoned blowjob and needed very little encouragement. But she was right, we both needed sleep and leaving wasn't going to get any easier. "You be careful too."

Reluctantly I left Presley's loft, taking the short drive to the apartment I shared with Tibbs. He'd be awake for sure, probably about a minute or two away from calling the chief to see if anyone had seen me.

"Jesus, Leighton, between you and my sister, not sure which of you is giving me the bigger headache. You want to answer your phone once in a while?"

Predictably he was annoyed, me going off radar for so long, not the usual. "Sorry, forgot to charge it," I lied. "Anything I should know about?"

"You first. Where the hell were you?" He glared at me, and part of me was worried he'd figured it out. After all, he knew I was driving Presley home . . . might not be a stretch to assume I didn't leave.

"I was with someone," I hedged, not willing to volunteer anything but not wanting to dig the hole too deep. "Things got a little intense, so I stayed the night."

Again, nothing out of the ordinary. While Tibbs occasionally did one-night stand drive-bys, I tended to stick around a little longer.

"So, what? You drove Presley home and then went and hooked up?" He scratched his head, completely oblivious that was *exactly* how it happened. Only thing he hadn't clued in on, that there wasn't another girl involved.

"Yes. I dropped Presley home, checked her apartment and then . . ." I left the sentence trailing, part of me feeling guilty I was deliberately being cagey.

He shrugged, usually not giving a shit about my sex life one way or the other. "Is that why you weren't into the girl at the bar? You got someone on the regular?"

"I'm hoping so, but it's early days. You know how it is."

It had been a while since we'd had girlfriends and it wasn't just the hours. Girls liked the uniform, the fanfare that went with it, and some even got off on the hero bullshit. Not too proud to admit I'd capitalized on it in my time, happy to accept the bountiful gifts the service gave me. But long term, it wasn't as exciting as it sounded. There were missed birthdays or anniversaries, and times when all you wanted to do on your day off was crash for a solid ten hours. And it wasn't fair to expect someone to wait around for the scraps you could maybe offer them.

That wasn't even taking into account the worry, the idea that when that alarm sounded sometimes not everyone would make it home. Fuck, it wasn't even just the fires. I'd had a gun pulled on me more than once, the last time three weeks ago attending a head on collision. The driver was obviously high, waving his 45 around and resisting medical assistance despite us needing to cut him out of his goddamn car. So yeah, a relationship was a heavy commitment you didn't want to ask of someone unless you were fairly sure they had the stomach for it.

"Anyone I know?" he asked, probably wondering why I hadn't already spilled.

Yep.

That was how it was going to go.

"You've met her," I offered, figuring it was the closest I could get to the truth without fucking it up. "Look, I know you have a lot on your mind with Presley. We'll talk about it after we see how it all pans out. Anyway, it's very likely she'll get sick of me and I'll be back to single status before ever making it official."

And as much as I hated to admit it, that wasn't necessarily a lie. Who knew if after a week or two, Presley wouldn't decide she wanted something else. Right now, we were both having fun and who even knew what the future held. All I knew was I wasn't going to get worked up about it, enjoying what we had while it lasted, committed to not fucking up our friendship even if the sex stopped. It was a longshot, but I'd seen it done. Fuck, Cole—one of our EMTs—was the best man at his ex-wife's wedding. He and his new wife even holidayed with the happy couple and somehow it had all worked out.

"Okay, but just because my head is tied up with my sister, don't think I can't shoot the shit if you need to. I already owe you with everything you've done, last thing I need is to rack up a debt from being a shitty friend too."

Perfect, because I didn't already feel like a jerk.

"Tibbs, it's all good man." I clapped him around the shoulder. "You're far from a shitty friend, and there is nothing I need right now. But if this little heart-to-heart is over, I could use some decent sleep."

He laughed, a smile spreading across his lips. "Gotcha, buddy. If the way you look is anything to go by, not a lot of *sleeping* went down last night. Make sure you set your alarm though, we both know I can't be trusted to wake us both up in the morning."

"Brother, I could be half-dead and still make it to work on time. I'll see you in the morning." And with a wave, I forgot all about the shower I hadn't taken and collapsed into bed.

"Jared."

My name moaned from her lips was the sweetest sound I'd ever heard, one last flick of my tongue making her come hard on my mouth. She'd made me promise to wake her when I got in, and I had spent most of the twenty-four hours apart thinking of exactly that. She was obviously tired, probably getting home only a few hours earlier and I'd finished what had been a largely uneventful shift. Calls came in, we went out and when it was time to finally clock out, I waved goodbye to my buddies at the stationhouse and went right back to Presley.

Going down on her was the highlight of my morning, her fingers still gripping my hair as the last of the tremors left her body.

"Good morning." I planted a kiss on her thigh, working my way up the bed. "It's still early though, so if you want to roll over and go back to sleep, I'm happy to join you."

A contented sigh spilled from her lips, closing her eyes as I shuffled in beside her. I'd already lost my clothes, stripping at the door, pulling her naked body next to mine under the covers. "Mmmmm, you feel so nice."

Her skin was soft, the faint smell of bodywash still lingering as I kissed her shoulder.

"That felt sooooo goooood." Her ass wiggled against my dick, the breathy moan and the ass action making me even harder. "I totally owe you a blowjob when I wake up properly," she giggled.

"Let's worry about my payment when you're more coherent. If I didn't know how tired you were, I might have been offended you just came and are ready to go back to sleep. But I'm a big boy and know how talented I am, so there's no way it was lack of technique."

She laughed again, grabbing my hand and shoving it up against her tit. "Lack of technique is so *not* your problem. But," she yawned, "you're right, I need sleep. Especially after that mind-blowing orgasm."

I liked holding her while she slept, dozing off with her and knowing she'd be there when I woke up. Hadn't really cared much about it before, not really concerned about cuddling. And if I hadn't already been a fan, I'd become a full-blown convert when she took her turn waking me. My cock between her pretty pink lips, a sight I'd never get sick of.

After more sex, because clearly we were fiends, we showered—separately—and then got dressed. I'd been more organized and packed an overnight bag, meaning I didn't have to head home to get a fresh set of clothes.

"You want to go get something to eat?" I asked, last night's dinner a distant memory. "I know you don't do breakfast, but surely it would count as lunch." I checked my watch, the display showing just past noon.

"I have a meeting at *Diablo* and can't be late. It's an important client. But if you want to go get something and then meet me later, I don't mind."

Not sure what she was thinking but me leaving after having not seen her for an entire day wasn't happening. I didn't care when or where we ate, committed to spending as much time with her as possible. It was like a sickness, the need to be near her probably not very healthy, but I was far from wanting a cure.

"Or I can drive you to your meeting and then go get us something for when you're done," I suggested, positive at some point she was going to have to eat. "Unless you don't want me cramping your style."

She rolled her eyes, grabbing me by the T-shirt and pulling me closer. "Just kiss me already, you moron. You could never cramp my style."

With our plans set we got into my car and drove to *Diablo*. Traffic was average, not taking us long to cover the couple of blocks between her loft and the club.

"So you're going to get lunch?" She looked at me with excitement, her hand hovering on the door handle. "Or was that just a ploy to come creep on me at work? Because I have to say if you're using food as a bargaining chip, that is not cool."

I scoffed, pretending to be offended. "Oh, so I see how it is. You're just with me for the services I can provide. Last time I checked, I didn't turn into Uber Eats, Presley."

"I know, I know, I'm terrible. But I get cranky when I'm hungry. You don't want me to be cranky, do you?"

Just one look at those big brown eyes and I'd do pretty much anything she asked. Go get lunch, drive to Utah, get a tattoo on my ass of *Diablo's* logo. She had to know the kind of power those babies wielded, willing to put myself through epic-level shit just to make her happy. "Fine, I'll walk you in and make sure Bennett is around, then I'll go get us lunch. You have a preference?"

"Anything, just no burgers. Proper food, okay? We can eat in my office when you get back."

Agreeing to get her *proper* food, I walked her to the door and waited as she unlocked it. We walked in, the place completely deserted except for a guy at the bar restocking.

"Hey Boss." He lifted his hand and waved. "Need anything?"

"All good, Hank, thanks."

It was obvious the staff loved her, something I'd seen whenever I walked through the doors. Every single one of them would volunteer to drop what they were doing if she needed something, just like Hank had offered to do. It was similar to what I had at the stationhouse with the guys, the sense of family that elevated what I did from just being a job. And I liked she had that too, albeit with a different pecking order.

"You doing an inspection? I think you'll find we're up to code." Bennett didn't bother with the hello, materializing from thin air before folding his arms across his chest. He really was an agile son of a bitch. Something else to be glad about, especially since one of his jobs was to protect Presley.

"Just dropping Presley off, I'll be back soon." I tipped my chin, knowing he was probably expecting some pushback. "You want some lunch?"

It would have been easy to get into a pissing contest, to try and assert which of us had more of a right to be there. I was almost positive he was more than a little territorial, and that extended to Presley as well. Didn't make me feel good to know he might've had designs on her. For all I knew, he was looking for the right time to make the jump from professional to personal. But if I was going to be with her, I was going to have to trust her. And regardless of whether he was just a meathead with a superiority complex or was in love with his boss, he'd take a bullet for her for sure. Something I could respect.

"Lunch?" he asked, his usual lack of expression MIA as he couldn't hide his surprise.

"Yeah, I'm going out to get us something. You want in?"

He considered it, shooting his eyes to Presley before responding. "Sure, I'll have whatever she's having, let me know what I owe you."

"All good, I've got it." I waved, taking a step toward Presley before stopping.

Shit, without thinking, I was about to kiss her. Put my lips on hers in front of Hank and Bennett and whoever else was around.

It would have been just that easy.

But being kissed in front of her employees wasn't only a bad idea but also stupid considering no one was supposed to know we were together. Fuck, as far as they were concerned I was the good "friend," playing errand boy, giving her a ride so her brother didn't lose his mind. So we were a hell of a long way from where I could just kiss her in public and it was okay.

With my reality in check, I gave her the same stupid chin tip I'd given Bennett, a weird wave and said goodbye. She looked amused as I retreated, no doubt laughing her ass off at my expense.

It wasn't until I was at the door that my phone buzzed, the incoming message from the woman I'd just said goodbye to. No words just a kissy face emoji, the subtext not all that clear.

She'd either been taunting me *or* had wanted that kiss as much as I had.

There was no way to know which.

So taking my fake role seriously, I went and got her, me, and the guy who may or may not be in love with her some lunch.

Because clearly, that made sense.

Chapter 12

Presley

SCOTT ARRIVED MINUTES after Jared left, his beaming smile unperturbed by the scowl Bennett was giving him. And without much fanfare, I welcomed him into my office and locked the door.

"So you and some of your friends want to open a club in L.A. and need a venue manager." He'd barely sat down when I started talking, the look of surprise on his face priceless.

"Smart as well as beautiful, that's a lethal mix." His smile edged wider, trying to recover. "But yeah, there is no one else who I'd like on my team."

He continued at my urging, trying to wow me with how much social influence he had which of course meant he could turn up at a yogurt bar and draw a crowd. He had no actual market research and no real theme setting himself apart, just the promise that money was no object and he wanted some of the creative control. "I mean, the place is going to have my name on it, it should look like I had a hand in it too."

Speechless, absolutely speechless.

It was only after he'd petered out—his *brilliant* and *compelling* pitch going for a full twenty minutes—that I attempted to speak. My words chosen wisely because what I wanted to say wasn't very polite.

"Scott, as flattering as the offer is," *where I did all the work and he took all the glory*, "I really don't think our interests are aligned. Working with the amount of partners you are talking about will be messy, too many cooks if you know what I mean. And while you seem to have a clear vision of what you want to achieve, it would cost millions and months to get a venue up and running with those kinds of operational requirements. I mean, hot tubs and massage rooms, it's a lot. Not to mention the possible violations it opens you up to."

"See, that's why I want you. You come in with your brainy stuff, make it all happen. Fuck it, I'll even let you pick a room we can include. What do you like? Puppies? Lipstick? Cupcakes? Woah... we could have a section where you dance in frosting, like those crazy foam parties in Ibiza. Shit, that would be brilliant. And let's face it, who the hell *doesn't* like frosting."

He had to be kidding.

Had to be.

Because no man in his right fucking mind would think anyone would want to dance in a vat of frosting and pay for the privilege. It was just too insane.

"Scott, I'm sorry, but that is a hard no from me. Your club sounds like a . . ." *disaster, shitshow, dumpster fire,* "interesting, but not the kind of project I want to be involved in."

I was just about to usher him out, and end what had truly been a waste of my time when he made one last attempt.

"I'll give you equity. Not just a salary but a share in the business and the profits. And we'll cut the bells and whistles in the main part of the club and have a private room just for me and my friends."

"Scott, I—"

"Come on, Presley. I *need* this." It was as if I was seeing him for the first time, the fake exterior completely gone as his walls dropped. "You know how hard it is to live in the shadow of my dad? Help me out here. I'll cut the bullshit, I swear, and we'll do it completely your way."

The confident swagger he'd came in with was gone, and in its place, desperation. He wanted this, and not just so he and his friends had a place to party. He was determined to have some kind of success that his father hadn't been a part of.

"Look, Scott, I get it." I stood, walking around my desk, genuinely feeling compassion however ill deserved it was. "But this *isn't* the way to do it. I'm sorry, but even if I could pick up and move across the country to set up this club for you, there are too many variables. It is a huge gamble, and I'm not just talking money. It could affect your career too, demolish your personal brand. Think about buying a vineyard, something social but where you can maintain most of the commercial control. You get the winemakers to do their bit, and you get a product you can sell to every licensed venue in America. It won't be your name on a door, but on the shelf of every club and bar across the country. And I don't need to tell you about the ridiculous marketing opportunities for promotional parties at all those bars and venues? It would be a non-stop party coast-to-coast."

It wasn't a new idea. Rock stars, actors, and celebrities of every kind of persuasion had been bottling booze and putting on a fancy label. And for good reason, most of the time, it was incredibly profitable.

So if Scott needed me to throw him a bone . . .

"Jesus, Presley, you're a fucking genius." He leaped out of his seat and stopped as he moved to hug me. It had surprised both of us, his hands out, his body inches from mine, the contact suspended in a moment of indecision. "Sorry." He dropped his hands, the apology written on his face. "I got caught up in the moment. I promise I'm not trying to hit on you."

I laughed, amused at the contradiction. It was a completely different Scott Collins to the guy I'd met the other night, and I liked the new version better. "If I hug you, are you going to make it inappropriate?" I asked against my better judgment.

"Well, considering I've given you enough material to seriously fuck me over, I'm a little scared." He chuckled as he moved closer and wrapped his arms around me. "Thanks, Presley. I owe you."

There was a subtle knock at the door, and I assumed either Jared was back, or Bennett was checking on me. And I knew how quickly the hug could be seen as something other than it was. I pulled away, feeling slightly guilty even though I had no reason to, and gestured to the exit. "Well, let me know how it goes and I expect a case of whatever when you go to market."

"Are you kidding? You'll get the first bottle off the line." He grinned, following me to the door. "And seriously, thanks. We both know you probably just saved my ass."

My hand went to the lock, the door popping open almost instantly. It was Bennett, and as much as I hated to admit it, part of me was glad.

Things between me and Jared were not only new but ambiguous, the terms of our new relationship not really discussed. It wasn't just sex, with real feelings there but the last thing I wanted was for something as stupid as a misunderstanding screwing it all up.

"Great timing, just wrapping up here." I opened the door wider, inviting Bennett in. "And it was great seeing you again, Scott. Make sure you keep in touch."

Scott nodded, putting out his hand as a final goodbye but unable to hide his excitement. "I will now I have your number." He winked, the old Scott making a reappearance.

I assumed it was for Bennett's benefit, pretending to be the playboy to keep up appearances. But I let it slide, choosing not to say anything as I waved him goodbye. It was only after Scott had left and the door was closed, that Bennett said what I was sure he'd been dying to say.

"You sleeping with him?" His brow popped.

"I could fire you for that," I deadpanned, knowing if it was anyone else asking it, they'd be gone without a second thought.

A smile broke across Bennett's face, ignoring the threat of unemployment. "You could, but you won't. So answer the question."

"Of course I'm not sleeping with Scott Collins," I scoffed, a little offended Bennett thought I'd be so easily charmed. "What did you think we did? Go at it on my desk?" *Ironic, because that was exactly what I'd done with Jared.* "He's not even my type."

He rolled his eyes, shaking his head. "Not the sock puppet, Presley. I'm talking about *Towering Inferno.*"

It was my turn to roll my eyes. "What does it matter?"

"So that's an affirmative. You going to make me start being nice to him?" he chuckled. "Because I have to say, Presley, it's more fun if I jerk him around. Especially now that I know you're sleeping with him."

My eyes went to the door half expecting Jared to burst in and I wouldn't be able to deny it. "I didn't say I was."

A loud baritone laugh escaped Bennett's mouth. "Sweetheart, it's written all over your face. Your brother know? Please tell me he doesn't."

"When did you turn into a gossip?" I punched him in the arm, my small fist barely leaving a mark. "And for the record, nothing is written on my face."

It was at that moment that Jared walked in, a bag of food hanging from his fingers as he pushed the half-open door. "Hey." He looked to me and then to Bennett, probably seeing something that wasn't there.

Great.

I'd avoided one possible misunderstanding and landed in another—karma was a complete bitch.

"Hey! Is that lunch? I'm starved." I moved closer to Jared, wondering if he was going to flat out ask or just assume the worst.

Bennett moved closer too, his huge body needing only two steps before he was standing beside Jared, his hand landing on his shoulder. "You hurt her and there won't be enough of you for a funeral. I made the mistake of not getting involved in her personal life once, not making it again."

Jared's eyes went to me, the confusion clear. But he didn't back down either, tipping his chin and meeting Bennett's gaze. "Guess that's something we can agree on. And I would *never* hurt, Presley."

"Talking about me like I'm not here, isn't doing either of you any good. Do I need to remind you that I'm more than capable of handling myself?"

I knew I should be annoyed, and part of me was, but not for the reasons I was advertising. I adored Bennett and knew if he ever saw Lewis again, no one else would. And with Jared, well, I had a hunch he'd do the same. But I wasn't going to be annoyed I had not only one but two men willing to stand up for me. What kind of idiot turns down that kind of support? I just wished I hadn't needed it.

Both of them turned, Jared locking eyes with me and ignoring the weird vibe in the room. "No need for the reminder. Just letting you know you have back up."

Bennett grinned like a moron. "Incidentally, if you don't want people to know you're sleeping together, you might want to lay off the ass kissing. Dead giveaway. *That* and that stupid look on your face."

"Really, B?" I glared, trying to hide my grin. "I thought you agreed to play nice?"

Bennett scoffed, "I didn't agree to shit." He looked over at Jared, his smirk barely contained. "And P.S. You might want to tell your boy you're screwing his sister. Now, what did you get for lunch? It better not have too many carbs, I'm watching my weight."

Jared didn't flinch, lifting the bag in his hand. "Well good news then, because I got you a salad. And I'll tell Tibbs when I'm ready."

"Okay, let's dial down the testosterone." I got between them, my body a makeshift barrier that could be snapped in two, if either of them got out of control. "And for your sake, Leighton, you better not have gotten *me* a salad."

Jared laughed, a smile of his own appearing. "Of course not. I got you a chicken and veggie bowl."

"Why the fuck do I get salad? Didn't I tell you to get me whatever you got Presley?" Bennett argued, annoyed his lunch was going to be on the light side.

"Yeah, you did. I might be kissing Presley's ass, but I'm sure as shit not kissing yours. Maybe next time be less of a jerk and I'll get you something decent." He smirked, pulling out the plastic clamshell container and held it for Bennett to take.

Cursing under his breath, Bennett took his salad and stormed out of the room leaving the door open so we could hear his displeasure even though he'd left my office.

"And here I thought you were a nice guy." I wrapped my arms around him, lifting my lips to kiss him.

"Oh, I am a nice guy, Presley. But don't think for a second I don't have the capacity to be a total prick." His smile edging wider as he leaned down and kissed me.

"YOU GOT HANK A FUCKING CHICKEN AND VEGGIE BOWL TOO?!" Bennett's voice boomed from outside the room.

"See?" He tipped his head to the door. "*Total* prick. Now, let's eat before Bennett comes back and tries to wrestle the bag from my hands."

My hand gripped his shirt, able to kiss him how I wanted to since we no longer had an audience. "I know I shouldn't like you mean, but it's kind of a turn on."

"That's kind of messed up, Presley. And considering how much I like it, not sure what that says about me."

He didn't hesitate, kissing me like he meant it as he walked me back to the desk. The door was still open so we couldn't get too crazy, but we were using the small amount of privacy the walls of my office afforded us.

I loved the way his lips felt, their teasing both demanding and urgent. Like nothing could be taken for granted, and he didn't know when he'd kiss me again.

Maybe, that was exactly it.

He was the first to pull away, the crumbling bag against my back reminding me he was still holding onto our lunch.

"Now, should I be worried about your meeting with Scott Collins?" His head tipped to the side, the curiosity simmering in his eyes.

Since he hadn't mentioned it earlier, I'd assumed he hadn't seen Scott. Obviously I'd been wrong, Jared either seeing him leave my office or *Diablo* on his way back.

"You're worried?" I teased, glad he was asking me outright rather than jumping to conclusions. I liked that, that he didn't just assume the meeting had been anything other than business.

"Presley, have you looked in a mirror? Of course, I'm worried. The guy walks into a room and ladies cream their pants. I'm confident, but I'm not stupid."

His grin told me otherwise, and I couldn't imagine him feeling inadequate. He'd always been larger than life, Justin's cocky best friend who always had a woman hanging off his every word.

"It was business. Buuuuuut," I figured it was as good a time as any, "you know, I could ask you the same thing."

He shook his head, dismissing the notion. "Presley, he seems like a nice guy, but I'm straight. Not interested."

"Oh ha, ha, ha," I mock laughed. "You're forgetting I've seen you with other women. In my club, Leighton." I pushed a finger into his chest. "Now, I'm not going to punish you for the stuff you've done before, because that would be dumb. But considering we haven't really talked about what's going on here . . . is this an exclusive thing?"

It had been me who initially said I could do casual, promising I wouldn't turn into the clingy girlfriend who demanded things. And, that was what I had intended to be. But I wasn't so sure I'd be able to share him, the idea of him with another woman driving me crazy.

"In case you hadn't noticed, Presley, the last few times I was in *your* club, I went home alone. That wasn't because I didn't have choices."

It *was* something I'd noticed, probably a little too much, but refused to read too much into it. "So what are your choices now?"

"You, and only you. I'm not interested in anyone else, Presley. And I don't want you with anyone else either."

Those words were exactly what I'd wanted to hear, both excited and relieved I hadn't been the only one feeling what I had between us. "Do you think it can work? Us actually date and be a regular couple?"

Things were complicated, and while we were in the bubble, we didn't have to really face the regular relationship stuff. It was fun, exciting, and completely isolated from everyone else. And while I was fully prepared to put up with whatever happened when my family found out, the last thing I wanted to do was force Jared to make a choice.

His best friend.

Or me.

"We can do whatever we want, Presley. We already tried keeping away from each other and that didn't work. I need to be with you, in whatever way that can happen." His finger grazed my cheek, giving me a small smile. "Trust me, okay."

I nodded, a lump forming in my throat. I'd promised myself after Lewis I'd never trust a man again, but with Jared, there wasn't even a hesitation.

"Good, now let's eat lunch before it's completely cold, and then we'll talk about Bennett."

"Bennett?" I asked, wondering what he wanted to know about the head of my security.

He took a step back, lowering the bag housing our lunch onto the desk before he looked back at me. "He seems very . . ." he waved his hand, "close to you."

I laughed, unable to help myself. "Bennett is a really good friend, not just here in the club, but outside of it too. He's seems like a hard-ass but he really is just a sweet teddy bear. But we're just friends, nothing has or ever will happen between us."

"Good. I wish I could tell you the idea didn't make me jealous, but it does. So his inability to remember my name isn't because he's pissed you're with me?" He tilted his head, asking in earnest.

"Bennett is a smart ass and will do anything to get a reaction. I threaten to fire him daily. But from what I can see, you're going to be able to handle him and his shenanigans just fine."

He nodded, taking me into his arms and kissing me. "I'd do a lot more than that for you. Now, let's eat and brainstorm. If he's going to be messing with me, it's only fair I get some payback of my own."

Chapter 13

Jared

ANY MAN WHO got bored spending a day with a woman clearly isn't with the right one. I didn't even notice the time, minutes and hours getting lost as day turned into night, and I felt like I hadn't even blinked.

We'd gone back to her apartment after *Diablo* and made love on her couch. It was slow and deliberate, a desperate need for me to look at her the whole time making me want to stretch it out.

I loved kissing her, loved the way her eyes would close and her breathing would slow, the trail of goosebumps under my fingertips when I ran my hand on her skin. It was easy when we were laying together to think she was fragile and soft, but five minutes in her club when she was in *Diablo* mode, and you'd see she was anything but.

Between those walls she was a machine, walking between the sections and knowing what everyone was doing and what was going on. Her beautiful eyes were restless, constantly scanning the crowd as she checked in with her staff and VIPs. She even made time for me, shooting me some flirty smiles whenever she strolled past.

And when I took her home, all bets were off. All the pent-up frustration of not being able to kiss and touch her manifested into an all-out assault.

It was around ten the next morning when my phone rang, the vibration on Presley's nightstand waking me up even though the ringtone had been turned off.

"Yeah?" I yawned into the phone, not bothering to check the caller ID.

"It's Tibbs. Do you know where Presley is?"

Even though she was sleeping safely beside me, the edge in his voice had me worried.

"Umm, at her apartment I assume," I pushed up in the bed, Presley groaning a little as I moved. "Why, what's wrong?"

"One of Shapiro's guys spotted the asswipe's TT last night around the club. He said it circled a few times but left. I don't want to freak her out, but she needs to know, and I've been trying to call her all morning but her phone's off. You still have her spare key, right? Any chance you could meet me at her place in twenty minutes?"

FUCK.

Presley rarely shut her phone off, the fancy piece of aluminum on 24/7. But for whatever reason she'd silenced it when we got home, determined to have a few hours without the barrage of emails, texts and social media alerts that usually came.

But at the moment it wasn't her newfound balance that had me concerned, it was that her brother wanted to visit her, at the apartment of which I was currently in, naked.

"Errrr." I looked around, trying to find where I'd left my clothes. "Twenty minutes?"

The words had no sooner left my mouth then Presley turned, reaching for me in her sleep. "Where did you go?" She groaned loudly when she didn't feel me beside her, my eyes widening as I lowered my hand to her mouth. "What?" The muffled word coughed out against my palm as she woke up with a jump.

"Ah, shit, Leighton. I'm sorry, I know you're with your girl, but this is kinda important. Hey, why don't you give me the address and I'll meet you at her place. Meet me down on the street, give me Presley's spare key and then you can go back to doing whatever you're doing."

What I was doing was his sister.

And I was positive he wouldn't want me going back to that.

Not to mention I couldn't exactly volunteer my location. Tibbs might not be the smartest man alive but even he would question why I was in Presley's apartment when I was supposed to be with my "girl."

Presley's head shook under my hand, probably wondering why I was muzzling her while I was talking on the phone.

"Tibbs," I said both into the phone and to her. "It's fine, you sure you want to go to Presley's? You know she's not usually awake before noon."

Like the smart girl that she was, her eyes flared in recognition. Her hand reached up to mine, pulling it away from her mouth as she stayed silent, shuffling up the bed as she listened.

"Dude, I know. But this is important. She'll get pissed and then get over it. Not a lot she can do when I'm on her doorstep."

Well, he clearly had his head up his ass because there was *plenty* she could do. But I was thanking the saints and angels that he'd decided to call before heading over wanting the spare key and not just turned up and pressed the fucking buzzer.

"Okay, give me twenty-five, I'll meet you there." I shook my head wondering what kind of shitshow it was going to turn into. "Bye."

"What the fuck?" I'd barely ended the call when Presley leapt from the bed. She was still extremely naked, which shouldn't have been as distracting as it was considering the circumstances.

What? I'd already admitted I had issues.

"Lewis was seen around the club last night, Tibbs tried to call you this morning. Your phone's off," I paraphrased, joining her off the bed while I pulled on my underwear. "He's on his way over to talk to you about it."

"Why can't he just leave a message like a regular person?" She tossed me my jeans while I pulled my T-shirt over my head. "It's like he doesn't trust a recorded message which will literally give me the information exactly as he says it."

We didn't have time to debate her brother's inability to leave voicemail, tossing on my pants as I tried to find my socks and shoes. "Presley, I've got nothing. But unless you want our grand reveal to be right now, I need to get downstairs to meet him, and you need to be suitably surprised when he arrives."

She nodded, grabbing a fluffy bathrobe. "What about your bag?"

"I'll take it down with me and toss it in the car." I moved to her, my hands resting on her hips. "I'll go back to my apartment with Tibbs so he doesn't get suspicious and then come back later."

"Do you promise?" She grabbed my arms, bringing me closer.

"I promise. I better go. I have no idea if he's walking or driving and the last thing he needs to see is me leaving here with a bag in my hand." I kissed her, wanting it to last longer but knowing we were on the clock.

With my socks and shoes located, I threw them on and grabbed the rest of my things. I did a quick sweep of the apartment, checking to see I hadn't left anything and then after one final kiss, I walked out of Presley's loft.

Not bothering to wait for the elevator, I ran down the stairs to the main front door, checking to see the coast was clear before punching open the glass and stepping onto the street. I jogged around back to where I'd left my car, tossing my bag in the trunk.

So far there'd been no sign of Tibbs, which meant I had time to go through the stupid charade of pretending I'd just arrived and was waiting for him. Shaking my head, I checked my phone, locking my car again and leaning against the hood. If I arrived at the front too early, he'd be wondering how I'd gotten there so fast. And since he had no idea where my mystery woman lived, I had to at least keep up the pretense that it had taken me the whole twenty-five minutes.

I waited thirty.

Chilling with my ride until half an hour had passed and then I slowly strolled back to the front of the building where surprise, surprise, Tibbs was waiting.

"Sorry, dude," I apologized, not in any real hurry.

Tibbs shook his head. "It's fine, thanks for meeting me. Things must be going pretty good with you and this girl if you were with her again last night. When are you going to introduce her to us?"

"Soon," I coughed out, wanting to change the subject as soon as possible. "So should we go up?"

He hadn't asked me for the assist, but like hell I was going to let him go up there alone. Last thing Presley needed was to deal with an overbearing Tibbs on her own, especially since I was partly to blame for his appearance anyway. Had to think if I hadn't been around, wearing her out with our extracurricular activities, she'd have probably not switched off her phone. And even if I wasn't feeling some residual guilt for his early morning visit, I wanted to know if there was any other information he hadn't shared yet.

Tibbs hesitated, putting in the code for the external door. "You don't have to, man, you can head back to your girl or home . . . I've probably asked more of you than I should."

"Hey, fuck that, Tibbs. You know I'd do anything for Presley . . . and for you," I quickly added. "Let's head up there and let her yell at you for a bit."

He nodded, heading to the elevator. "Right? I'm surprised she hasn't taken a chunk out of you yet, that charm of yours must really be working."

You have no idea.

"Must be."

We took the ride to Presley's loft in silence, the metal doors opening with a ping on her floor.

He knocked on her front door, giving her a chance to answer before he unlocked it with his reacquired key. I was probably going to have to get it back, the idea that he could drop by unannounced, not one that sat well with me.

"Who is it?" Presley sounded suitably annoyed, her voice coming from behind the door.

"It's me and Leighton," Tibbs responded, oblivious she already knew as I played along. "Open up or I'll let myself in."

We heard the lock disengage, followed by a few curse words and then the door opened.

She looked amazing, her mess of brown curls no tamer than the thirty minutes before I'd left, her fluffy bathrobe covering those amazing curves. Her eyes were wild, shooting her brother a murderous look while she played her part being annoyed.

God, I wanted to kiss her. Right there in front of Tibbs and not give a fuck what anyone thought.

"You were just going to burst into my apartment, uninvited?" She pointed to the key in his hand. "What if I'd had a date spend the night? You might've got an eyeful more than you bargained for."

I raised my brow, trying to hide my smirk.

She was being naughty, and I loved it.

Tibbs rolled his eyes. "Well, *were* you? Because if you were and he's already gone, not much of a man, is he?"

Ouch.

That fucking stung.

And he had a point.

I was just about to open my mouth and set Tibbs straight on exactly the kind of man Presley was with when she answered instead. "No, I was alone. But seriously, you can't just come in anytime you want. Family or not, this is my place and I'll control who has access to it." She held out her hand, tipping her head to the key. "I want it back."

Tibbs laughed, looking at his sister like she was insane. "Pres, you're being unreasonable. What if you lock yourself out? Or worse, something happens to you and we need to get in? You have my key."

"Tibbs, this isn't up for discussion. I'm going to control what I can, and this is one thing I get to decide. I want my key back."

There was so much confliction in her eyes, I wasn't positive it was an act, her words hitting me right in the chest.

She was right, there was a lot going on she didn't get a say in, but she absolutely had a right to decide who entered her home. Especially when some asshole had already invaded what should have been a safe space. Hell, even I had muscled my way in that first morning, using the spare key to let myself in under questionable circumstances.

"She's right, Tibbs." I snatched the key out of his hand and handed it to Presley. "No one will ever come in without your explicit permission or consent. And if they do, I'll deal with them."

His brow scrunched in confusion, taking a step back. "Jesus, Leighton. Dial it down, okay. Fine, keep the key. And I promise I'll always knock. Now, are we done making me feel like the asshole? I came over for a reason."

Presley directed us to her couch, which incidentally I'd fucked her on when we'd originally gotten home. She bit back the grin, her attempt to not smile telling me she was thinking about the same thing.

Yeah, we were a couple of sex fiends. And there probably wasn't a lot of places in her loft that hadn't been desecrated. And it gave me a warped sense of pleasure to know she liked it too.

"So what's so important? You guys might have the day off today, but I'm still working tonight." She moved into her kitchen, turning on her coffee machine and pulling out three cups.

Tibbs parked his butt on the sofa, leaving me room to join him. "Lewis did a drive-by last night. There were no uniforms in the area at the time, and the guy who was tailing him lost him in traffic when he crossed into Brooklyn. You know any of his friends who live out there?"

"If it wasn't the cops, who was tailing him?"

She was a smart woman, and even though he hadn't exactly signposted the additional help, she picked up on it right away.

The coffee machine was left as she spun around to face us. "Tibbs, what did you do?"

He shrugged, probably not planning on telling her right away. "There's an old cop we're friends with. He's no longer on the force. He's doing some digging."

"Wait, you knew about this too?" She narrowed her eyes, the venom that had previously been reserved for her brother now directed at me.

Shit.

"Tibbs had mentioned it." I rubbed the back of my neck, knowing I probably should have told her. She had a right to know but to be honest, there wasn't a lot to tell. Shapiro hadn't found dick, and who knew if he would. "He was doing some behind the scene stuff."

Even to me it didn't sound good, the intentions getting lost in the heavy handedness of it.

She took a breath, exhaling slowly in what I assumed was an effort to stay calm. "I can't be an outsider on this, it's literally my life. I get what you're trying to do, what you're *both* trying to do.

But if your guy finds anything out, you'll come to *me*, Justin. You don't get to make the call."

It was a lot more rational than I was expecting, not blaming her if she wanted to cuss us out. Not sure I'd be as cool being handled.

"Pres, of course." Tibbs nodding his head, his voice softening. "But I'm not sorry I did it. Between Shapiro working the backend and Leighton keeping an eye on you, I feel a lot better. And you know I'd be fucking driving you around and doing the other stuff if you'd let me. I get why you don't want your big bro around cramping your style, but I can't sit around and do nothing either."

It was an impassioned speech, and I could tell it came straight from the heart.

And I hated he didn't know the truth.

"God, Tibbs, and Mom always accuses *me* of being dramatic." Presley shot him a smile. "Is there anything else I should know?" She looked between us, inviting me to volunteer any intel if I had it.

"That's it. Unless you want to know about Chief's new woman. The guy is hardcore for her, totally smitten. He didn't even look half as happy when he was married to Melinda."

Presley's eyes widened as she went back to the coffee, "Oooooo, you need to spill. The chief deserves someone nice for a change, I want to know everything."

She turned, returning her attention to the coffee she had started making. "Well, come on. You've got me awake, the least you can do is come up with the goods."

Her brown curls bounced as she moved, my hand itching to walk up behind her, push that hair out of the way and kiss her on the neck. She was beautiful, stunning in every fucking way and she'd been under my nose the entire time.

"He's been baking," I added, keeping my hands and lips right where they were. "Walking around with a goofy look on his face."

Tibbs elbowed me in the ribs and snickered. "Sounds like someone else I know." He cleared his throat before announcing loudly, "And Leighton has a girlfriend."

Presley spun around, the cup of coffee in her hand splashing a little on the side. "Wow, really? You been holding out on me, Leighton? You're dating someone?"

God she was adorable, going along with Tibbs when she knew exactly *who* he was talking about.

"Yeah, I really like her too. She's different than the others, special. It's early days and things aren't going to be easy, but I'm hoping she feels the same way."

Last thing I intended to do was tell her how I felt while her brother looked on. And what was worse, it wasn't half as much as I wanted to say. But every single word of it was true. And whether the timing was right or not, it didn't matter. I would've tapped it out in Morse code if it were the only way.

Her beautiful eyes softened, giving me a smile. "I'm sure she feels the same way. But make sure you tell her. Women like to hear that kind of thing."

"I will," I promised, swallowing as she walked over and handed me a cup. "I'm going to tell her the first chance I get."

Tibbs laughed, rolling his eyes. "Now who's being dramatic."

And you know what, he was right. I was. But I no longer cared.

Chapter 14

Presley

HEARING JARED SAY I was special was something I hadn't known I needed.

It was unexpected, his declaration happening after my brother had almost caught us, and somehow that made it a little more exciting. His little code, the words said publicly but meant just for me, and I loved hearing them.

Of course, it took *hours* before we were back to being alone. Tibbs insisted we go out and get breakfast, and hang out like old times. I'll admit it was nice, Jared slipping right back into Leighton as we sat side-by-side and ate pancakes and bacon.

He was so sweet too, remembering I preferred blueberry syrup instead of the regular stuff and passing it to me without even asking. I wasn't even sure how he'd remembered, the last time we'd eaten breakfast together probably when I was still in college.

But later in the day, when he came back, Leighton didn't immediately disappear. He kissed me slow, his lips gently pressing against my skin as he told me again how much he liked me and how special I was to him.

I'd assumed we'd have sex, but we didn't, laying on my bed fully clothed as we watched stupid daytime television and cuddled. And then when it was time for me to go to work, we left together. I went and did another night like I always did, and Jared sat at a table lazily drinking a beer and making me crazy.

It had been just over a week and Jared and I had fallen into a comfortable rhythm. And other than Raelle and Bennett, we hadn't told anyone we were dating. Staff at *Diablo* had their suspicions, wondering why he was hanging around without his sidekick that was my brother. But they were too smart to say anything outright, choosing to keep their mouths shut and their heads down. It was the way it worked between those walls, we did our job and left the commentary to everyone else. Except for Raelle of course, who had plenty to say.

"Girl, just out this relationship already. The pressure to keep the secret is too great." She groaned, tucking into one of the bagels she'd brought over for brunch.

Jared was working, having left early in the morning which meant Raelle had come over. I'd finally caved, telling her about my plans for *Diablo* after she found a property flier on my desk. I'd been careless, too blissed out from my personal life and warned her that it was one thing she could *not* gossip about.

She'd been hurt for a second, and then got over it, wanting to know everything she could. She'd even argued her current visit was to "help me" pick an outfit for my meeting with David. But what she really wanted was to talk about Jared and was unable to do it freely at work where other people might hear.

"How is my relationship affecting you? And you know, don't think I haven't noticed your lingering hugs with Bennett. Something you want to tell me?" I held my black shift dress against me before alternating to a white one.

"I wish I could say it was more than hugs, but it's not." She sighed, brushing bagel crumbs off her hands before coming to stand beside me. "I really want to do more, but we work together. Soooooo risky. Besides, our boss is a hard ass and could totally fire us." The last bit said with a smile.

"Rae, your lives outside the club are your business. I would never begrudge anyone happiness. I trust you both to keep it professional, if it was my blessing you were looking for, you have it."

Maybe it was because I was feeling good, confident my meeting with David was going to be a success. Or maybe it was because Lewis hadn't been seen since that drive by near the club and I'd assumed he'd found some other sucker to con. Or maybe it was that I had a guy who was amazing, who I literally couldn't believe I was dating. And other than us keeping it to ourselves, it really was the perfect relationship.

He was kind and considerate, and so goddamn sweet. He always made sure I had lunch or dinner, looking after me for a change. He even cleaned up after himself, never leaving towels in the bathroom or dirty socks on the floor. And the sex . . .well the sex was off the charts. His body was incredible, every inch of him toned to perfection with a determination to drive me crazy. He knew exactly what to do with it, able to get me off in seconds if he wanted. Or draw it out for hours, just to see me squirm. And if all of that wasn't enough to prove I'd won the boyfriend lottery, he never once complained about my hours or the fact I worked almost every single night of the week.

Rae shrugged, lost in her deliberations while I celebrated my good fortune. "I don't know, Pres. Maybe. I think you should go with the white, it does amazing things for your skin."

Ordinarily, I'd agree with her because the white dress did look better. But I also knew white was a color frequently worn to Asian funerals, and I hoped I wouldn't be walking into mine.

I tossed both dresses aside and settled for a red pencil skirt with a matching thin twill sweater. It was both conservative as well as being a "lucky" color, and I was willing to take all the help I could get.

"I'll change into the white one later and wear it to the club. Make sure you save me a bagel." I called over my shoulder and went to change in my bathroom.

I wasn't nervous for the meeting, more excited, butterflies fluttering in my belly as I slipped into my skirt and sweater and looked at my reflection. I'd wanted to tell Jared all about my meeting but was worried about jinxing it, keeping my plans and the two o'clock appointment a secret in the hopes I could surprise him with good news later.

When I emerged from the bathroom, I was feeling pretty confident. Raelle had saved me a bagel, helping herself to some orange juice while I took tentative bites not to mess up my makeup. "You sure you don't want me to drive you? It's not like I have anything better to do."

"It's fine." I chewed, the need for someone to play babysitter surely over. "No one has seen Lewis in days, and there's no way he'd know about this meeting. Besides, instead of driving me to the Plaza, you could go see Bennett. Strategize which parts of the team should stay in Midtown and who should go across to the Meatpacking district. Maybe it's time for you to step up and be my bar manager at the new site? I know you're more than capable, and poor Hank doesn't do well with change."

I knew I was getting ahead of myself, but it was exciting to think about the future. Everything was going so right, the idea that David would be anything other than supportive, just didn't enter my mind.

"You'd let me be the bar manager at the Meatpacking district?" Raelle's eyes lit up, her usual cool exterior sidelined with excitement.

"Who else am I going to trust. Annnnnnd if you and Bennett are at two different sites, there really isn't a conflict anymore is there?" I tossed out casually, pretending it wouldn't be one hell of a sweetener.

Raelle stilled, lowering her juice and grabbing me by the shoulders. "You go into the Plaza and you fucking wow the shit out of David Cheng. You hear me. Use that big brain of yours and hypnotize him with your profit margins."

"But no pressure, right?" I joked. "Just remember, out of all of us, I have the most to lose. He could think I'm insane for wanting another site so close, giving me my walking papers at the end of my contract."

There was a slight possibility he wouldn't love it, thinking I was greedy instead of ambitious, something Lorena had warned me about. And while I was confident, I also knew that nothing came with an iron clad guarantee.

"Yeah, he could totally do that. And a big fucking asteroid could come out of the sky and obliterate the planet and we all die. I'd say your chances are about the same." She blinked, like she was actually being serious.

I hugged her, willing to take my ego boost however I could get it. "Thanks. Make sure if you see that asteroid, you give me a head's up. I want to be naked in bed with Jared when it happens." I winked, pulling back and giving her a smile.

My bagel was only half eaten but I didn't bother finishing it. Instead I gathered my handbag and keys, walking Raelle out before hailing a cab.

It was nice to be feeling independent again, the fear from a couple of weeks ago almost completely gone. I knew Tibbs and Jared were still keeping an eye on things, but the whole time the police had been investigating, they'd literally found nothing. So I felt completely justified in trusting my instincts, and going it alone.

The drive to The Plaza didn't take long, the cab driver dropping me off in front of the beautiful landmark hotel. David always stayed there, insisting on the same suite every time, and enjoying lunch in the Champagne Bar as he gazed at the Pulitzer Fountain.

I took a deep breath as I entered the glass doors, a text message from Jared reminding me he was thinking of me, the last piece of luck I needed.

It was hard not to be overwhelmed by the blatant opulence, the polished marble and the gold. But with my shoulders pushed back I walked confidently to where David was already sitting, his coffee and pastry still untouched.

"David." I put out my hand and greeted him, watching him smile as he stood. "I hope your stay in New York has been fruitful."

His hand grasped mine, the pleased look on his face, genuine. "Always. And even better when I see your numbers. Not sure how you turned that old warehouse into a diamond, but you've yet to pass the point where I'm not impressed. Please take a seat."

"I'm glad." I took the chair opposite him, a waiter delivering a glass of champagne I didn't order. I assumed David had, his tendency of not wanting to be interrupted when a meeting started, prompting it.

But it was too soon to celebrate, moving the champagne flute to the side as I readied myself for our conversation.

"Before you start, Presley. I have to ask if you're here to tender your resignation. I can tell you have some speech worked out, and if that's what this is about, I would rather we pay each other the respect of skipping through the pretense."

"My resignation?" I asked, unable to hide my surprise. "You just gave me a fifteen percent pay increase, why would you think I want to quit?"

"Scott Collins?" His head tilted like he was gauging my reaction. "It's the worst-kept secret in the business. He was looking to open something up in L.A. and I know he was in town recently. I believe he even visited *Diablo*. Tell me, and be honest, did he make you an offer?"

Since the minute Scott had walked past those big black doors of the club, he'd been a huge pain in my ass. And while we had met, me barely entertaining the idea of helping him for a second, I hadn't spoken to him since he'd left. I'd assumed he took my vineyard idea and ran with it, forgetting all about his disaster-waiting-to-happen.

"Yes, I met with him. And he offered me a lot actually. Artistic control, a salary and equity."

"Equity?" David's brows shot up, no doubt surprised Scott had cashed in such a big chip.

"Yes." I took a breath, deciding to go all in. "David, I know you're a busy man so I'm not going to waste your time by pretending to be modest. *Diablo* has made a name for itself, we are at capacity every night of the week and are constantly listed in social blogs and magazines. And I don't have to tell you that above all of that, we're making money."

"And . . .," David urged me, knowing I had more to say.

"And I've worked my ass off to make it that way. I like my team, and the brand, and I'm not going to leave them to chase someone else's pipedream. Especially when I have my own. You trusted me once, now I'm going to need you to do it again. But this time around as a partner instead of just an employee."

I laid out my plan, my ideas for the expansion and the second site, and even some rough expenditures I modeled on the data I already had. I did it without my notes, minus spreadsheets and with no fancy graphs. It was straight business, keeping as much of the emotion as I could out of my voice even though I wanted it so desperately.

"You've been working on this for some time," he nodded after I'd finished, tenting his fingers in front of him. "You flat out rejected Scott's offer?"

"Yes, I did. Feel free to call him if you want to verify it, I have his number." I picked up my cell and tilted it in his direction.

He waved his hand, dismissing my offer. "No need. But I am impressed not only by your ingenuity but your loyalty as well. I have no doubt you could have turned Scott's toy into something of a success and reaped the benefits for yourself. And I'm almost positive I'm going to see you on the cover of *Forbes* before you're forty."

"I say before I'm thirty-five, but let's not split hairs."

David laughed, shaking his head as he reached down to get his coffee. "Yes, Presley. We will partner in this venture. But," he warned, my heart almost stopping from both the excitement and the sheer terror. "Not a word to anyone until our respective lawyers iron out an agreement. With anything of this nature, you need the element of surprise. And I don't want anyone else hearing about it, especially other developers until we are locked in, understand?"

"Of course." I nodded, having kept the secret for what felt like an eternity. "Two staff members know, but that's it. I haven't even told members of my family."

"Good, keep it that way. I'm sure they can celebrate with you once we've both signed on the dotted line. More deals have been ruined by loose-lipped relatives than I'd liked to admit." He sighed heavily, his father probably the implication.

I nodded, willing to take an indefinite vow of silence if it helped. "My lips are sealed. I won't breathe a word of it until it's finalized."

With the business out of the way, David flagged down the waiter and we ordered a light lunch. It was hard keeping my excitement under wraps, my heart beating a million miles a minute. After he'd agreed, I'd wanted nothing more than to run onto Fifth Avenue and dance like a lunatic. But I didn't, keeping the crazy simmering while we talked KPIs.

When David finally announced he had another meeting, my body almost sagged in relief. I tried to not look too ecstatic when he rose from his seat and waved me goodbye, my feet doing their best to keep even steps and not skip out the door to a cab.

It was only once I was safely back in my apartment that I kicked off my heels and literally screamed. I was so excited, the smile so wide on my face I was probably going to develop laugh lines. I didn't even care, squealing and dancing in the wide space of my living area with a feeling of happiness so huge I thought my heart might burst.

And that was it, wasn't it.

I was happy.

Not just content, but happy, all the pieces of my life finally falling into place all at the same time. And it wasn't the job and the new expansion, or that I'd proved I didn't need to be a forty-year-old man to be successful. It was that I had *that*, and finally someone who was worthy to share it with.

Jared.

God, I'd always thought he was just the guy I had a crush on, wanting to sleep with him because he was my older brother's hot best friend. The forbidden fruit. And even though the sex had been beyond anything I could've imagined, he was sooooo much more.

He was kind and gentle, and never once told me I should do something else. Hell, it couldn't be easy for him, us spending almost every night at the club instead of doing fun stuff like other couples. We'd barely even dated, catching a lunch or dinner either in between my schedule or his. Not a lot of guys would put up with that. In fact, the long list of my ex-boyfriends was pretty much the testimony.

But he was different, and when I got my good news, he'd been the first person I'd wanted to tell. Not Bennett or Raelle. Not even my parents or Justin.

Nope, it was him.

The guy who I could let into my heart and trust not to break it.

The guy who had been there all along.

Chapter 15

Jared

COLLISION.

A family sedan had played chicken with a semi just outside the Lincoln Tunnel.

We'd responded, expecting the worst, the scene the kind of stuff nightmares were made of.

"Get the kids," yelled Cap, a toddler and a baby still strapped to their car seats were crying in the back. The mother was unconscious, trapped behind the steering wheel, the hood of her car wedged under the grill of the truck.

Rev and North took the front, using the piston-rod hydraulic Hurst, most people knew as the jaws of life. We had no idea if she was still breathing, our priority, getting the kids out of the car ASAP and I could already smell gasoline.

"Locked," Tibbs cursed, the door not budging.

I shook my head, pointing to the front passenger side. "Smash the front, it's too risky to do the back." He nodded, popping out the front passenger side window, giving us enough access to reach the central locking.

"Mommy," howled a little girl, her face stained by endless tears as she reached out in fear. "Mommmmmmyyyyyyyy."

There was no time to get emotional, our objective to secure the two kids while the others took care of their mother. Cranking open the door, I reached inside, doing a quick visual check for injuries before cutting loose the tethers for the car seats. With no idea what we were dealing with—and until one of the EMTs could make sure one or both hadn't snapped their spinal cord—we were moving them as little as possible.

"Take the baby," I hollered at Tibbs, the smallest of the two screaming so loud he or she was literally gasping for air. "I'll grab the other."

We each took a kid, ripping their seats out from the back and carrying them away from the wreck. The driver of the semi was already out, dazed and in severe shock.

Darcy, one of the EMTs, took the toddler while Cole took the baby. Both were doing their best to calm the kids while North and Rev were getting closer to slicing a hole into the car's metal.

We'd barely left the kids when Cap yelled, "Get some foam down on that gas," the small leak of gasoline quickly spilling onto the street. All it would take was one fucking spark and the whole thing would go from a really bad accident to a fucking disaster, so we wasted no time in getting the AFFF out and smothering it.

North got the ram, using it to push the dash back so they could finally get to the mom. She wasn't breathing, North starting CPR the minute she was on the ground, yelling for the EMTs.

McGee was at his side, bagging her while North continued with compressions, not stopping until she finally gave a cough.

"We've got a pulse. Faint, but we need to move her." McGee pointed to a stretcher.

Without waiting to be told, Tibbs and I grabbed the stretcher, helping to lift her on while McGee's hand kept squeezing the BVM. She was far from out of the woods, but at least she was free and breathing, the rest of it completely out of our hands.

It wasn't until the family had been loaded into the ambulance that I stepped back and finally took in the whole scene. It was intense, the Honda the family had been traveling in was almost unrecognizable. The silver metal was twisted in directions that shouldn't be possible, while the semi looked like it had eaten a car, and then vomited from indigestion. All the while traffic had backed up, the stream of cars wanting to get into the tunnel extending farther than we could see.

"PD are handling the diversions. And I have a hazmat team on the way. Good work out there." Cap nodded his head, pointing to the engine. "You guys head back, and I'll keep the second unit here just in case. I'll radio it in to the Chief."

Cap was hanging back with the second unit, North, Tibbs, Rev, Evans, and me climbing into the engine and heading back to the stationhouse.

"Fucking crazy," Tibbs shook his head. "It's not even raining."

Traffic accidents were common, most a fender bender or two that people usually walked away from. And while it was inconvenient, and racked up insurance premiums like no other, if you had to have a wreck, that was the kind you wanted. Then there were the others. The ones like we'd just left, or worse, the ones where you pull out corpses.

North's parents had died in a wreck. Both high and drunk, they'd left to go find their next score while their eighteen-year-old kid was home trying to be the adult. He didn't hide it, but I could never understand how it hadn't messed him up beyond recognition. His ability to tune out all the bullshit and do his job better than anyone else, something that I fucking admired.

"How's Quinn?" I asked, tapping his shoulder as I leaned forward in my seat. "Must be getting close."

The guy turned, biggest smile I'd ever seen beaming from his face. "She's doing great. Man, I can't wait."

And that was all it took, the conversation turning to North and Quinn instead of the horror we'd just left. It was the only way you could keep doing what we did, finding a little part in your head to lock it away and go on with a life you were lucky to be living.

We got back to the station, restocked the truck, and then showered and changed. We hoped to have time to eat dinner between calls, feeling confident when we sat down at the table while Chief dished up spaghetti.

"Hey, you want to do something tomorrow night?" Tibbs asked, tearing off a piece of garlic bread before handing it to me. "We haven't hung out in a while. Feel free to bring your woman along too, I'm beginning to think you made her up."

He laughed as did Cole, the rookie not knowing what was good for him. "She exists, asswipes." I flipped them off. "But tomorrow's my niece's birthday. My mom is having everyone at the house. And even if I didn't love Maddy and want to see her turn two, my ma would kill me if I didn't show up."

Ironic how I could be excited and disappointed at the same time. Maddy was my sister Deanna's youngest, and I fucking loved the hell out of that kid. So the fact she was getting to blow out two candles was a big deal and I wanted to be there. But it also meant I wouldn't get much time—if any—with Presley. Kid birthday parties usually happened during the day, with my mother insisting on a family dinner after the extended relatives had left. Celebrations were a big thing, and I didn't like disappointing my mother. Which meant by the time I'd get back to Midtown and Presley, she'd already be at *Diablo*. I'd have to wait hours before I'd be able to touch her. Having to sit and watch from a distance instead of pulling her into my arms and kissing her like I wanted.

"Maddy is turning two?" Tibbs scratched his head, taking a forkful of his noodles. "Fuck, how the hell did that happen? Seems like yesterday Jeff and Deanna left the hospital with her."

I shrugged. "I know. Crazy shit. So yeah, I'm out."

It should have been the end of the conversation, but that would've been too easy. Tibbs chewing his mouthful before adding, "so, we'll hang out later. Actually, here's a plan. Why don't you leave your car at your mom's and I'll come get you. Then we can go do something, and I'll drive so you can have a few beers. Trust me, after a few hours with a bunch of kids, you're going to need it. I'll drop you back in the morning to pick it up."

"Is this your way to try and score birthday cake, Tibbs? Because if you want some, I can just bring some home." I tried not to panic, my throat feeling tight.

Tibbs laughed, not noticing I couldn't breathe. "Dude, your mom loves me. I'm like the son she never had."

"She has a son, me," I pointed out, not in the mood for the famous Tibbs logic.

"Exactly, which is why she needs me." He waved his hand, not bothering to hide his grin. "Listen, tell you what. I'm heading to Long Island anyway in the afternoon to see my folks. Mom needs to fuss over Presley and make sure she's okay. So, I'll be out there anyway."

Mention of his sister had my immediate attention, especially since I hadn't spoken to her in the last few hours. I knew she had some kind of meeting at the Plaza, and I'd told her about my family thing tomorrow, but other than that, nada. "You both should stop by. Dinner is always early or the kids get cranky and my mom hasn't seen Presley in forever. Annnnd, since we'll have to leave to take her to work, I'll have an excuse to leave."

Oh, I knew I was being shady. Using Tibbs as the middleman so I could see Presley. Did I give a shit? Not even a little. Not to mention I liked the idea of her being with me and my family, the opportunity too good to pass up.

Tibbs nodded, oblivious to my ulterior motives. "Yeah, sounds good. You bringing the girlfriend to Maddy's birthday?"

"No," I answered truthfully, after all, *I* wasn't bringing anyone. Presley was coming with Tibbs, so as far as breaking one of the commandments, I was free and clear. "I show up with a girl and my mother is going to be planning the wedding. I like this girl, I don't want to scare her off."

That was also true.

I wanted nothing more than to take Presley to my house and introduce her as my girlfriend. One, because my family already *loved* Presley, and two, because I didn't want to hide it anymore. But that came with consequences, ones that would see my mother calling Mrs. Tibbs and the two of them already naming the grandkids. And that was pressure I didn't want to put on either of us, especially since everything had been so great. So we compromised and got creative. I'd get to have my girlfriend with me, by my side, and we wouldn't have to deal with the family drama that would surely erupt.

It was a win/win.

"Good plan. Let me know what Maddy wants and I'll pick something up tomorrow. My mom will kill me if I show up without a present. Never thought I'd be excited to go to a kid's birthday party, but your mom's cooking is the best. I actually can't wait."

I barely kept the grin from my face as I agreed, "Yeah, me either, buddy. Me either."

My mom's family was Irish, which translated to a lot of fucking people. Even though most of them hadn't set foot on the Emerald Isle, they popped out kids like it was their job. And don't even get me started on religion. They lived their lives like Jesus was watching, and prayed to the saints and angels in an effort to cover all their bases. You'd be hard pressed to walk into any of their houses and not see a crucifix, the chance of a devoted holy wall, better than average.

But unlike my mom's seven brothers and sisters, she'd only had us three; Deanna, Sarah and me.

Deanna was the oldest, and already had two kids. Mason was seven—who she'd had with her deadbeat first husband— and the birthday girl, Maddy. And Sarah—the middle kid—had a three-year-old son named Sammy. So, as you could imagine, my mother—whose family was huuuuuge—loved nothing more than getting the gang together and feeding everyone until they thought they were going to die. The woman was literally incapable of catering small, the idea that someone might go hungry as sacrilegious as taking the Lord's name in vain. Which was why we were all crammed into Casa Leighton on a chilly Saturday afternoon.

"Baby, you look tired." My mother shook her head as I helped clean up the balloons and streamers from earlier in the day. "You getting enough sleep? Just last week I read an article that said lack of sleep was as dangerous as cocaine."

"Orla, leave the man alone. He works long hours, he's fine," my dad piped in, trying to play interference. I wasn't just my mom's only son but her "baby" as well.

"Mom, I can assure you I'm fine, and I'm getting plenty of sleep. Would have preferred a little more today but couldn't miss Princess Maddy's big day."

The princess in question was passed out on her father's chest. She'd been hyped up on sugar and cake, crashing hard once the last of her little friends had left. Sammy was also taking a nap, dangling like a stunt dummy from my mom's two-seater. "Should we move him to one of the spare bedrooms?" I asked my sister, Sarah, who was sitting in her husband's lap. I swear if they didn't make another baby before they left the house, it would be a fucking miracle.

She laughed, showing a complete lack of concern. "He sleeps like that all the time. It's worse if you move him."

Mason—who apparently was too old to nap—was checking out his little sister's present haul. He was quietly entertaining himself on the iPad I'd given her—because I rocked as an uncle and was determined to be their favorite—while his mom was uploading the three thousand photos she'd taken to her social pages.

Content that I was getting enough sleep, my mother moved on to other pressing matters. "What time are Justin and Presley coming? I'm so glad you invited them over, you should have told them to come earlier for the party. Justin loves my cooking."

"Tibbs, Mom, call him Tibbs." I shook my head, my mother hanging on to *Justin* even though no one hardly called him that. Hell, even his old man was calling him Tibbs, as was most of his family. "And they were hanging out with their parents earlier. Trust me, he'll eat enough when he gets here to make up for whatever he missed earlier."

She shot me a stern look. "I'll call him the name his mother gave him. And don't you go making him feel bad. I love him like another son."

Rolling my eyes, I finished filling the trash bag in my hands and carried it out to the garage. I'd barely put the bag into the trash can when my phone buzzed with an incoming message, an announcement from North that he was a new daddy to a little girl named Ava. Quinn and the baby were doing fine, Mack already at the hospital with him. Gave me a warm feeling in my chest to hear his good news, and doubly excited there would be a new princess to celebrate next year on the same day as my niece.

"Quinn and North had a baby girl, Ava," I announced, walking back into the house.

My dad laughed, pointing to Tibbs and Presley who were already in the living room. "Gotta be quicker than that, Son, Tibbs already told us."

"Can you believe North is a dad?" Tibbs shook his head in disbelief. "We definitely need to go out and celebrate tonight."

It was funny, his voice fading out even though he kept talking. Because whatever he had to say was no longer important when she was in the same room.

Jesus, she was beautiful.

Dressed down in a pair of jeans and a T-shirt, her face was makeup free and her hair pulled back. She was perfect, every inch of her breathtaking as I fought the urge to go over and kiss her.

I'd never get tired of looking at her, or wanting to touch her, the idea that I couldn't, driving me crazy. And if her smile was anything to go by, she knew exactly what I was thinking.

"Sweetheart, you want to go put your bag in Jared's room? You can change in there before you need to go." It was my mother's voice that pulled me from my daydream, my eyes blinking as I thanked God no one saw me staring.

"You need to go to my room?" I asked obviously having missed part of the conversation.

Tibbs mock punched me in the ribs. "Her bag, you moron. She brought her clothes and stuff so she can get ready for work."

Presley lifted a small overnight bag, her brow rising with it. "You want to show me to your room? Probably best if it's out of the way so no one trips on it."

I didn't even hesitate, nodding my head so fast I almost got whiplash, thankful for the opportunity to get her alone for a minute if that was all I had. "Sure, I'll show you where it is. We'll be right back." My head tipped to the hallway, hinting to her that she should follow.

"Show her the upstairs bathroom as well. It's been a while since she's been here," my mom called after us, my heartbeat kicking up a notch as we made it to the bottom of the stairs.

"Will do, Ma," I yelled back, unable to peel my eyes from the hottest woman I'd ever seen. "I'll give her a quick tour."

Presley bit back a grin, running a hand slowly down my chest. "Take me to your room, Leighton. We wouldn't want to disappoint your mother."

Fuck.

I was definitely going to hell.

Chapter 16

Presley

THE MINUTE THE door closed, Jared had me pressed against the wall. His mouth on mine as his hands moved down to my ass. I was dying, anxious to kiss him from the moment I'd walked in. And when I finally got the chance, I felt like I was going to explode.

"Fuck, Presley." His mouth moved from my lips to my neck. "We're both going to end up in a lot of trouble."

My hand slid down his chest and landed on the front of his jeans. He was hard, rubbing himself against my hand. "I've wanted to sneak into this room for years, who knew it would be that easy to score an invitation."

"You thought about being in here with me?" His hand moved to the front of my jeans, popping the button. "Thought about all the things I'd do to sweet little Presley?"

"Hey, I was never sweet," I moaned, his fingers slipping into my underwear.

We didn't have much time, five minutes or maybe ten, before someone would come looking and wondering why it was taking so long. But I didn't care, taking those stolen moments and precious touches, breathing out a shaky breath as his thumb circled my clit.

"I want to make you come so badly," he panted against my skin. "Right here, in this room where I've jerked off to you more times than I can count."

"You jerked off thinking of me?" My body tingled as his thumb continued to move. I was positive it wasn't possible to orgasm in a minute, but my body was completely up for the challenge.

His head nodded slowly, kissing me hard as he plunged in a finger. "Enough to make me think I was a deviant."

As horrible as it was to admit, it was hot making out in Leighton's old bedroom, getting fingered while his family was downstairs. Maybe I was a deviant too, my body bowing against the wall as he added another finger.

"Go faster," I begged, burying my head in his shoulder, his twists against my clit picking up speed as my hips rocked against his hand.

My breasts strained against the soft cotton of my T-shirt, wanting to be touched as I grew wetter. I'd assumed we wouldn't get the chance, his family commitments mixed with my work schedule meaning we'd be lucky to even kiss.

"Oh my God, I'm so close." My body shook, his fingers pumping inside my slick center as his thumb circled. I was so turned on it felt like I was buzzing, my body vibrating like a tuning fork that had just been struck.

It wasn't enough, needing more contact as I bucked against his hand. My head banged against the wall. His free hand reached up, cupping my mouth as I whimpered, the sensation, a war of pleasure and frustration as I chased the high.

"Shhhh," he laughed, kissing my neck as his voice deepened. "I can feel how close you are. Feel your greedy pussy clamping around my fingers. You want more of me, Presley? You want my cock buried inside of you? Have me fuck you right against this wall while people wait for us downstairs?"

It shouldn't have turned me on, shouldn't have been so hot, but as he growled against my neck, I felt more worked up than was rightly appropriate. "Yes, I want that. I want you so badly."

My words were muffled, lost against his palm as my eyes widened. He pumped into me, nodding in an unspoken promise that he'd give me whatever I asked.

His hand against my mouth slipped, his lips stealing my heated moan before it could escape.

We were so close, everything touching and yet barriers of clothes separating us. But it didn't matter, my body splintering into a million pieces as he kissed me feverishly, taking my pleasure into his body like it was his own.

"God, you're beautiful." His kisses slowed, his hand still buried in my underwear. "I love watching you come, Presley."

I kissed him back, hungry for more as I reached down and rubbed against the bulge in his jeans. I knew he'd be hard, wanting to give him exactly what he'd given me.

"Yeah, that's not going to happen." He brushed my hand aside, sliding his fingers out of me. "We've already tempted fate, let's not get totally stupid."

He was right. Of course, he was right. It had been how many minutes? Ten? More? I had no idea how much time we'd spent in that room, but I knew it was longer than it took to drop off a bag and show me the bathroom.

"I want to blow you so bad," I ground out in frustration, my voiced irritation making him grin.

He groaned, pressing his forehead to mine. "And I'd like nothing more than to have you suck me. But not right now, it's going to have to wait. You remember where the bathroom is up here? Or do you really need me to show you?"

"I remember," I pouted, watching him adjust himself in his jeans.

He lifted his fingers—the ones that had been inside of me—to his lips and sucked them. His eyes flickered, savoring what was in his mouth before returning his gaze back to me. "Not even close to the taste I wanted, but it will have to do. I'm going to do the best I can to hide this," he pointed to the hard rod pressing against his fly, "and then meet you back down there."

"Okay, I might just go ahead and get changed. Save me time in case dinner is running late." I glanced back at him, my fingers teasing the bottom of my T-shirt.

He coughed, that bulge he'd readjusted probably needing additional attention as he took a step toward the door. "Sure, whatever you want."

"Maybe I'll make myself come again before I do." My hand moved from the hem of my top to my waistband. "You know, since I'll already be naked."

His look was heated, almost murderous, as he froze. "You are *not* playing fair."

I laughed, unable to help myself.

Of course, I'd been kidding. Because not only was my body still limp from the orgasm he'd given me, but I wasn't perverted enough to get myself off while everyone else was downstairs. Sure, that was pretty hypocritical since I'd seemed to have no problem at all when he was doing it, but logic was funny like that.

"Go," I motioned to the door, "I promise I was joking."

With one final kiss and a heated huff, he left me alone in the room. I heard the faucet running from the bathroom down the hall, waiting until I heard his footsteps descending the stairs before I finally allowed myself to take off my clothes. I didn't trust myself. Or him either to be honest, knowing how easy it would be to pull him back into the room and finish what we started.

Uh, so much for not being a pervert.

Shaking my head and reminding myself his entire family was downstairs including his mother, I got my clothes out of my bag and started to change.

His room hadn't changed much since he'd moved out. It was painted the same slate grey, just with a fresh coat, his old queen-sized bed pushed against the wall. But the energy was different, the smell of him gone when he'd walked out the door instead of lingering in the room like it used to when he slept there. I liked it, the fresh scent of his cologne or deodorant, the thought of it making me smile. The memory of sneaking up to his room with the excuse of looking for my brother flashed in my mind. He'd smelled delicious back then too, the urge to bury my face in his pillow still very vivid even though it had been years ago.

It was ridiculous to be so excited about how someone smelled. Surely that wasn't normal. And yes, I knew the perfume industry had banked millions on the idea of being able to entice us with concoctions designed to send us into a frenzy, but *frenzied* wasn't what I felt.

I felt happy, safe, content. Like my heart was expanding in my chest as my lungs drew it in. It wasn't sexual. Okay, it wasn't *just* sexual. It was more.

Oh.

My.

God.

It wasn't just sexual.

And not in the same friendly way I used to appreciate him either. It was different.

Fuck.

Fuck.

Fuck.

I paced nervously around the room, my pulse quickening as I padded around in bare feet. It was waaaaay too soon to be having those kinds of feelings. Not only did I have my bad-news ex still trying to fuck up my life, but I was literally on the verge of the biggest move of my career. I didn't have time for a serious relationship, not one that attracted the L word.

Had I ever been in love? Like *real* love, and not just infatuation or lust. Maybe? I didn't know, my chest tightening as I tried to talk myself off the ledge. It wasn't the time. It was NOT the time. And it wasn't like I could just confess to Jared I was tangled up in feelings. I mean, obviously we'd cared about each other for a really long time, but this was so incredibly different.

I was in love with a guy—and other than Raelle and Bennett—no one knew I was even dating.

Fuck.

"You okay there, Sweetie?" Leighton's mom rapped at the door. "We're just about to sit down and have dinner, you find everything you need?"

Yes, unfortunately I did, Orla, but the fucking timing sucks and now I'm in love with your amazing son and I don't think he loves me like that.

"Yes," I croaked out, trying to clear my throat as I pulled open the door. "I'm sorry, I just thought since I was up here it was just easier to get changed."

Her smile spread, looking me over from head to toe as she crossed the threshold and entered the room. "Oh, Presley, you look stunning."

"Thanks." I nodded, not wanting to correct her that I was actually a hot mess and wasn't even taking into account my shoeless feet and smudged makeup. I was so far from stunning in every single way and my head was spinning out of control.

She clasped my hands, tapping them with hers as she took in my outfit. It was my Stella McCartney cocktail dress which plunged low at the front so I couldn't wear a bra. Which probably wasn't appropriate when I was going to be sitting around children, and something I should have considered before changing.

Fuck.

"I should probably put something else on." I reached down to my discarded T-shirt on the bed, thinking Jared's nephew was going to get more familiar with boobs than his parents were probably comfortable with.

"Nonsense. You look lovely. No need to cover up. My heart might belong to the Lord, but I'm not a prude," she chuckled. "So come down and have dinner. I set a place for you and Justin right beside Jared."

Great.

"Thanks so much, Orla. That's so kind. I'll just be another few minutes, but you can go ahead and start without me."

She shook her head, watching as I shoved the clothes I'd arrived in back into the bag and pulled out my black patent leather pumps. "You take your time. We'll get the grandkids started."

Leaving me to my panic, she closed the bedroom door behind me. Then I was a whirlwind of arms, cleaning up my face and reapplying my makeup as I slid on my shoes. I was so *not* ready to go down and face Jared. Having to look at him and smile like I hadn't just discovered I loved him after he fingered me in his old bedroom.

Because who even thinks like that.

Harnessing the bravado of Presley past—the woman who could run one of the biggest nightclubs in the city and negotiate deals with multi-millionaires—I walked out of the safety of the room.

It was fine.

No one could read what was going on in my head, and I certainly didn't need to be advertising it. Especially not to Jared who was probably expecting a blowjob, not declarations of love and other complicated feelings.

Heads turned when I walked in, eyes focusing on me and my ill-suited dinner attire as I took a seat in between Jared and Tibbs and pretended I didn't feel the stares.

"That dress is amazing." Deanna, Leighton's oldest sister, was the first to talk. "If you weren't so busy all the time, I'd totally take you out shopping with me to be my personal stylist."

"As long as you sdon't mind waiting a while, I'd love to." I smiled as I took a seat, Jared's eyes wide as I shuffled toward the table. His leg pressed against mine, one of his hands disappearing under the table and squeezing my knee.

Blowjobs, I reminded myself. *He was thinking about blowjobs.*

Thankfully the awkwardness didn't last long, Maddy—the birthday girl—squealing she was hungry. Then like a huge and unexpected sinkhole, conversations started around the table, ignoring me and my dress.

"So, after we take Presley to work, where do you want to go?" Tibbs asked Leighton, ignoring the heated looks his best friend was giving me.

"I thought we were hanging at *Diablo*." Jared cleared his throat, sliding his hand slightly up my leg before extracting it.

I breathed out in relief, thankful he wasn't going to hitch higher up my leg and tease me as payback for what I'd said to him in the room. Little did he know, I had my own torture happening. Didn't need any extra from him. "You guys don't have to stick around. Bennett and his team are more than capable of handling security and have been doing it since we opened. And a drive-by a few days ago doesn't mean anything. For all you know it could've been someone else's car."

Ordinarily, I loved Jared spending time in my club. Even though my time was limited, I selfishly liked having him there. I liked those stolen kisses in my office. Those flirty glances he threw at me when I walked by. And then the hungry grab of his hands the minute I was done. It was completely unreasonable and greedy, but it made my night infinitely better.

But that was before.

And while I still wanted all those things, since my heart had gotten involved, I was going to need a minute.

Just a break to sort things through and work out what the hell I was going to do.

"You don't want us to stay?" Jared asked, the subtext saying something entirely different. He wasn't worried about security or Lewis or even my brother. He was asking me why I wouldn't want *him* to stay, to steal those precious moments when we could.

"Presley's right." Tibbs loaded his plate with roast beef, agreeing with me for the first time in forever about backing off. "Bennett has it under control and we'd probably be more useful somewhere else. And of course, we'll pick her up when she's done. That's not even an issue."

I shook my head, shooting that idea down too. "Not necessary. Rae can drive me home. You both just go out and have a good time."

Jared couldn't hide the confusion on his face, probably wondering how we'd gone from flirting in his old bedroom to me telling him to go have fun elsewhere. But I needed the space, even if it was just for the night so I could sort through my feelings.

He'd understand. He was the most perfect man anyone could ever ask for. And when I untwisted all my thoughts and worked up the courage to tell him, he would know why.

At least, I hoped he would.

"Are you sure?" he asked, his heated look asking me to reconsider but I wouldn't be swayed.

"Yep, it's fine. Now let's eat. I need to get to *Diablo* early for a staff meeting, so we either move this along, or I'm going to steal Elena." I laughed, attempting to lighten the mood and teasing him about his beloved car.

"Hey, you leave her out of this. She's done nothing to you." He returned the playful banter, hopefully moving from his concern back to our happy flirty place. "No one drives my baby but me."

"Then it's settled. We eat, then leave, and Rae drives me home." I forked some of the roast beef on my plate, spreading a smile across my lips.

"Whatever you want, Sis." Tibbs nodded, heaping more food on his plate. "And then, maybe I'll finally find out more about Leighton's woman. I swear, I'm beginning to think you're ashamed of either her or me."

My eyes widened, praying to God dinner would go quickly. "And it sounds like your evening's set too."

I was so fucked.

Chapter 17

Jared

FINGERING A WOMAN in my childhood bedroom probably wasn't my finest moment. It had been hot, making her come in the same room I'd jerked off in a million times, juicing me up more than it should. Those saints and angels my mother had mounted to almost every wall were definitely judging me. The amount of Hail Marys and Our Fathers I'd need to get back into their good graces, more than I was able to offer.

And yet, I didn't regret it.

Watching her come undone, the desperation in her eyes as I took her right over that edge was well worth the price of giving up the salvation of my soul. Hell, I'd even contemplated taking out my dick and making her come a second time, but wised up before I did something stupid.

No, what we'd done in that room hadn't been stupid. Reckless, sure, and probably a little seedy, but not stupid. Because nothing I ever did with her would ever be stupid, even if there was a risk of me getting excommunicated from my family and a broken nose from her brother.

I loved it.

Loved those whimpers of desperation when she was right there. The way her eyes would widen as she tightened around me, those little tremors against my hand, mouth or cock, the best reward for a job well done.

And I'd assumed that appreciation was a two-way street, my commitment to making her scream my name as many times as possible something we both could agree was a good thing.

But.

She'd been weird when she came back down the stairs, her eyes slightly clouded as she appeared in what had to be my new favorite dress. It was a tough call and changed daily, the outfit I liked best usually the one she happened to be wearing at the time. Didn't matter if it was a sexy black dress that stopped her from wearing a bra—like she'd been wearing—or a faded college hoodie and an old pair of jeans. She wore everything like it belonged in a magazine, my senses feasting over every inch.

And the change in her mood hadn't been the outfit. My initial assessment was she'd been self-conscious about her outstanding cleavage on display. But that was sidelined when she told Tibbs and me not to come to *Diablo*.

It had nothing to do with the dress. And while she attempted to joke, smile and pretend like everything was fine, I had a hunch that maybe what we'd done in my old bedroom was responsible.

"You sure you don't want to leave your car here?" Tibbs asked, watching as I climbed into my Mustang. Presley was already sitting in his car, the need for me to drive her redundant. "I'll bring you back in the morning."

"Nah, it's fine. I'll drop it off at the apartment and meet you at *Diablo*. Then we can leave from there." I tapped the roof of my car, watching as he nodded in agreement.

"Yeah, good plan. Okay, I'll wait for you inside. It will give me a chance to tell Bennett what Shapiro saw, keep him in the loop too."

With Tibbs happy with the plan, he hopped into his car and backed out of the driveway. I said another quick goodbye to my parents—the rest of my family still inside—and did the same in my car.

It ate at me the whole drive back to Manhattan, wondering if what we'd done had made her feel cheap. Sure as shit hadn't been classy, even if she'd been the only person who'd come in that bedroom other than me.

I hadn't done *the sneaking girls* into my room when I was growing up. Two older sisters who had better hearing than an FBI wiretap was the first problem. Followed closely by religious icons at every turn, neither of those really conducive to getting busy with a girl. So the first time I'd ever taken a girl home had been when I'd been paying my own rent. Meant I didn't have to worry about St. Peter giving me the evil eye or my Ma getting a briefing from Deanna or Sarah.

But she didn't know that, maybe assuming it was something I'd done in the past. Or worse, that she'd somehow felt disrespected in some way.

Yes, she asked me to touch her.

Hell, she begged me to fuck her too.

But saying shit when you're about to explode and making rational decisions with a clear head are two very different things.

Jesus, I'd probably hand over the keys to my car right before I blew my load, that's how clouded my judgment could be. Which was why I had to face the possibility that maybe our actions— while hot as all fuck—might not have made her feel good.

Which was why I needed an excuse to go to *Diablo*. Her insistence that we go "hang" somewhere else, taking the opportunity I might have had through the night.

I did what I said I was going to do, dropped Elena home and then walked to Presley's club. It was still early for the public, the big black front doors still locked when I yanked on one.

"Look at you coming through the front door like a good boy." Bennett grinned as he opened up for me. "We just need you to sit and roll over and you'll be all trained up."

I flipped him off, not really in the mood for his shit. "You gaining a little weight there, B? Looking a little rounder in the middle. Maybe add some cardio to the lifts, dude. Also, might want to skip the birth control pills, I hear they cause water retention."

He laughed, stepping aside so I could come in. "Your boy is at the bar, clearly no wiser you're doing his sister. And Presley is in her office. You going to tell him tonight? I spent the afternoon with my mother at the pediatrist, could use some comedic relief."

"No one is saying shit," I warned, not even joking. "I'm serious, Bennett, this is mine and Presley's decision and I won't have you fucking shit up because you're bored."

He rolled his eyes, not giving me the satisfaction of a comeback. "Go see her, I'll keep him busy. You have five minutes though. That's the limit of my small talk, and I'm not making exceptions, even for you two."

It was more than I'd hoped for, the big guy coming through for me in a way I hadn't expected. And while I was under no delusions he was doing it for me—his loyalty to Presley—I was grateful for the chance.

Tibbs was at the bar talking to Hank with his back to the door. Even though he was on the other side of the club, without a wall of bodies, there was a good chance he'd see me sneak in. But the wall of bodies wasn't necessary when you had a three-hundred-pound giant blocking the view, enabling me to stroll past and get out of Tibbs' sightline before he'd even noticed I was there.

I wasn't expecting Presley's door unlocked, the fancy block of wood that separated her from the rest of the club left ajar when I reached it. I didn't bother knocking, not giving her the opportunity to blow me off.

"Hey," I walked into her office, my voice making her spin around, "I've only got four minutes, Bennett is entertaining Tibbs. But I needed to know you were okay."

I didn't ask permission, moving toward her and taking her into my arms. She didn't hesitate, letting me hold her as I kissed her forehead gently. "Presley, if what we did made you feel uncomfortable in some way, I need to know. And I get how it might have looked, but I've never had a girl in my room let alone did anything like that. I respect you, Presley. You're not just a piece of ass."

She blinked back in surprise, her eyes searching my face. "You've never had a girl in your room?"

"I mean, like a girlfriend. My sisters, my mom, like family and shit have obviously been in there, but not like that. I didn't want you to think I was—"

"I was the first?" She cut me off, not letting me finish.

Not sure if that was excitement or horror in her voice, and not sure which was the better option. "Well, yeah. But it doesn't matter. I get how weird it was, especially after and having to go downstairs and eat dinner. So, if that's why you didn't want us here tonight—"

"I love you."

She'd cut me off again, but this time around it was me who was confused. Because either my hearing was fucked or she'd just told me she loved me.

"You saying that because you're the first girl I had in my room or because you can see us being long term, Presley? Because this is the one thing I won't joke about. Not even with you, Baby."

I'd never said those words to a girlfriend.

Never even been tempted.

To me those words were sacred and there hadn't been a woman I'd been with who came close to earning them. So rather than be an asshole, and say them because it might get a woman into bed quicker or something else equally as shady, I chose to not go down that road.

But, Presley.

Fuck.

I hadn't only been tempted to say those words to her, but actively had to stop myself. It was supposed to be just sex, but if I was honest, it hadn't *ever* been like that. Even if I'd been trying to convince myself that it was the whole time. I'd almost fooled myself into thinking it was just about her body, but deep down I knew it was more.

"I mean it. I'm not joking, Jared. I'm in love with you. Me acting weird at dinner wasn't about what we did in the bedroom. It was about what I'd realized after you left. About how much I love you. This isn't just sex for me. And the timing is horrible because I'm trying to—"

It was my turn to cut her off, stopping whatever bullshit excuse that didn't matter, as I pressed my mouth against hers. She moaned, returning my kiss as she fisted my T-shirt. And whatever she was going to say was forgotten, opening her mouth and letting me inside to explore like I wanted.

She nibbled at my lips, my own teeth fighting back as we kissed, sucked and bit. It was hot and deep, and probably not romantic enough considering what she'd just said but I didn't care. It was us.

"I love you, Presley." I pulled away from her mouth so I could say the words and leave no doubt. "In love with you. *Love* you. I don't know the best way to put it, but I know that these feelings are bigger than anything I've ever had. And the thought of being without you makes me fucking crazy."

"Wow, that's a relief. I was so worried you were going to say thanks but no thanks. I told you I wouldn't make things more, and here we are. To be fair, you did warn me, and I *did* get attached." She laughed.

"Just as well, because the feeling is mutual. You want to go out there and tell Tibbs? I think we should celebrate this loving feeling by stopping the sneaking around. I don't want to lie to him anymore, Presley. And I want to be able to kiss you whenever I want without worrying about who is going to see it."

It had been on my mind since I'd left the house, disappointed that she'd been with my family, but they hadn't known she was actually *with* me. My mother would have lost her goddamn mind, been on the phone to Angela Tibbs and planning the fucking wedding. And while the idea had originally scared the hell out of me, I no longer gave a shit. I didn't see a future without Presley in it, and if picking wedding cakes made our mothers happy, then who the hell cared?

"Can you give me a few days?" She winced, her hand on my chest slipping right across my heart. "My dad just left for Chicago for business, and I want to tell them all together. I know he's your best friend, but I need to tell my parents first. After everything I put them through with Lewis, I think they deserve to know I've finally found a good one."

Hearing the asshole's name jacked up rage in me that wasn't healthy. There wasn't a doubt in my mind that he was going to pay, and if Shapiro couldn't find him, we'd track him down some other way. But none of it was ever going to land on her, Presley's days of dealing with cocksuckers over.

"I will never hurt you, Presley. I need you to know that. Never. I don't even know the full extent of what that shithead did, and I already want to kill him. But I can promise you right now, I'd die before hurting you."

"I know." She smiled, the light in her eyes enough to quell whatever doubts I might've had. "Which is why I want my parents to know and for them to see us together. Because there isn't a doubt in my mind that you mean every single word."

There was a buzz on Presley's desk, her cell blasting an alert of an incoming text. She mouthed an apology, picking it up before flashing me the screen.

Big bro taking a piss and I'm done being social. Get lover boy out here for the handover or I'm telling him you're pregnant and naming the kid after him. Choice is yours. And P.S. Yes, you could fire me but you're not going to. Not tonight. B

"Guess you should go out there." Presley rolled her eyes. "It's too late to find more security for the night so I will have to keep him on my payroll."

I kissed her, hating I had to leave her but unable to see the situation as anything but positive. "I'm going to come back and get you in the morning when you're done here. Then I'll drive you home and we can make whatever plans you want to, work out when we can go over and tell your parents. And then go tell mine."

"Okay," she kissed me quickly, holding my shirt despite telling me I needed to leave. "Have fun tonight and see you in the morning. And Leighton," she kissed me again. "I still owe you a blowjob."

"Mmmmmmm," I groaned, the anticipation of those lips around my cock making my balls ache. "You're still not playing fair, Presley." But I didn't care, loving the fucking torture that woman put me through.

Knowing I was already down to the wire, I stopped myself from kissing her again—because that wouldn't end well—and walked backward toward the door. I liked that satisfied grin on her face, waving her goodbye as I headed out of her office. "Bye baby, see you in a few hours."

I'd made it to the bar just before Tibbs got back. Bennett tapped his watch, looking less than impressed. "You boys find your own way out."

"He's so weird, Dude." Tibbs laughed, watching Bennett disappear. "For the longest time I thought for sure he and Presley were together. But nope, they're just friends. And either she's telling the truth or she's the best liar I know. Kind of glad she's not in a relationship at the moment. I love her, but Jesus Christ, does she have the worst fucking taste in men. Hoping she stays single for a while, if you know what I mean."

It didn't give me a warm and fuzzy feeling knowing not only had I'd been lying to Tibbs about mine and Presley's relationship, but we were also talking about her behind her back. And yes, I understood what he was saying, she had made some questionable choices about who she'd dated. But fuck, so had both of us and we weren't getting judged for it.

Presley was far from a damsel in distress. And while she didn't need me defending her honor or telling her big brother to stop being a jackass, I felt the need all the same. "Listen, dude, don't talk about Presley like that. Yeah, Lewis wasn't her best choice, but you want to take a look at the long line of airheads and bimbos you've slept with? That one girl you went out with three months ago had a criminal record for fuck's sake."

Irritation ate at my gut, the idea that anyone could think she was anything but perfect was beyond me. And nothing Tibbs or anyone else said was going to convince me otherwise.

"Yeah, but I only found out later. And notice I'm no longer with her." He shrugged, like it somehow made it better.

"Because she stole a car and broke parole." I pointed out, their break up made a lot easier by the fact she ended up back on the inside for a few months.

He waved his hands, dismissing the evidence. "Circumstances don't matter. We're not together, end of story. And it wouldn't have lasted anyway, it wasn't serious. Presley has a big heart, she deserves better."

That was one thing we could agree on, she sure as hell did.

And I'd spend every last waking moment making sure she got that. What was between us wasn't just a passing flirtation.

It wasn't even just sex.

It was more.

"She's going to be okay, Tibbs. Trust me." I made a promise I couldn't qualify, and I hated it.

Just a few more days, a week tops, and her dad would be back, and we'd come clean. And I couldn't wait.

"Now let's get out of here before she tosses us out."

Chapter 18

Presley

CONFESSING I'D BEEN in love with Jared hadn't been as scary as I'd thought.

It hadn't been scary at all.

One minute I'd been resigned to hiding it, seeing where things went over the next few weeks and then maybe—if I thought I'd get an I love you too—I'd tell him.

And the next minute, I decided that I'd never lived my life in the safe zone and I wasn't going to risk losing the most decent, caring guy I'd ever met.

If he didn't say it back or thought I was too needy, or even if he wanted to stop what we had going on because of it, so be it. I'd rather know.

But he did say it back. And not only did he say it back, but when I looked into his eyes, I believed him. Knew he felt the same things I did, and whatever reasons we'd had for not being together, they were no longer valid. He was the guy for me, the one who I could honestly see something long term with. Someone who'd be my partner and not just someone to pass the time with. And I wanted to do it right.

Jared's arms were around me, his warm body pressed against mine, and he'd done exactly what he promised. He'd gone out with Tibbs to some other club, then returned to *Diablo* just before I closed. Then we drove back to my place where we made love before falling asleep.

At first, it was hurried and hard, both of us needing the connection. I'd wanted to touch him since he made me come in his old bedroom, desperate to make him feel as good as he did me. But after the initial edge was taken off, we slowed down, taking our time and drawing it out, telling him I loved him over and over as he looked me in the eyes.

And then we slept, my body and mind completely relaxed as he held me all through the morning.

"What do you want to do today?" Jared kissed the shell of my ear. "I'm back on rotation tomorrow, but today, I'm all yours."

Usually when I was in a relationship, I was the one with the crazy schedule. The one who was always apologizing for the insane hours. The lack of nights off where we could go be a "regular" couple, my fault. But I hadn't had to do that once, neither of us had.

"Can I ask you a question about your past girlfriends?" I turned in his arms so I could face him.

His eyes narrowed, frowning a little. "Presley, you can ask me whatever you want. But they're in the past for a reason. No point to even think about them anymore."

He was more contemplative than usual, and I assumed it had been because we'd done the whole *I love you* thing. "I promise this isn't me trying to bait you or using it as something to get jealous over." My lips brushed gently against his. "But with the other girls you've been with, did they complain about your hours?"

It was obviously not what he was expecting, his brow scrunching as he focused on me. "What do you mean? Like when I have to work?"

"Yeah, were they pissed if you had to go on a Saturday or couldn't do something on their birthday or something like that?"

He blew out a long breath, and while I was sure he didn't want to talk about it, he wasn't going to avoid it either. "Presley, I haven't dated in a while. But sure, when it came up, it would sometimes piss them off. Who wouldn't like dedicated weekends off? But that's not the job I signed up for, and I sure as hell don't want to be doing something else. Why?"

From the hesitation in his voice he had possibly—and wrongly—guessed it was going to be an issue for me. And rather than let him play out the scenario in his head, I decided to set him straight right away. "My ex-boyfriends always said that about me. That I worked too many hours, didn't take weekends off. That the club was my first priority."

"Well, of course it was." He scrunched his brow like it hadn't occurred to him to be any different. "It had to be, right? You were building something, and if it succeeded or failed, it was on you. What were you going to do? You're one of the youngest successful club managers in the city, you don't get that way by taking off work to cuddle."

No one had ever said that to me.

No. One.

Not even my amazing parents who supported everything I did. They still thought I worked too many hours and were worried I was going to end up in my thirties alone with an ulcer.

"I love you."

He chuckled. "And I love you. Is that what you're worried about? Our schedules? Baby, we'll make it work."

I shook my head. "That's just it. I'm *not* worried. You are the first person who hasn't made me feel like I have to choose. Like I can have you and keep doing what I want with *Diablo*. And I can't imagine you doing anything else either. I don't care that there are nights we can't be together, because when we are, it actually *means* something."

"Presley, I love you, and I love my job. And fuck yeah, we can have both. And I'd rather spend a night sitting in your club waiting for you than wasting time with someone else."

He was so sure, no doubt clouding his beautiful blue eyes as he brushed the hair off my face. "Is there something else you want to tell me? Or do you just need me to tell you that I love you and no matter what happens in the future, that isn't going to change. Because I can do that."

My teeth played with my bottom lip, the internal deliberation raging out of control. David had told me not to tell anyone about *Diablo's* second site, swearing me to secrecy until the contracts were signed. But I needed to tell him, wanting to share it, even if it meant breaking my word to David. "Jared, I'm going to be investing in another site for *Diablo*. I'm not even supposed to talk about it yet but I'm really excited. It will be mine, not because I'm running it, but because I own a stake in it. And it might mean I'm gone more hours, but it's what I want."

His lips spread into a grin. "Did you not hear what I said less than a minute ago? I love you; nothing is going to change. If you need something from me, all you have to do is ask. And yeah, I'm going to miss you when you're not around, but I know where you are, Presley. And I'm so fucking proud of you. You're amazing, way too good for me."

"Stop that," I pushed against his chest, "you are amazing too."

We were right in that moment when his weight shifted. I stared at him puzzled watching as he lifted himself off the bed, and then without warning, pulled me off the mattress and hauled me over his shoulder.

"What are you doing?" I squealed, my head hanging down his back as he smacked my bare ass.

"We're going to go celebrate. I'm taking you out to breakfast even though you say you hate it, and then we're going to work out when we're telling our friends and family. I'm talking pulling out schedules, checking when your dad is back in town, and setting up a phone tree. Because the first chance we get, we're doing it, Presley. I'm not hiding this anymore."

And for once, I didn't argue.

He was absolutely right.

It had been amazing spending time with both Leighton *and* Jared. The line between them was blurring, making me feel slightly undeserving and insanely lucky. Either of them would have made an amazing boyfriend, but together, it was like winning the boyfriend lottery. And more than I could have ever hoped for.

We went to breakfast like he wanted, went to the grocery store and even went home and cooked ourselves dinner. He watched as I got ready for *Diablo*, making me promise at least five times that I would get a ride home with Raelle before he agreed to drop me off at work and then go spend the night at his apartment. He'd even offered to get up early and pick me up but that wasn't practical, and I didn't want to be blamed for him being exhausted.

I hated being responsible, wanting to be selfish and have him meet me early in the morning like he'd suggested. But what he did was important and in order to keep being at the top of his game at work, he needed sleep. I would never forgive myself if he put himself or anyone else at risk because of me. And I was totally capable of spending one night alone, even if I knew I was going to hate it.

Never had my bed felt so empty as it did that night, the sheets feeling cold as I slipped between them, my arms reaching for a body that wasn't there. It reaffirmed what I already knew. I might not *need* Jared, but God, I really wanted him.

The next morning, I woke early. It was ten-thirty and I wasn't even mad. I got up, ate breakfast—who was I anymore?—and went about my regular routine.

I traded text messages with Jared, smiling like an idiot with each exchange. I didn't even care how cliché it seemed, loving hearing from him even if it was just words on a screen. I was still wearing my girly over-exaggerated smile when another message came in shortly before five.

Meet me at the stationhouse. It's important. Tibbs.

Seriously? He wanted me to go to the stationhouse? While he'd said it was important and he didn't usually exaggerate, a few weeks ago I'd have totally blown him off. I was already dressed, ready to go to *Diablo* and wanted to get in early so I could meet with my staff. David had messaged me earlier in the day, saying he was emailing me contracts to send to my lawyer, and I could almost taste the opening of *Diablo 2.0*. But, going to the station meant I would also get to see Jared, which was something I also wanted. And if I was a little late to the club, what was the big deal?

I quickly typed out a message I was on my way and that I'd see him soon. Then I grabbed my purse, keys and phone and left my apartment.

Raelle was still on driver duty, picking me up or driving me home whenever Jared didn't. I still thought it was unnecessary, convinced that Lewis was already bored or found another sucker to con. And while I appreciated the company, I was hoping I could go back to walking to the club or catching my own rides. I'd still go with Jared when he was available because . . . well, I really liked driving with him.

"Rae," I had the phone pressed to my ear as I walked out of my apartment building and onto the street, "change of plans. I need to go see my brother at the stationhouse before coming into work. I'll meet you there."

Rae laughed, making it clear she thought I was full of shit. "Your brother, huh? What's so important you need to see Tibbs right now? Or is it a different fireman that you have a rendezvous with? So saucy. And with your brother around too."

"I'm going to the stationhouse, Raelle. It is literally filled with people. What do you think I'm going to do? Jump into one of the trucks and screw Leighton in the back seat?" I mean, I'd had the fantasy, but I'd never actually do it.

She sighed, seeming to be disappointed. "Fine, don't screw him, but you have to at least kiss him. If you're going to defile our place of business, it's only fair you do the same to his."

Well, she had a point. And while getting down and dirty with Jared with an audience would not be happening, I couldn't see myself leaving there without kissing him either.

"Just meet me at *Diablo*," I chuckled, not volunteering any more information. "Get Hank to check when we're getting our next liquor delivery. Our old driver is still off sick and the new guy comes really late. I want to make sure I have cover at the bar if he has to go help unload."

"Want me to call in Cherry? The girl smokes ten packs a day and is lazy as shit, but can mix drinks when she's chained to the bar. I have some handcuffs in my purse I'll be happy to loan to the cause," Raelle volunteered.

I shook my head, not wanting to know why Rae was walking around with handcuffs in her purse or what else was in there. "Sure, tell Cherry she can do four hours. The delivery should be done by then."

Ending the call, I walked the rest of the way with a smile on my face. I knew I was going to see Jared in the morning, his big warm body crawling into bed beside me after he finished work. But I was glad for the extra opportunity, the happiness I was feeling almost too ridiculous to contain.

"Hey!" Leighton saw me first, stopping himself from pulling me into a hug. It was difficult for me too, my hands twitching at my side pretending I wasn't affected.

Rev and Evans weren't far away, both of them raising their hands in a wave.

"Hey yourself!" I popped Leighton playfully in the arm feeling like an idiot. "Tibbs sent me a message, telling me to meet him here."

Jared's eyes rolled over my body, following the curves of my tight bodycon dress. If he was trying to be casual, he was failing, biting his lip as he cleared his throat. "Yeah, he . . .errr. . . got a call . . . from Shapiro."

It was adorable how much he was trying to act normal, swallowing hard as he yelled out for my brother. He leaned in closer, whispering in my ear so no one else could hear. "This week, Presley. This week we're telling everyone whether your dad is back or not. I'm fucking dying here, and that dress isn't helping the situation."

"Oh really?" I arched my brow, folding my arms across my chest which inevitably pushed up my boobs. "You want me to leave it on? Let you peel it off me when you get home?"

It wasn't even a threat, the idea of his hands unzipping me and working me out of that dress enough to make me wet.

His eyes darted to the hall, the footsteps which probably belonged to my brother making their way closer. "Yes. Leave it on. And more than taking off that dress, I'm dying to kiss you."

"Hey, guys." Tibbs came around the corner, not giving me the chance to tell Jared he was getting that kiss before I left. "What's going on?" His eyes darted between us, either feeling the sexual tension or guessing it was something else.

Leighton shrugged, shoving his hands in his pockets. "Nothing, just talking to Presley. You done with Shapiro?"

Tibbs nodded, his eyes getting huge. "The dude really came through. Listen, Lewis—"

He was cut off, the alarm sounding and getting everyone's attention.

"Shit," Tibbs swore. "Can you stick around? It might be a quick one and this is really important, Pres."

"I don't know, I have to get to the club," I started to argue, not really wanting to hang around indefinitely. "Maybe for an hour or so but then I have to go."

"Presley!" Mack was already in his turnouts, dressed like he was joining the crew. "What are you doing here?"

"Look at you." I wolf whistled, winking at the chief. "Looking pretty sexy. You're going out on a call?"

"North is home with Quinn and the baby, so we're down one. Couldn't fill the spot for tonight, so I'm up." He looked pretty damn pleased with it too. "Hey, if you're going to stick around, can you do me a favor? Hayden was supposed to meet me for dinner and she doesn't really know anyone. Think you could let her know I've gone out on a call and I'll be back?"

There wasn't a lot I wouldn't do for the chief, and waiting around to give his girlfriend a message was the easiest favor I'd ever do. Not to mention, it gave me the chance to see what she was all about, find out what I could about the woman who'd captured the chief's heart.

"Of course, it will be my pleasure. You guys go and I'll be sure to let Hayden know. I'll message you if our plans change," I offered, not knowing if they were going out to a quick call or a building fire that was going to take most of the night.

"See you when we get back," Tibbs gave me a quick hug before jogging away to go get in his turnouts.

With most of the guys busy, Jared pulled me into his arms and gave me a quick kiss. "I love you, see you soon," he whispered, reluctantly letting me go before leaving to change as well.

Butterflies flittered in my stomach, the urge to call him back for one last kiss so overwhelming I had no idea how I'd kept my mouth shut. But I'd see him soon, concentrating on meeting Hayden, who'd be my distraction for a while.

The bay doors opened, and the trucks left, leaving me mostly alone in the stationhouse. There was another crew lingering in the rec room but they kept to themselves, using the time while I waited to check my emails.

It wasn't long before she arrived.

She was pretty, big grey eyes staring at me bewildered as she pushed open the door. She'd obviously dressed up, her blond hair styled to tame her curls while the stunning fitted dress showed off some pretty dangerous curves.

"Hey, you must be Hayden. I'm Presley." I smiled, welcoming her into the building.

"Tibbs' sister?" she asked, her eyes checking me out just as I'd done to her. "Wow, you're gorgeous."

"Thanks, and yeah, the jerk is my brother, but don't hold it against me. Mack told me you were coming and wanted you to wait." I hooked a hand on my hip, wondering what else she'd heard about me.

"Oh, did he need to go?" She looked around, surprised he wasn't there. "He doesn't usually go out with the crew."

I nodded, a small smile edging across my lips as I looked at her outfit. "Chief is riding with them tonight because Riley's home being a daddy, and they got called out. Probably just as well you didn't get here early, would have been harder for him to get into the truck after he'd seen you."

"Well, thanks." She blushed, like she wasn't used to the attention. "I thought it might have been too much, but I just got this and wanted to wear it."

I could tell she was nervous, her hands fidgeting with her dress as she tried to look confident. Without trying to sound condescending, it was actually adorable. She seemed so incredibly nice, Mack deserving someone decent after the nightmare that was his ex-wife. Maybe Jared and I weren't the only ones destined for a happily ever after.

"Oh no, it's not too much. And his eyes are going to launch out of his head, trust me." I laughed, trying to reassure her. "If I didn't have to go to work, I'd stick around just to see it."

"You need to go?" she asked, looking a little nervous.

"Yeah, I like to be at the club early. Meet with my front of house and security before it gets busy. Once the doors open, I like to be on the floor." I checked the time on my phone again. *Shit.* It was already well after six. "And I'd have already been there if my pain-in-the-ass brother hadn't texted me to meet him here. Not sure why he couldn't just have left me a message. Weekends are insane for me."

"Is it as exciting as it sounds? Running a nightclub." Her eyes warmed with kindness, but nervously flicked around the stationhouse like she wasn't looking forward to being left alone. And to be honest, I hadn't really found out anything interesting, so I wasn't ready for the conversation to end either.

I laughed, already deciding to invite her to come with me. "It has its moments. You want to come hangout with me until they get back? It's not far, and at least there I can buy you a drink."

She couldn't agree fast enough, the, "Yes, I'd love that," flying out of her mouth the minute I'd asked.

"Then let's get out of here. I'll text Tibbs and let him know you're with me. Mack can call you when he gets back." I tossed the phone back into my handbag, motioning to the door as I smiled. "I should probably let you know I have ulterior motives. Chief hasn't dated anyone seriously since he split up with his wife. Well, not anyone we've seen. And considering the amount of time he spends with my brother—who no shit couldn't keep a secret if his life depended on it—we would've totally known if he had. There's been no one. Well, not until you. So, naturally I want to know everything."

She smiled too, a breath of relief escaping her lips as she nodded her head. "Hey, if you're buying me drinks, I'll tell you anything you want to know. I'm pretty much a lightweight these days."

"Oh, we're gonna have some fun tonight." I pulled open the door and led us back out to the street.

It wasn't far, *Diablo* only two blocks from the stationhouse which made it a really quick walk. Hayden still seemed a little tense, her gray eyes widening as we walked inside the club.

"The owner is an investor from Hong Kong. As long as I keep up profits, he doesn't care what I do with it. It's a rare thing, usually they want to interfere or assume I need my hand held because I'm a woman. Doesn't matter I have a business degree and worked in clubs all through college. In this world, unless you have a penis, they want you either serving their drinks or dancing on a pole, and they can kiss my ass if I'm doing either of those things."

I hoped by sharing a little information it would help her relax. Last thing I wanted to do was make her feel uncomfortable, and judging by her body language she was way out of her comfort zone.

"So what about you? What do you do?" I asked as we settled at the bar.

Staff had started to come in but were largely ignoring us. It wasn't uncommon for me to take meetings just before opening, and they knew enough not to bother me unless it was urgent when I had company. Bennett looked over nodding his head in greeting, while I grabbed some bottles from behind me and waited for Hayden's answer.

"I'm a sales associate at Target. And do some medical transcription at home. It pays the bills." I could hear in her tone how much she hated her job, almost as if she was ashamed of it. I hated that for her.

"Well, I sure as hell wouldn't turn down that discount." I shrugged, lowering two glasses on the bar. "I can't go into the place without spending like a hundred bucks. Last week I went in for a throw rug and ended up with a cart full of stuff I didn't need. Oh, and I totally forgot the throw rug so had to go back."

Hank asked if I wanted him to take over, but I assured him we were fine, Hayden and I laughing about how much money we unnecessarily spent in Target while he continued to set up the bar.

"They have a lot of respect for you. Lots of bosses would have sat down, asked for drinks, not caring about what they had to get done." She nodded to Hank. "I bet they love working here."

I looked over at my bar manager, smiling because he was ignoring us. "It's not hard to treat people with respect. And just because I have a degree doesn't make me any more important than any of them. You can replace a club manager fairly easily, but good staff are hard to find. The place would fall in a heap. And I'm not above making my own drinks. I said I wouldn't make them for misogynistic assholes, but for us is a different story." I grinned, pouring the vodka, topping up with soda then dropping in some of the freshly cut lime. "So tell me, Hayden. You like working at Target? And I say that with no judgment. But I did warn you I was going to pry, and I get the feeling it wasn't the dream job you had in mind."

She sighed as I handed her a vodka and soda, telling me she'd dropped out of college her second year and her life got stuck in a rut. She'd done odd jobs here and there where she could, landing in retail because it was reliable.

"Wow, this is really good." She nodded to the drink.

"Thanks, but it's hard to mess up a lime, vodka and soda. I leave all the fancy stuff to the professionals. And you still haven't answered my question. All you did was justify why you're there."

I wasn't trying to put her on the spot or make her feel unwelcome. But as someone who was finally about to realize her dream, I wished that for other women too. So many times we were asked to settle. To wait our turn, to be happy with the scrapes we were given. And that wasn't close enough to what we deserved. I could already tell Hayden deserved more too.

"It's okay. Am I happy? No, not really, but I'd be less happy if I was unemployed and living on the streets." Surprisingly she didn't stop there, giving me a detailed explanation of the type of work she'd do if given a chance. She was incredibly analytical, very clear in the operational requirements of businesses, and what was involved in risk assessment and compliance. It was so refreshing, lacking the starchy, boring language that came from someone usually in the field.

She was clearly smart, her current retail role not even close to reaching her potential. And just like David had taken a risk on me, I'd easily hire someone who didn't necessarily have the "right" qualifications if they had the right attitude and could think on their feet.

"It's not too late." I took a sip from my glass, enjoying the tartness of the lime. "You could take night classes. Online college."

She laughed, probably assuming I was joking. "Or I could stay at Target and keep my amazing discount."

There was something about her that was different, and I was pretty good at reading people. She was more than what she was showing on the outside, bottled-up potential that reminded me a lot of . . . well, me. Not sure why I even felt so strongly about it, I mean, we'd just met. And other than knowing Mack was crazy in love with her, I didn't know a whole lot else. But I wanted to. I wanted to help her in some way, and had a hunch she'd be an amazing part of my team.

"True, but if you ever change your mind, decide you want to do something else? Give me a call. No one says you have to stay on the road you're on, just remember that." I tried to play it off casually but really meant it, hoping she would see what I saw, and would someday give me a call.

She cleared her throat nervously, as she took another drink.

"So if you're allowed to pry, then I am too. What do you know about Mack's ex-wife?"

Great.

Mack's ex-wife.

Next to my own ex, she was another one I didn't like talking about. Melinda had been frequently coming to *Diablo*, probably hoping to bait Mack or piss me off. And while I hated her, she hadn't done anything wrong—yet. She even kept her distance from Jared, leaving him alone since her original proposition of a blowjob. But I could understand the worry, the shadow of a crazy ex was something that followed me too. I wondered if Jared worried about it, and if sometime later it might become an issue.

Just saying her name was distasteful, unable to hide my disgust as I answered her question. "Melinda? Enough to know she's bad news. In any case, you're here and she isn't, so I wouldn't worry about her."

Deciding a change of subject would be better for everyone, I instead asked about Ava, Riley and Quinn's new baby girl. Other than a photo Riley had sent everyone, I hadn't had a chance to visit but knew Mack and Hayden had been at the hospital when she'd been born.

After Hayden gushed about how sweet she was and filled in a few more details, I decided I needed to get back to work. As much as I wanted to stay and chat some more, I had some things I wanted to go over with the team. "You going to be okay around here for a bit by yourself? I have some meetings I need to take, but it shouldn't take too long. I can come and chat in between my tasks until Mack gets back."

She nodded, waving her hand like it was no big deal. "Of course, I'm fine. And thanks so much for the drink. If I'm not going to be in the way, I'd love to just hang around. I'd rather wait in here than sit at the stationhouse."

"You're welcome to stay as long as you like, and I don't blame you. That place is made for function but isn't as sexy as *Diablo*. I totally picked the color scheme, the designer almost having a heart attack." I laughed, remembering the pushback I'd gotten. And in a few short months, I was going to do it again, this time with even more authority.

Instructing Hank to look after Hayden at the bar, I took my drink and headed to my office. I tried not to look too happy, the smile I usually tried to contain when I was at work, beaming off my face.

"You screwed him." Raelle was sitting on my desk waiting for me as I entered my office. "All that talk about not wanting to do it with an audience, and there you go. Such a dirty girl, I fully approve," she laughed, with a little too much joy in her irises.

I rolled my eyes, sinking into the chair behind my desk. "I didn't. And if I did, I wouldn't tell you about it."

"Well, if it wasn't sex then he did something equally as good." She pointed accusingly. "You better keep him around, smiles like that on you are hard to come by."

"I'm in love with him, Rae," I admitted, not wanting to hide it any longer. "In. Love. With. Him."

It was her turn to roll her eyes, grinning. "Girl, tell me something I *don't* know. Now, move in together already because you've wasted enough time."

And she was right.

Usually I dated a guy for months before I'd even consider moving him in, but Jared was different. And not just because I'd known him forever.

It was different because I couldn't see another guy ever taking his place.

Because he was the one.

And I'd wasted enough time.

Chapter 19

Jared

I WASN'T GOING to make it.

Presley had shown up in that dress and tested whatever resolve I had left. How I was able to 1. Stop myself from kissing her and 2. Not tell everyone she was my girlfriend was a mystery for the heavenly Father. I wasn't even sure how I'd made it onto the engine, my arms and legs doing what they needed so I could pull on my turnouts and leave with the rest of my team.

It had been a shop fire, Mack riding shotgun on account North was still out. He'd made some bullshit excuse that he couldn't find cover but deep down I think he missed it and wanted back in. Can't say it's something I could walk away from, but the chief was a different man.

We'd partnered up, sent into the basement on a rescue or recovery. It had been an intense few minutes, but we'd located the guy, Chief showing he still had what it took as he hauled him out without an assist needed by me.

After we'd gotten the patient to the EMTs, Cap ordered us back on lines. Nothing could be done to save the structure, letting the fire and water fight its way to conclusion until we were finally standing in front of the rubble.

It had been at least a couple of hours, and any hope that Presley was still going to be waiting was gone. She would be at *Diablo* in *that* dress, and I'd have to do my best not to jerk off in the shower. We were definitely having wake up sex the minute I got to her apartment, my dick hardening in my uniform just at the thought of it.

And surprise, surprise, when we got back not only was Presley MIA but Hayden as well. Tibbs grinned as he checked his phone and saw his sister had taken Chief's woman to the club with her.

"Poor Hayden," Tibbs laughed. "I think I'd rather have an interrogation from Shapiro than one from Presley. Chief is gonna be pissed."

"Well then, you should go tell him, better he hears it sooner than later." I grinned, liking the idea of a Presley interrogation probably a little too much for my own good.

Not that she would have to try too hard, all she'd have to do is look at me with those eyes and I'd agree to anything.

Tibbs left to go find the chief while I grabbed my phone and hoped to find a message of my own. She hadn't disappointed me, unable to contain my grin as I opened it.

Thinking about you and can't wait until tomorrow morning. Love P xx

She wasn't the only one, the countdown to the end of my shift happening as I sent my reply.

I'm considering getting paperwork from Chief and sneaking out to see you early. Not sure I can wait. Love you more xx

I shoved the phone back into my pocket, grinning like an idiot as I heard the chief yell. And not just the regular kind of yelling when one of us pissed him off or something. It was different, a roar that would make a wild animal back the hell off.

Without even thinking I ran to Mack's office, Tibbs busting through the door just as I joined him.

"You okay, Chief?" Tibbs asked, followed by my, "We heard you yell."

"What the hell did your fucking sister say?" Chief blasted, looking angrier than we'd ever seen him. "You get Presley on the phone right now!"

Presley?

I looked over at Tibbs wondering if he had any idea on what she had to do with Mack's combustion, but he looked as clueless as I did.

"What's going on?"

"Hayden sent me a message." He looked down at his phone, shaking his head. "It's just. . . she's. . . said she was done."

"What?" I coughed out in disbelief thinking it had to be a mistake. "You sure you didn't read it wrong?"

"Did I read it wrong?" He barked out a humorless laugh as his jaw tightened. "You tell me." He tossed me the phone, letting me read it myself.

Mack,
It's over between us. We clearly want different things and if we continue, someone is bound to get hurt. Please, don't try and call me, I won't answer. Trust me, this is for the best. Goodbye.
Hayden

I could feel Tibbs behind me, his eyes reading the same thing I was. "Chief, this has to be a mistake. She doesn't seem like—"

"Get your sister on the phone now." The words strangled by his clenched jaw. "She was probably the last person who spoke to her, and I want to fucking know what the hell was said."

Deciding to do what Mack asked, Tibbs dialed Presley while I handed Chief back his phone. I had no idea what was going on, but there was no way Presley could be involved. She loved Mack like all of us did, and there was no way she'd do anything to hurt him. Her text to me hadn't been anything unusual, and if something had gone down, surely she would've mentioned it. And while I was worried for the chief and the state of his relationship, my need to find out if Presley was okay was higher on my list of priorities.

Something didn't add up.

We watched while Tibbs relayed the info to Presley, Chief stalking like a caged animal as we waited for more intel.

"Presley said she left the club a little bit ago, so she assumed she was with you. Bartender saw her go outside to check her phone and didn't come back." Tibbs held his phone from his ear, taking a swallow before adding the next part, "Chief, apparently she'd asked about Melinda."

"Fuck!" Mack roared, his fist hitting the desk. "Ask Presley if Melinda is there, I have a hunch I already know the answer."

Tibbs brought the phone back to his ear and asked Presley, his head nodding when he got the response. "She's sitting at the bar."

"Good, tell Presley to keep her there if she tries to leave. I'm on my way." He grabbed his keys and phone, calling in a replacement for himself as he walked out the door.

"We should go." I pointed to the doorway, the chief already telling Cap he was leaving. "Whatever the fuck is going on, Presley doesn't have anything to do with it."

Tibbs shot me a funny look, my concern for his sister a little more than friendship. "Of course she hasn't got anything to do with it. But we just can't leave. Mack's pissed, but he'd never hurt her. Jesus, why do you look like that? You're starting to freak me out."

I wasn't exactly sure how I looked, and really didn't give a shit how it made Tibbs feel. But something in my gut was telling me it was all wrong and I needed to see her.

It was my turn to talk to Cap, leaving Tibbs in Mack's office as I went to find him.

"I need to leave too," I said, not hesitating as Cap lifted his head.

He popped a brow, probably wondering where I got the balls to make those kinds of demands, but I'd deal with the paperwork later. "Want to run that past me again, Leighton? Because I know you saw the Chief just leave and we're down North too."

Tibbs appeared at my side, not saying a word as I continued, "Cap, I'll take whatever punishment you give me. But I'm walking out that door with your permission or without it. I need to go see Presley."

"Why the fuck do you need to see my sister?" Tibbs shoved my shoulder. "And what the hell does it have to do with Mack storming out?"

Presley was going to be pissed.

But much like Cap's fury, I'd deal with all of it later.

"I have no idea about Mack, but something about this doesn't feel right. And I need to see Presley because I'm in love with her."

It was like a bomb had gone off; the room pitched into silence as noise ceased to exist. Tibbs blinked—like he couldn't register the words—unmoving, while Cap's gaze ping ponged between us, probably lost as well.

Tibbs narrowed his eyes, his expression unreadable. "What did you say?"

"I said I'm in love with Presley. I love her. And whatever the hell is going on over there with Mack or Hayden, I don't want her to be alone."

His head snapped up, taking a step back as he held up his hands. "Wait a minute. What about this girl you've been dating?"

"Presley *is* the girl. I've been dating Presley. I've been with her this whole time."

Didn't know if that made it better or worse. Sure, he'd seen me turn down any other girl who'd even looked my way, my interest in anyone else nonexistent. But he also knew how many nights I'd spent in "my girlfriend's" bed; my time at our apartment so limited he'd started to think I was moving out.

Which meant . . .

"You're *fucking* my sister!" Tibbs lunged, his voice booming. "What the fuck is wrong with you?"

"Hey!" Cap yelled, standing up and throwing his weight into the mix. "Both of you need to calm the fuck down. There will be no fighting in here, understood?"

I hadn't even raised my fists, willing to take a punch if that was what it took because honestly, I couldn't blame Tibbs. And I'd take whatever Cap had to offer too, neither of those things changing the situation.

"Wait!" Tibbs pointed a finger in my chest. "When you met me with her key, you'd been with her the whole time? I was going out of my mind trying to get a hold of her, and you'd been there the whole night fucking—"

"I love her, man. LOVE her. I'm not with her because I was bored or to use her for sex. I could *never* do that. Not just because she's your sister, but because I've always cared and respected her. But it's different now, and I can't be without her. She's in here." I tapped my chest, my words not even close to how much I felt for her. I couldn't back down, my chest rising and falling with each heavy breath as I stood my ground. "You know me,

Tibbs. Look me in the eyes and tell me you think I'm capable of ever hurting her."

Cap was in between us but hadn't said another word. Not sure if that was because he didn't know what to say or was waiting to see if Tibbs was going to take another swing. I didn't know either, looking at him and hating the way he'd had to find out.

But I refused to fight my best friend.

I just wouldn't do it.

Even if he wanted to lay me out for no other reason than lying to him, I'd take it.

"We were going to tell you." I ran a hand through my hair in frustration. "We were waiting till your old man came back because Presley wanted tell your family all together. This isn't just a fling, dude. It's the real deal. And I only have two regrets about this whole thing. One, that I hadn't made her mine sooner, and two, lying to you."

"Fuuuuuuuuuuuuuuuccck," Tibbs huffed out a breath, squeezing the bridge of his nose with his fingers. "You're making it really hard for me to be pissed at you right now."

"I won't hurt her, Tibbs. Ever," I promised, knowing it was the easiest promise I was ever going to make. "I'm not Lewis."

"Shit, shit, shit. I forgot about Lewis," Tibbs cursed out, turning back to Cap. "Sorry, Cap, but we both need to go."

Cap hadn't even had a chance to argue when my phone rang, it was Presley and I didn't even hesitate to pick it up. "Presley, are you okay?" The words out of my mouth before I could even say hello.

"Jared, he's got Hayden." I could tell she was trying to keep calm, her voice wavering all the same. "Lewis grabbed her from the *Diablo* parking lot, and he's taken her somewhere."

"Lewis did what?" I asked, the words not making sense.

Tibbs yanked my arm, the mention of the cocksucker's name in connection with his sister getting his attention.

"Presley, I'm putting you on speaker. I'm here with Tibbs and Cap, tell us exactly what happened."

Hitting the speaker button, I lowered the phone. "Go ahead, Presley, we can all hear you."

"Mack came to the club to set Melinda straight, thinking she'd said something to Hayden. But it wasn't her. They hadn't even met. I was checking the surveillance footage, seeing if maybe I could work it out. That's when I saw him grab her near the staff entrance and force her into his car. I've called the cops, and they've put a trace on her phone, and Mack stormed out of here like a bat out of hell."

"Pres, it's me," Tibbs piped in. "Lewis is in deep. Gambling debts. At least fifty K. He needs money, a lot of it and fast. We haven't been able to find him because he wasn't just dodging the police but loan sharks as well. He's in serious trouble so I guess he got desperate."

"Then why didn't he just take me? Why would he hurt her? I swear if anything happens to Hayden, I'll never forgive myself. I brought her *here*. It's my fault."

Even though I couldn't see her, I could hear it in her voice how hard she was trying to keep it together. But she wouldn't allow herself to crumble, fighting back tears and panic, trying to keep her voice normal.

She was so strong, but I hated that she needed to be. And the mention of Lewis potentially taking her instead made me so fucking angry I couldn't see straight. "None of this is your fault. You didn't do this. This is on him, Presley. They're going to find her and she's going to be okay. Stay where you are, Tibbs and I are coming."

There wasn't even a question of whether I was leaving. Short of Cap and the entire crew holding me down, I wasn't sticking around. They could even threaten to fire me and I'd still be walking, my need to get to Presley at an all-time high.

But Cap didn't fight us, tossing us a scanner, pointing to the door, and telling us to go. "Keep your radios on and me posted at all times."

With no way of knowing what else we were dealing with, walking to the club was sidelined. If for no other reason than to have the means to go find the chief, the idea that it was going to take longer to get to *Diablo* killing me as I fisted my keys.

Tibbs and I raced out of the station without saying a word, both of us sprinting to my Mustang without a discussion. As much as he loved his Impala, Elena could leave him in my exhaust fumes at the lights, and speed was something we definitely needed.

Doors slammed either side of my car, the ignition on and the engine revving before we'd even fastened our belts. Tibbs turned on the scanner, his phone in his hand already dialing as I left rubber in the parking lot.

"Rockefeller, it's Tibbs. We're on route to *Diablo*, any word on Hayden's location?"

Rockefeller's impatient voice boomed out of the phone. "We're handling it, Tibbs. You and your boys keep out of our way. Shit is more complicated than it looks."

"What does that mean?" I yelled back, changing lanes whenever I caught a break. We'd have already been there if there wasn't so much traffic, but sitting behind a bumper and laying on my horn wasn't happening either.

"It means you guys will stand down. Let PD handle this. And for God's sake, find Mack."

"Fuck this." Finding a narrow opening, I hammered on the gas and slid in front of a delivery truck. We almost traded paint, the bastard cursing me out as I drove by him like a maniac.

"Anything goes down with Mack, you don't take him in, okay. Fuck procedure, Rockefeller, this piece of shit deserves whatever is coming to him," Tibbs warned, hanging on as we skidded into the parking lot of *Diablo*.

"Don't tell me how to do my job, asshole," Rockefeller spat back. "He's one of ours, doesn't need to be said."

Ending the call, we both ejected from the car and hit the staff entrance of Presley's club. She was with Bennett just inside the door, her eyes wild, red because she'd either been crying or was trying not to and wringing her hands like a junkie looking for her next hit.

I couldn't even talk, pulling her into my arms and kissing her the minute I got close enough. "We're here, Presley. We're right here."

A racked sob bubbled up her throat, fisting my shirt as she lifted her head. "Have you heard anything?"

"No, but everyone's looking."

Fuck.

If Mack didn't kill the son of a bitch, I sure as hell would, pulling Presley back to my chest as I nodded to Bennett. "You guys secure? We have no idea if he's working alone or if he's got some other agenda."

Bennett didn't even bother with his usual bullshit, tipping his chin as his voice barreled out. "Eyes on all entrances and roving guards on the floor. And Presley has a new fashion accessory tonight, me."

If I couldn't be the one to keep her safe, Bennett would be the guy I chose for the job. The man could take down a tank with his bare hands and wouldn't flinch, and right now, I needed her safe more than I needed my pride.

"Shots fired, active shooter. Target, West 225th Street. Bronx. All units please respond." The announcement from dispatch echoed from the scanner Tibbs was holding. *"Please maintain perimeter and wait for SWAT."*

"Jesus Christ, is that where Hayden works?" Tibbs asked, speed dialing Mack. He hadn't answered the last few times but if ever there was a time to call in a miracle, that would've been it.

I gave Presley one last hug, hating myself already for needing to make the choice. "Bennett," I nailed him with a stare, "I need you to do this for me, dude. We've got to go and it's too dangerous to take her with me."

He nodded in understanding. "They'd have a better chance at getting to the President tonight. Go, I've got it covered."

Whatever control Presley had before was gone, her beautiful brown eyes pooling with tears as she hugged me first and then Tibbs, telling us both to be safe.

"I love you, Presley." I turned to Tibbs and pulled out my keys. "We've got to go."

Chapter 20

Jared

ITHER WE'D MANAGED to cash in that miracle or one of the angels was intervening, but we finally got through to Mack. He'd gone to check out Hayden's apartment in Inwood when he'd heard the 9-1-1 call from the store manager come through dispatch. Tibbs rapid fired his additional information, letting Mack know we were on the way as we hit the FDR.

The phone wasn't even on speaker, the roar coming down the line as clear as if he was sitting in the car with us. I could only imagine how he felt, the idea that it could've been Presley, still very much on my mind.

Which was why I called North.

I knew his wife had just had a baby and the last thing he needed was to be tangled up in this mess. But if shit went down, Mack was going to need his family. And as much as I liked to think Tibbs and I could be there for him, there was only one of us he saw as a son, and that was Riley.

By the time we'd pulled into the Target parking lot, the active shooter situation had turned to shit. SWAT had stormed in and gotten the gunman down, but not before he'd shot a female victim. And I didn't need to hear the description to know it had been Hayden.

We met Mack in the parking lot, the guy half out of his mind as Rockefeller tried to talk him down. I didn't like the detective's chances; the stare Mack was giving him lethal. Not sure if it was an effort to keep Mack calm or he'd finally decided to throw us a bone, but Rockefeller shed some light on Lewis.

It seemed the cocksucker hadn't only been Presley's ex-boyfriend but was also related to Hayden. In what had to be slim-to-none chances, Lewis Goodman, AKA DJ Lewis G, was actually Lewis *Wright*, brother to Cooper Wright, Hayden's ex-husband.

There'd been some family issues, all of them disowning him—something I completely understood. So, by the time he'd started dating Presley, he was a completely reincarnated fuckface. Between that, the gambling and the debts he owed, he was a man ready to do anything to save his own ass. Even if it was taking someone he once shared a last name with at gunpoint.

By the time the EMTs entered there was no holding Mack back. And he'd either pulled rank or everyone was scared to tell him no, the chief pushing through the crowd to reach Hayden while Tibbs and I followed.

It was intense.

Cops were everywhere, collecting evidence, securing the scene, and a couple had taken the shithead into custody. Why they hadn't just taken him down with a bullet to the head instead of the leg was beyond me. But I guess that was why I was a great fireman and would have made a lousy cop.

There was blood on the floor, Mack begging Hayden to stay awake as we looked on, unable to contribute any help. It was tough to watch, EMTs working on Hayden while Mack hovered like he was ready to rip out someone's spine if they didn't do everything they could to help her.

With so much blood, it was hard to see where exactly Hayden had been shot. It looked like a chest wound, the fact she was still semi-conscious a good sign and probably the only reason Mack hadn't lost it completely.

"Her pulse is stabilizing. We need to move her," Maree—one of the EMTs shouted, Taylor—the other—helping roll Hayden onto a stretcher.

As much as I sympathized with Mack, he was getting in the way, making Maree and Taylor's job ten times harder because they had to contend with him as well.

With a silent nod, Tibbs and I each grabbed a side and held him back, Mack blinking back in genuine surprise. Either he'd forgotten we were there or he didn't think we'd try and stop him, his death stare just as lethal as his tone.

"I'm going. Move your arms or I'll rip them from their sockets."

"You're no good to her if you're getting in the way." North got in between the chief and the stretcher. "I'll take you to the hospital, but you're riding with me."

Never had I been so glad to see Riley, his hand pressed against Mack's chest with a single focused determination. Considering the guy had a newborn, probably hadn't slept much, *and* had made a mercy dash from Brooklyn, he looked surprisingly calm.

"What are you doing here? Why aren't you home with Quinn and Ava?" Mack focused on North, not having seen him arrive.

"Because I was needed here. Now stand down, Mack. You might be able to take on one of us, but not even you can take on all three." North wouldn't back down and we all knew it, the best chance of Mack getting to the hospital was to comply.

"Fine, you drive. But you drive like you have a purpose, North." He fingered him hard in the chest. "And someone find out where the hell they're taking her. We also need to call her family."

"I can do that. Her brother is her emergency contact. I'll call." A blonde woman who was apparently the store manager had appeared, trying to reassure Mack. "Go, just get one of your guys to let me know which hospital."

I was already on the phone as North and Mack left, finding out which hospital the ambulance was going to so I could pass on the information.

"She's going to New York-Presbyterian Allen on Broadway," I told the manager, Tibbs texting the info to Mack as I ended the call. "They're probably going to need to take her straight to surgery."

The manager nodded, grabbing her own phone as she left me and Tibbs with the cops. It was crazy to think how close Hayden came to dying; the only thing saving her was that Lewis hadn't just been the worst person alive, but a lousy shot as well. He'd grazed a couple of ribs, hitting her in the chest but missing anything vital. It was the kind of luck you prayed for, and more than often didn't get delivered.

"We need to get back to Midtown." I nodded to Tibbs, fisting my keys. "Presley."

Her name had been enough of an explanation, Tibbs nodding as he followed me back outside to my car.

"You really love her, Jared?"

It was the first time he'd said my real name in years. The sound of it so foreign in his mouth, it almost felt wrong.

"More than I ever thought was possible." I stopped short, looking him in the eyes before getting into the car. "She's the one for me."

He nodded. "Good, because she's going to need you now more than ever. This shit isn't going to be over for her even if Lewis is out of the picture. You saw her back at *Diablo*, she blames herself and she's going to need someone who is going to stick around. She's going to say she's fine because that's what Presley does, but Brother, she is going to be so far from fine."

He wasn't telling me anything I didn't already know, seeing the weight of responsibility in Presley's eyes before we'd left the club. It was why it had been so hard to leave, even though I knew she'd be safe.

"I'm in this for the long haul, Justin. I'm not going anywhere."

He shot me a look of relief. "Then let's go."

Chapter 21

Presley

"FUCK, FUCK, FUCK." I paced back and forth in my office, Bennett perched on the desk, watching me.

I'd been going out of my mind until Jared called, every worst-case scenario flashing before my eyes as I imagined poor Hayden with the monster I used to share my bed with.

And then when Jared called, my mental roulette just got worse.

Lewis shot her.

SHOT HER.

Never would I have believed he could do that to someone, let alone a person who was once his sister-in-law. I still couldn't believe Lewis and Hayden's ex-husband were brothers. That we were somehow connected by a sad and tragic thread of terrible men.

God, I'd been so stupid.

So fucking stupid.

"Stop doing that. I'm getting fucking seasick," Bennett grunted. "You heard what they said. She's going into surgery, she's going to be fine."

My feet stopped moving.

Not because I was worried about making Bennett sick, but because he was being so casual. And yes, I knew he didn't do drama, his resting heart rate rarely getting elevated except when he worked out. It was one of the reason's I'd hired him in the first place. He was clinical, precise, solution orientated, and basically unflappable.

But Hayden had been *shot* by my ex-boyfriend.

"You don't know she's going to be fine. She could code on the table, she could die from sepsis, she could—"

"And monkeys could fly out of my ass." He folded his arms across his chest and pointed to the empty chair behind my desk. "Sit down. You don't want to believe me, believe *Smoke Alarm*. You think he'd lie to you?"

"You know his goddamn name," I groaned, giving up my commitment to wear a hole in the floor and sitting in the stupid chair.

Bennett laughed, not concerned in the slightest that tonight might be the time I actually followed through with firing him. "It's more fun my way. And you didn't answer my question. Do you think—"

"Jared. Jared or Leighton, say it," I spat out, frustrated.

"Jar-ed," he elongated his name unnecessarily, "would lie to you?"

His eyes were on mine, forcing them to connect with his, and I cursed under my breath because he was right.

"No, no he wouldn't lie."

Jared had assured me she was still breathing when Hayden had left in the ambulance. And that she was going to get the best medical care. And that he loved me and would be there soon.

Bennett was right.

I needed to trust him.

My head fell into my hands, the weight of my skull feeling too heavy for my own neck. "If anything happens to her—" I couldn't finish the thought.

Hayden might have once been related to the guy, but he was in the parking lot because of me. He was there for money. *My* money.

"Then the asshole who did it will wear the blame. Not you."

The sound of his voice snapped my head up, Jared standing in my doorway flanked by my brother. "This isn't your fault."

I didn't bother answering, out of my chair so fast that I didn't even realize I'd ran until my arms were around his neck. "If—"

He didn't let me finish, kissing me in front of Bennett and Tibbs and pulling me closer to his body. And I was kissing him back before I realized that, while Bennett might've known we were together, my brother sure as hell didn't.

"Oh my God," I pulled back, my mouth struggling for words. "Tibbs."

He rolled his eyes, not wearing the same shock I was as he smiled. "I know you two are together. Leighton told me."

I didn't even care about the circumstances; glad he didn't seem angry and that I could go back to kissing Jared.

My lips found his again, my emotions bubbling to the surface as I sought out more of him. His hands wrapped around my body while my fingers yanked at his shirt, both of us lost in each other as his kiss said everything he needed to say without uttering a word.

Tibbs cleared his throat. "Hey, I said I knew you guys were together. Not sure I want to see you make out. You guys want to save that for later? Like when I'm not around and when we don't have to get to the hospital."

"The hospital," I nodded feeling like a selfish bitch making out with my hot boyfriend while Hayden was in hospital. "We need to go now."

I had never left the club before closing.

Even when I'd been sick, half dead and tired, I dragged my animated corpse to work and limited my contact with everyone else so I didn't give them the plague.

But I was always there.

"B, can you close for me?" The words I'd never said before fell from my lips easily. "I'll handle all the reports in the morning, just get everyone out and lock up."

His brows popped in surprise but recovered quickly. "Sure thing, Boss. You need anything else before you leave?"

"Nothing, and thanks." I let go of Jared briefly, heading to my desk and collecting my handbag. "We should go."

"Okay, let's go." Jared nodded, looping my fingers through his as I joined him at the doorway.

There was no hesitation, walking through *Diablo*—that was still filled with bodies—and leaving, like it was the most natural thing to do. I knew it would be okay, and my presence was required somewhere more important.

Jared's Mustang was parked in the same lot Lewis had taken Hayden, a shiver running through my body as we walked toward the car. Tibbs offered to sit in the back, the idea of him folding himself into the tiny space so ridiculous I just shook my head. I popped the passenger seat, sliding into the back bench seat before Jared and Tibbs both climbed in.

The engine roared to life, Jared flying out of the parking lot and into the street, before I'd even done up my seatbelt. He'd been patient in *Diablo*, not rushing me, but I understood the need to get to the hospital. God, Mack must be a mess.

"Is someone with Mack?" I asked from the backseat.

"North," Tibbs offered over his shoulder. "Leighton called him and he met us at Target, he drove Chief to the hospital."

The tightness in my chest eased knowing Riley was with him. I hated to think he was alone, and could only imagine what he must be feeling.

The trip to the hospital was made in silence. Tibbs giving Cap a status report while trading text messages with North who was with Chief, both Jared and I listening as he relayed information. My hands were knotted in my lap, watching traffic pass in a blur until we reached New York-Presbyterian Allen.

We were ushered into a waiting room. Hayden's brother and sister-in-law, along with a blond I didn't recognize, were already waiting with North and Mack. Chief looked terrible, like he hadn't slept in a month, his hair ruffled at weird angles from having his hands run through it too many times.

Like I was on autopilot, I walked up to Mack and offered him a hug. He gave me a weak smile, circling me with his big arms as I told him I was sorry again.

"It's not your fault, Presley." He dropped a soft kiss on the top of my head. "So stop apologizing."

It was hard to agree, my nodding more to placate everyone than because I actually believed it. I took a seat, feeling useless as I waited like everyone else.

Jared slung his arm around me, pulling me closer as he kissed my forehead. I needed to be touched, wondering if it would raise too many eyebrows if I crawled into his lap and snuggled against his chest.

I'd never been *that* girl.

Never needed a man to be my anchor, happy to fill that role for myself.

But it was different with Jared, it just felt less like an emotional dependency and instead, a partnership of support. And at that moment, it was support that I needed.

When the doctor finally came to tell us Hayden was out of surgery, I almost wept in relief. Her vitals were strong, but she was still in recovery, the doctor letting Mack know he'd be able to see her soon.

I'd never seen Mack so grateful, shaking the doctor's hand like he was going to dislocate the poor guy's shoulder.

"I'm going to get some coffee," I whispered to Jared, needing something to do other than sit around and feel terrible. "I'll be right back."

"I'll come with you," he offered, standing up before I'd had a chance to agree.

His fingers linked into mine, North raising a brow when he saw our joined hands, but he didn't say anything. Even if he didn't guess what our hand-holding meant, I wasn't exactly going to make an announcement.

Hey guess what everyone, Hayden didn't die annnnd I'm dating Leighton! Woo-hoo!

Yeah, that was going to have to wait for another day, hopefully one that felt less shitty.

There was a vending machine next to the coffee one, Leighton pushing in some dollar bills and getting some candy bars while I got some coffee. I'd planned to get some for everyone but was stopped from pressing the button again by Leighton's hand after the first two.

"Why don't we take a minute, sit out here, and then we'll go back in." His head tipped to a couple of random seats by the machines. "It's going to be a while before we'll be allowed to see her."

I nodded wordlessly, letting my weight sink into one of the plastic chairs as Jared took the one beside it. The coffee was terrible but hot, the brown watery liquid burning my mouth when I tried to sip it.

My eyes stayed hypnotized on the paper cup, concentrating so hard on the swirling patterns in the coffee that my eyes started to water.

"I have to ask, Presley. I need to know what you need right now. I don't want to push you to talk about it, but if you do, I'll listen."

"I don't know," I shrugged, feeling like it was the first time in my life where I didn't have a plan. "I don't know what I need."

Kinda ironic that someone who could run a multimillion-dollar business with all its moving parts, couldn't decide what she needed at a single point in time. But that was where I was, too many foggy thoughts to sort through and no idea how to start organizing them.

"Then I'll wait until you tell me." He wrapped an arm around me and took a sip from his cup, not at all concerned there was no timeline for how long that was going to take.

I was glad someone wasn't worried, because even if I didn't admit it out loud, I was rattled.

And that wasn't something I liked or aspired to be.

Great.

I was flying blind, hoping that at some point, my instincts kicked in and I'd know what to do.

Because the current, uncertain and indecisive version of myself, sucked.

Chapter 22

Jared

IT HAD BEEN a week since Hayden had been shot.

Mack had proposed to Hayden the minute she was out of recovery, and we'd all packed into her tiny room to congratulate them. It was good to see her awake and smiling, Mack making it his job to make sure she wanted for nothing.

He was finally able to take her home to his condo in Midtown, taking some personal time to be with her while she recovered. It was good to see Chief so happy, his beaming smile, the kind of thing that made you believe that everything was going to be okay.

But for Presley and I, it was a different story.

I'd gone home with her that night after the hospital and stayed at her apartment. She'd spent most of the time in my arms, unable to sleep as she stared off into space. I knew what trauma looked like, having seen it firsthand on the job. And it didn't present with visible scars.

She'd said she was fine, shaking off my concern with a promise that a decent night's sleep and getting back into her routine would fix it. Because that was *how* it worked, her version of dealing with it as effective as slapping a Band-Aid over a gunshot wound.

Determined to keep my word and not push, I let her set the pace while keeping a close eye on her. With our relationship out in the open, it had made things easier, except for at the stationhouse where Cole was confused why I was allowed to date Presley, but he apparently wasn't.

"You hear from Presley?" Tibbs was still wearing a towel, both of us having just returned from a house fire. "Don't you think she should've taken some time off? Not like they couldn't have managed for a couple of days without her."

"Why don't you tell her, Tibbs. I'm sure she's itching to have someone else tell her what she needs." I laughed, the suggestion she take a vacation shot down the minute I'd suggested it. "And no, I haven't heard from her tonight."

Presley didn't like being told what to do.

That wasn't anything new.

But I'd hoped the next day when she woke up and evaluated the amount of stress and shock she'd gone through, she might have taken a day or two. Or at least not taken off my fucking head for suggesting it.

Instead, she was right back at *Diablo* the next night, wearing a dress that made me impossibly hard and acting like nothing had happened. She was flawless, her smile almost looking sincere as she moved through the club, greeting everyone and letting them get their face time like it was business as usual.

She even let me tag along, pulling me into her office sometime around two a.m. and begged me to fuck her on that huge desk of hers. And while I'd never turn down sex with Presley, there was something about it that felt all wrong.

It was the first time we'd made love since the shooting, the night before spent in bed cuddling rather than fucking.

So I'd wanted it to be special. Not like rose petals on the floor and fucking *Bruno Mars* playing on the stereo. But slow and considerate, making sure that every single part of her body got the attention it deserved.

Instead she'd unzipped my jeans, hiked up her dress and told me to fuck her.

Not make love.

To. Fuck. Her.

And because I wasn't sure I could say no to her, even if I wanted to—and I didn't—I did exactly that. Laid her down on the smooth wood of her desk and pounded into her until she was screaming so loudly I wasn't sure where one orgasm finished and another started.

And that was about it.

She didn't withdraw or push me away, it was really the opposite. Since we no longer had to sneak around, she loved me hugging her in front of her staff before the doors opened or kissing her when the last person left.

Instead she pushed *it* away.

The shooting.

Lewis.

The whole thing.

Digging herself back into her life like NOTHING had happened.

"She's okay, though, right?" Tibbs echoed exactly what had been on my mind.

I sighed, refusing to lie to my best friend and honestly just wanting someone to talk to. "Tibbs, I don't think she is *okay*. How can she be? It's a lot for anyone to process and she hasn't. Like at all. She won't talk about any of it. It's like that part no longer exists. And while I know I'm no shrink, repressing it can't be healthy. One way or another, it's going to work its way to the surface, and she won't be ready for it when it does."

He blew out a low whistle, shaking his head because, deep down, I think he already knew. "Shit, maybe I need to talk to my parents. See if they can get through to her."

"No," I fired out, waving my hands in the air. "Last thing she needs is a fucking ambush. I won't have her thinking—however inaccurate—that we're all ganging up on her. It's about control, Tibbs. She needs to have it. We take that away and all of it will implode."

I didn't want to even think about it, knowing she could easily shut out every single one of us or even leave all together. That club owner would kill to have her move to fucking Hong Kong, and while they were still ironing out the particulars for the second *Diablo* site, no papers had been signed. One wrong move and she'd be on a plane, flipping us all off and miles away. And then what? Not only would I lose the fucking love of my life, but she'd be fucking alone.

Wasn't happening.

Not on my watch.

"I'm not sitting around, Leighton and waiting for her to have a nervous breakdown, if that's what you're suggesting. She's my fucking, sister." Tibbs warned, clear that he wasn't happy with the situation either.

I nodded, agreeing that one way or another it was going to come to a head. "So let's think about this logically. We're firemen. How would we treat this if it was a fire?"

Women were complicated. And as much as I liked to pretend I understood them, most times I was just guessing. Fire was complicated too, but I knew the fucking rules. And if you knew the rules, the conditions, the circumstances—there wasn't a blaze you couldn't extinguish. But you go in not knowing—or at least with a good estimation on—the variables you're going to end up hurt, and worse, the fire wins.

"Presley's a warehouse. Internal fire. No idea if there's additional accelerant, or how many individual fires are going. We need to stop the flames before they compromise the structure."

Tibbs thought for a second. "Multi-lines, roof access, containing the blaze is more important than putting it out. Once that shit is burnt, it's done. And if you keep it back, stop it from spreading, you can still salvage the building. Easy to rebuild a room that is charred rather than have to start from the foundations."

"You forgot the most important part, Tibbs." I shook my head, knowing he was only half-right. "You do all that, but you need to ask the owner of the building what the hell was in there burning first."

Keeping the fire to one room is smart. Like Tibbs said, once it's burnt, it's burnt. It can't reburn, and eventually once it runs out of accelerant, it puts itself out. But what if there's rocket fuel in that *one* room. The place will be blown to bits regardless of how much you try and contain it. Which is why warehouses usually have those fancy signs letting us know what the flammable liquids or chemicals are inside. And if we don't know, Cap is on the horn finding the hell out.

"She's going to have to help us put out the fire, Tibbs. No amount of surrounding and drowning will work unless we have an ironclad guarantee that shit isn't going to level the block."

You had to know.

Or have a really fucking good estimated guess.

And with Presley, we didn't.

She was asleep when I got to her apartment.

I'd spent more time there than I had my own place, already out of my uniform and sliding into bed beside her. She was warm, the comforter doing its job, covering her naked body until I was able to take over. My lips pressed against her shoulder, a small moan escaping her lips as she leaned into me, and it was easy to believe everything was okay.

"I missed you." She turned in my arms, her long lashes opening to reveal her beautiful brown eyes. "How was work?"

"Good. Long. And I missed you too." I kissed her, my mouth fusing to hers as her lips parted for me. My tongue moved in, massaging hers as she groaned and gripped me tighter.

Her nails grazed against my back just enough to sting but not to draw blood, and I loved the feel of it. She shuffled underneath me, her tits pressed against my chest as she arched. "Mmmmmmmmm, I love morning sex."

"I thought you didn't like waking up before noon?" I teased, my dick hard and pressing against her lower belly.

She shuffled higher up the mattress, parting her legs so I could settle between them. "Exercising my prerogative to change my mind. Now do you want to discuss it, or do something else?"

"Discuss," I said drily, pretending like sex wasn't what I wanted.

Part of me wished I didn't. That I'd be that guy who'd hold her and tell her that it was more important to cuddle. But I couldn't, and not because I was a selfish bastard, or because I loved how it felt when I was inside of her.

I knew she was using me.

Using the sex to hush the demons and to lose herself, forget whatever else was going on in her head that she didn't want to discuss. And I wasn't even mad.

If that was what she needed, then I'd give it to her. It was that simple, not bothering to ask the question whether it was right or wrong. And no, I wasn't being taken advantage of. I was having sex with the most beautiful woman I'd ever met, who I also happened to be in love with. Are you kidding me? It was nooooooooo fucking hardship.

And I wanted it too, because whether I was fucking her hard or making love to her slow, she was always with me, and *only* me.

She smiled, her beautiful lips parting as her tongue slipped out of her mouth. "Fine, let's discuss then." She leaned into me, dragging her tongue up my neck as her nipples hardened against my chest.

"Fast or slow?" I asked, the only discussion I wanted to have.

Her hips tilted, using my length to rub up against her clit. "Fast."

I kissed her, grinding against her to give her the friction she wanted. She whimpered, seeking more contact as her hands slid down my back and grabbed my ass.

"Please more."

It was like a chant and a prayer, both of them desperate as she bucked underneath me. I assumed those demons had been louder last night, feeding her need for a quicker release. And as much as I wished I could take them away permanently, I'd settle for an hour or two.

She protested as I lifted off her, trying to pull me back. "Condom, Presley." I kissed her gently, "Give me a second to put one on and then I'll give you what you want."

"What if we didn't?" she asked, her body underneath me going still.

"Have sex?" I clarified, because surely she wasn't suggesting me not wearing one.

She shook her head, stopping me from going into the drawer of her nightstand and grabbing a condom. "What if you didn't wear one."

Look, given a choice, any guy would rather go bare.

I'd done it three times ever, and it was fucking mind blowing.

You feel everything.

Her hot, wet center.

How tight she contracts.

And everything just feels . . . well, more.

So yeah, if you're in a relationship where you're not screwing around, and you're taking other precautions so nine months later you're not rocking a baby carrier, then fuck the condom.

But Presley was a control freak, and she wasn't the kind of woman who'd take that kind of a risk. And 99.9999 percent wasn't good enough.

Which was why she took the pill every single day like clockwork, and I wore a condom.

"Presley, don't you think we should have this discussion when we're both thinking straight?"

I had to give her the chance to reconsider. Because so help me, God, if it was left up to me to decide, I was going to be buried inside of her—bare—in the next thirty seconds.

"No, I don't want to think straight. Just do it. Please, Jared."

There was so much need in the way she said my name that if I had any doubts whether or not I was going to do it, they were tossed out the window. I didn't even care how fucking stupid it was, convincing myself that if I got her pregnant, I'd probably be ecstatic with that too.

I lowered my mouth to hers, crushing her with a kiss. My teeth pulled against her bottom lip, sliding in my tongue as the blunt of my cock settled at her opening.

She lifted her lips seeking me out, but I didn't budge, feeling her coat me in her juices as she slid up and down my shaft. It was delicious and sadistic, each drag of her hips making *me* harder and *her* wetter.

"You like using me to make yourself come, Baby?" My eyes focused on the juncture between her thighs where she was getting herself off.

"Yes," she rasped, the word trapped on an exhale. "It feels so good."

My hand reached down to my dick, giving myself a long hard stroke as I circled her. "Well, *good* just won't do. I want you to feel great."

I pushed in an inch, the head of my cock buried inside of her as she squeezed around it, both of us panting. And however mind-blowing it had felt those other three times I hadn't worn a condom, it wasn't even close to how fucking amazing it felt with her.

"Jesus," I groaned, unable to hold back as I sunk all the way in. It was too good, the slick and tight way we fit together so phenomenal I was fighting the urge not to come. There was no way I was blowing my load so soon, conjuring up every unsexy thought I could to stop it from being over before it even started. My balls ached, a tremor traveling along my shaft as she squeezed against me.

"That feels sooooooo good." She arched her back, her tits pushed up high and tight as her head dipped.

It was too much of a temptation, my mouth capturing one of her nipples as I slid out and then thrust back in. I'd already decided *good* wasn't working for me, and her saying it again just strengthened my resolve.

I pumped into her again, getting myself deeper each time as her mouth opened and only wordless whimpers fell out.

But it still wasn't enough, rolling us over so she was on top, adjusting her body as I held onto her hips. "Fuck me," I said, looking into those beautiful wild eyes. "I want to see you get off with my cock inside of you."

Her hands landed on my shoulders, fingernails biting into my skin as she used the leverage to rock. Her thigh muscles tightened, lifting off me before impaling herself on my dick.

The plan had been to let her give herself one orgasm and then I'd give her another, but I'd seriously over-estimated my patience. There was no way I could lie there and not be involved, the sight of her fucking me enough to drive me insane.

My hands guided her movements, picking up speed as I thrust in from under her. I didn't give her the chance to fully retreat, pushing myself back in so deep, her eyes were rolling back into her head.

It was beyond good.

Hell, it was beyond great.

Every muscle in my body coiled so tightly, I was sure something was going to snap.

"I'mmmmm sooooo close," she groaned, the words unnecessary as I felt her contract. "Jared, oh God."

I lifted my head higher, getting my mouth on one of her nipples and sucking, her body trembling as I fucked her hard and fast.

She cried out, a jumble of syllables that didn't sound coherent spilling from her lips as she detonated. The tiny spasms gripped my dick enough to send me over the edge with her, chasing the high. I couldn't stop, pumping harder as she continued to shake as I filled her.

Our mouths met somewhere in the middle, pulling her down on top of me as my back hit the mattress. Our tongues tangled as our hot skin pressed against each other. I didn't want to move, wrapping my arms around her and deepening the kiss, feeling myself still buried inside of her.

There was a chance she'd regret it. That once the initial buzz wore off, she'd realize the fraction of a possibility was too much and she'd beat herself up. Or worse, she'd blame me. But until that happened, I wasn't willing to ruin what had been possibly the best sex of my life.

"You want to go shower?" I suggested lightly, thinking we could wash off and then crawl back into bed. There was still time for her to get more sleep but the mess we'd made was unavoidable.

"You want to shower with me?" she asked softly, which made me realize in the whole time we'd been together, we'd never done that.

We'd had sex all over her loft, and I'd showered in her fancy bathroom a plenty.

But we'd never done it together.

"Yeah, I do." I nodded, brushing my fingers over her skin. Giving her a quick kiss, I gently pulled out of her and moved from the bed. She turned onto her side, watching me as I strode naked to her bathroom door. "Let me go start the water, come in when you're ready."

She hesitated at first but then nodded, and I had to wonder if the lack of condom was going to come up sooner than later. "You good?" I asked, waiting for her to say what I assumed was on her mind.

"Yes, I'll be right in." A small smile spread across her lips. "I'd really like to shower with you."

It felt like more, like she was agreeing to something else, the shower the least of it. But she looked happy, relieved almost and I didn't want to say anything that was going to take that away.

"Good, then come with me."

Chapter 23

Presley

MY BATHROOM WAS my sanctuary.

The place where I could literally strip bare.

I didn't have to pretend in there, didn't have to the wear the expectations of anyone else, and didn't have to put on the brave face.

When Jared went back to work and I'd gone to *Diablo* solo for the first time, it was where I sat in the bottom of the stall and cried. It was stupid really, curled up in a corner and letting the water wash over me while I sobbed for no reason.

I was fine.

Hayden was fine.

And Lewis was in custody.

Why I was obsessing over it and letting it control my thoughts and feelings made no sense. I was a smart girl, why couldn't my brain accept that everyone was safe, and I didn't need to feel those feelings anymore.

But as much as I rationalized it, I couldn't make it stop. The endless loop of my bad decision, and the blame that I should've known.

I'd lived with Lewis.

How didn't I know about the gambling, the debts, the way he was manipulating not only me, but everyone around him? But I didn't. Because he was hot, and I was busy. And well, it was just easy to ignore the signs.

I felt stupid.

Angry at myself.

And so goddamn guilty that no one could convince me otherwise.

I brought Lewis into our lives, so for better or worse, I was partly to blame.

But I wasn't in my sanctuary where it was safe to have those thoughts, I was in my bed. And Jared was in my shower waiting for me to join him.

I'd never had a guy in there with me before, managing to avoid any intimacy in that room by careful and creative dodging. Sure, they used my bathroom when they stayed over, but never with me in it. The line of separation was maintained, keeping the integrity of my safe place.

Until Jared asked me if I wanted a shower.

With him.

The "no" had been right on my tongue, ready to give him one of the hundreds of excuses I'd given everyone before him. But for some reason, I didn't. Because for the first time ever, I didn't want to.

My feet slid to the floor, hearing the water already running in the other room. He'd left the door ajar, the steam barely spilling out. It was ridiculous how nervous I was about going into a room I'd been in a million times before, but it was different.

Wiping my hands down my bare legs, I took a tentative step and then another, holding my breath as I walked in. He was already in the shower, his blond hair saturated as his piercing blue eyes looked at me from under the spray. He was hot, rivulets of water snaked its way down, hugging each muscle on his chest and torso before falling to the floor.

Two large towels had been put conveniently close, his eyes raking up and down my body as I neared the stall. "You look pretty content in there," I asked, opening the glass door and stepping inside. "You sure you want company?"

He didn't respond, wrapping his arms around my waist and pulling me close. "I don't want company, Presley. I want you."

I wasn't sure if it was him or me that started the kiss, his hands moving to my face as his mouth continued to move.

It was hot, the water cascading between us as my fingers explored his slick chest, our bodies pressing together as we touched each other everywhere. I was turned on, and even though we'd just had sex, I was surprised when I reached for his hard cock that he shook his head.

"We did it once without a condom. But if that's something you want to keep doing, we need to talk about it when we're not about to have sex." A small smile edged at his lips. "And trust me, I want to. But I want for you to be sure."

It had been a snap decision on my part, so worked up and needy for him that I just didn't want him to stop. And then, when I thought about it—about having him inside of me with no barriers—it turned me on even more.

I trusted him, and I was so regular with my pill the chances were almost zero. No other medication to interfere with it and I hadn't been sick, so I was comfortable I wouldn't end up a statistic for carelessness. But he was right, normally I would have had a discussion about it. Weighed the pros and cons, and then decided.

But I didn't.

And part of me didn't care, wanting to feel something else, and so addicted to the high, I'd take the risk.

What was I doing?

I was supposed to be getting back to normal, not throwing out common sense and becoming reckless.

"Presley." He caught my chin in his hand, not even realizing I'd taken a step back. "Don't."

Water fell into my eyes as I blinked, unsure of what he meant until I looked down between us. I hadn't just taken a step back, but I'd completely let go of him too, my arms wrapped around my middle.

"I know, okay. I know you're using sex to cope." His voice was soft, his fingers skimming my jaw. "Baby, I'm not angry. I just need to make sure you're okay."

Hearing it out loud was so jarring I gasped, the idea that I was treating him like a sex toy, horrifying. "No, no, no. I love you." I tried to make excuses, not willing to believe I could be so selfish. "I love you."

He smiled, his eyes lacking the anger they probably should have. "I know you do, and I love you too. Which is why I haven't said anything until now. But you raised the stakes and I need to know this isn't a knee-jerk reaction that ends up taking you away from me."

My head shook, none of it making sense. "I'm not going to leave. Why would I leave?"

He sighed, his big shoulders rising and falling with the breath. "Because that feeling won't last, Presley. It will get to the point where it won't be enough. What I can give you won't be enough. And I can have sex with you until we're both raw, that isn't the problem. But in the end . . . you're going to need more."

"How can you say that?" I reared back in horror, wishing I hadn't agreed to the shower. It was exactly what I'd been afraid of, the air around us thick with steam, while the hurt seeped into the walls. "And more importantly, how can you just accept it?"

"Because this isn't about me." He reached behind us, switching off the water. "And deep down, I'm hoping I'm wrong."

My body shivered, the temperature in the room dropping dramatically and not just because he'd turned off the water. But he wasn't angry, why the hell wasn't he angry?

I would've been furious. Annoyed even if it was someone I cared about, that they'd been using me as therapy. Because that's what I was doing. Using one emotion to tamp down another. And yet, he wasn't even mad.

"You should leave," my voice broke, a sob hitching in my throat. "Because I'll probably end up hurting you too. And I just can't, Jared. I just can't know that I was responsible for one more person being hurt. I won't survive that."

It was like the dam broke, emotions I'd been holding back bubbling to the surface as I crumbled to the base of the stall. Tears I promised I wouldn't cry, leaked out all the same as every breath came out in a ragged burst that tore my lungs in two.

Jared dropped to his knees, grabbing the towels, wrapping them both around me before he pulled me in his arms. "Presley, you haven't hurt anyone, and you won't hurt me. I won't leave. I *can't* leave. There's only one place for me to be, and that's with you."

My head shook, wanting to believe the words he was saying but knowing different. A breath hitched in my throat making it difficult for the words to come out right. "I should've never been with him. I should've left him sooner. I should've filed a police report when he pulled that gun on me. What the hell was I thinking? I knew he was volatile . . . and I let it go. Glad he was gone, thinking he'd only done it to me. I didn't even think . . .that he'd do something like that to someone else. I was so caught up in myself . . . that I let it go. I could have done more. If I hadn't been so focused on *Diablo* . . . and everything else. I'd have seen exactly who he was. And I could've stopped it." The words came out in between sobs, my ability to keep it together falling apart at the seams.

It was too late to stop, tears streaming down my cheeks as my body shook. I hadn't wanted this, for him—or anyone—to see the mess I'd become. To witness how someone who'd had it all together could unravel so fast and so far. It was just another thing to be disappointed in myself, my inability to keep my shit together and deal like I'd always done before.

He pressed his lips to my forehead, kissing me as he softly rocked us. "Those are lies, Presley. A voice inside your head that has created this alternate reality where you are blaming yourself for shit you couldn't have known. You're smart, Pres, but last time I checked, you weren't fucking psychic." A small chuckle vibrated against my temple.

"But if I . . . I don't know . . . something," I choked out words, unconvinced.

One thing different.

That would have changed the outcome entirely.

He had to be cold, dripping wet and naked in the cooling bathroom while I was covered in both the towels. But he didn't shiver, not even the slightest wobble of his chin as he rubbed circles on my back.

"No, Presley. You can't play that game. You're going to end up in a circle of *what ifs* that will rob any happiness you have. He was clearly fucked up, and when I think about him being with you, it makes me want to break shit. Not because I'm jealous you had a past, but because that sick fuck didn't deserve you. And that wasn't or isn't your fault. The same way North couldn't control the assholes who were his parents, or the chief, his ex-wife. Do you blame Mack for Melinda being insane and propositioning every guy in your bar?" he asked, all the words missing the sharp edges I thought I deserved.

I swear all those holy pictures his mother had on the wall had a new contender, because Leighton had the patience of a saint.

Not only was he not angry, but he wasn't even bitter, which was crazy since he was paying for the sins of someone else. When our relationship had started, I'd promised sex with no drama. Too bad I'd just towed a boat load of fucking drama right to his port.

"Presley, do you blame North or Mack?" he asked again, the question having gone unanswered the first time.

"Of course, I don't. Riley didn't get to choose who his parents were, he was completely innocent. And Mack, well, Melinda charmed him, let's be honest. She was just really good at hiding that train wreck. It wasn't his fault he fell in love with her and then chose to believe she wasn't all bad."

His head dipped, meeting my eyes. "Do you hear yourself? What you just said about Mack? Why does he catch a break and you don't? Why would you treat yourself with any less compassion than you would the chief?"

I was ready to argue, to tell him how it wasn't even close to the same thing, but I stopped. Was it the same thing? If it had been someone else, in my *exact* situation, would I have blamed them?

It's not the same, my subconscious argued, but I couldn't land on why.

"I'm confused." I shook my head, the thoughts feeling like they were taking up too much space in my brain. "I honestly don't know anymore."

"Let me help you, Presley. Let your family and friends help you," Jared begged, his arms squeezing me tight. "No one is going to think less of you because you need help. This doesn't make you weak, Baby. It makes you human."

Human?

Funny that I felt anything but.

"I can't lose myself, Jared. I can't lose everything I've worked so hard for." My eyes shone with new tears, as I said words I never thought I'd feel, let alone say. "I'm scared."

The pads of his thumbs brushed underneath my eyes as he smiled. "If you can even think that—let alone believe it—you have no idea of the woman you are, the woman I know."

I wasn't sure who he was talking about, but it couldn't be the pitiful mess huddled in the shower stall. Had to be some other girl. And probably someone who deserved him more. But whoever she was, I wasn't just going to hand him over. Not after I'd waited so long to get him.

I blew out a long shaky breath, feeling completely out of my depth.

"I need help."

Chapter 24

Jared

THE FIRST THING I did was turn the shower back on, dump the wet towels and get her back under the warm water. And unlike when we first got in, there wasn't an agenda other than getting clean. She sat on the floor, letting me wash her as she blinked silently.

It was hard to watch, the light that used to be so bright in her eyes almost completely gone as I rinsed her off and got dry towels to wrap around her. She didn't fight me once, first letting me get us both clean and then when I dried us off, carrying her to the bed.

I'd never seen her so quiet, missing her fiery spark. But unlike her, I wasn't scared. That inferno we'd had to attack—with no idea what was inside—could be taken from each side. She'd finally let down those walls, and shown me exactly what kind of hell she'd been living in, and I wasn't walking away. Not a chance, not until we saw that turmoil snuffed out entirely. And fuck, was I proud. So unbelievably proud that she'd finally let me in.

We curled up together under her blankets, ignoring the world as she cried off and on for a while. Sometimes she'd talk, sometimes she didn't—and I did nothing but held her for as long as she needed. I wished I'd something smart or enlightening to say but nothing that came to mind seemed like it was good enough. So rather than pretend to know what I was doing, I let her cry it out.

By late afternoon she'd decided that she probably shouldn't go to the club. I'd wanted to suggest it but figured it was better if she came to that conclusion on her own. It was a gamble, the chance she'd get dressed and head out the door still fairly high. And if she did, I wouldn't fight her, following and being ready to catch her if she needed. Not sure how many prayers of thanks I offered the Virgin Mary when she called Raelle and asked her to cover. It was the first time since *Diablo* opened that she wasn't going in. Raelle assumed the conversation had been with Presley's ghost since the only conceivable way she'd miss work was if she were dead. And I think in a way, she was half-right. Still, the shift was covered, and while I knew it was a temporary fix, we had one night where neither of us had to work.

The way I saw it the next twenty-four hours were critical, and while she was talking, we needed to come up with some kind of plan. I didn't have a psychology degree, and I wasn't going to pretend I did, which was why I called Tara Roswell.

She was the shrink we went to see if ever things got too much in our heads. Traffic accidents, bad burns or close calls on the jobs—all of which can mess you up if you let it fester. So instead of ending a promising career over something that usually wasn't our fault, we'd talk to Tara and work it out. And while I assumed Tara couldn't technically treat Presley since she wasn't serving with the FDNY, she did have some good starting points as well as a name of someone who could.

And after we'd done all of that, we went back to bed and not had sex. Never thought there'd be a time where I was *glad* Presley didn't want to sleep with me, but given the circumstances, it was a good thing.

The next few days, we settled into a new normal. She made an appointment with the new doc, managing to score a session the following week. And in the meantime, we took things as they came, not looking too far ahead.

It was on my next day off that she decided to go and see her parents. Like Tibbs, they'd been concerned but hadn't known how hard to push. Presley was notoriously independent. She'd been working in clubs and juggling her course load at college for a solid year before her parents even found out how she'd been spending her nights. She didn't even apologize, moving off campus and able to afford her own apartment regardless of what anyone thought. So when it came to knowing her own mind, and doing things her own way, Brett and Angela Tibbs knew that better than anyone.

Even more promising was that she wanted me to go with her, the two of us making the drive to the Long Island house I knew almost as much as my own. I'd spent a lot of time there, especially over the summers, so it was weird to be slightly nervous. Of course, the last time I'd been there I hadn't been dating their daughter, so that was probably why.

"Presley, Leighton." Angela ran out to greet us before I'd even killed the engine. "I'm so glad you're here."

"Hey Angela, Brett," I waved, Presley's dad standing at the door. "Happy to be here."

Angela ushered us in, fussing over Presley as we went to sit in the living room. They knew—along with my family—that Presley and I were seeing each other. We'd taken turns telling our parents. But after everything that had happened, we hadn't gotten the chance to experience the insanity that was sure to follow.

Brett looked me over and nodded, which I assumed meant he approved, while Angela was practically levitating. Still, she was more subtle than my mom. When I'd told my mother that Presley and I were dating, I thought she was having a heart attack. Tears, screams, and inaudible noises which I couldn't really decipher—all ending with both her and my dad telling me how happy they were. Needless to say, if we ever broke up, I was going to be looking for new parents, so lucky for everyone involved I was *really* in love with her.

"Presley, it's so good to see you." The concern in Angela's eyes was palpable, her voice doing its best to stay even.

Tibbs had told me she'd been struggling, guessing her daughter was going through hell but shutting most people out. It was hard for them—well for everyone really—to believe Presley was fine even if on the outside she looked it.

Presley settled on the couch beside me and I could sense she was nervous. Vulnerability didn't come easy for her, even with those she loved, but she was trying, and I was so fucking proud of her for that.

"So, I'm going to start seeing a psychologist," Presley announced, not bothering to make small talk. "I have an appointment in a few days. I know you guys have been worried, but I'm going to be okay."

Angela's eyes shot to Brett's, the surprise evident. "Sweetheart, you know we love you, and we'll do anything we can to help. It's understandable that," she stopped trying to choose her words correctly, "it's been a challenge."

Brett nodded, holding onto his wife's hand. "Yes, it's been a big challenge."

"Please don't do that," Presley closed her eyes, letting out a sigh. "I know you've been walking on eggshells, watching what you say around me. And honestly, it's worse than if you just said what you wanted. I don't want to be treated differently."

Vulnerability was one thing, but one of Presley's fears had been losing who she was. Or who she used to be. Two months ago, no one would have bothered to censor. If they had something to say, they would have said it, even if it was difficult for her to hear. And that was the way she liked it, wanted it, and needed it.

"This is why I didn't want to come here." She shook off the arm I had around her and stood. "Because I didn't want to see that look. Please, if you want to help me, don't treat me differently. I'm not a baby."

Angela was also on her feet, looking at Presley like she was a bomb that might explode. "Presley, we know you're not a baby, we're just so worried about you. Maybe you could come live at home for a while? We'd love to have you back in your old room, think of how fun it would be."

And even *I* knew that wasn't the right thing to say. Presley's eyes peeled open, her fists locking at her sides as the tense words fought to get out of her clenched jaw.

"Are you kidding me? Your solution is to have me move back home? I haven't lived at home since I left for college. I've got my apartment in the city and that's where I'm staying."

She was angry and lashing out, looking at both her parents and then to me. "I need some air, I'm going for a walk."

"I'll come with you," I offered, getting to my feet.

"No," she bit back. "I just want to go by myself."

She didn't wait for the reply, stalking to the front door we'd only just come in through and walked out, slamming the door behind her.

"That didn't go well." Brett stood, shaking his head. "She'll come around, Honey, you know she has always wanted to do everything by herself."

Angela sniffed, clearly upset. "I just want her to be happy."

"She knows that. She knows you both love her, and despite her walking out, she loves you guys too. You just have to give her some time." I looked to the door, my gut telling me to follow anyway. "I'm going to go too. Maybe we can try this again later?"

I was positive it wasn't what Angela wanted to hear, possibly even hoping I might be able to talk Presley around. But I knew better than that, and changing her mind wasn't my job.

Angela nodded silently while Brett came up behind her and gave her a hug. I could imagine how hard it was, the strain written all over their faces. But as much as I loved them both—almost like an extra set of parents to me—my first priority was Presley.

Brett grabbed my arm as I turned to leave, stopping me before I could get to the door. "I'm glad she has you." He put out his hand, meeting my eyes. "If she won't let anyone else get close, I'm glad she has you."

I took his hand and shook it, wishing it were under better circumstances. "She'll have me for as long as she needs, and every second after that. I love your daughter, Brett. This isn't going to scare me off if that's what you're worried about."

He nodded, our goodbyes silent as I went to the door, hesitating just as I was about to go outside. "She's stronger than she looks. I know it's hard to believe it right now, but she is."

And with those words of wisdom, I left.

I wasn't expecting Presley to be outside waiting. When she said she wanted to do something, she did it. Which meant she had taken that walk. I wasn't worried per se, her parents lived in a nice neighborhood and it was early in the day, so my need to be with her was selfish. So that I could put *my* mind at ease, and not because she wasn't capable of a stroll around the block.

Deciding to try her phone, I sent her a text asking her if she wanted company. It was the one thing I knew she had with her, her purse still sitting in the front seat of my car. The message went unread and unanswered, so I shoved my phone back in my pants and decided I'd take a drive instead. Sure, it *might've* been a slick way for me to look for her while pretending I was just cruising around, but I wasn't going to *not* look either.

And it didn't take too long, finding her sitting on a swing in a park not far from the house. I drove up alongside, watching as she pushed slowly back with her feet while staring off into the distance. She was so much in her own world that she might not have noticed if I'd had a more environmentally friendly car, but a roaring V8 was a little hard to hide.

Her head turned, spotting me and the car and took a visible breath. "You here to talk sense into me?" she asked, pushing back and continuing to make herself swing. "I know I was harsh back there, and I'm going to apologize."

"Actually, I was wondering if you wanted to drive her. Thought it might be nice to sit in the passenger seat for a change."

She stopped swinging, dropping her feet to the ground to keep her still. "You'd let me drive, Elena?"

"Awww, you know her name." I grinned, petting the steering wheel. "And yeah, as long as you promise not to leave my transmission on the LIE. What do you say? Feel like taking her out?"

No one had ever driven my car.

Not even Tibbs, and the bastard had begged me since I'd gotten her. And it wasn't just the price tag, which would've been reason enough. It was just—well, she was like my woman. And no, I wasn't a sick bastard who fantasized about fucking the tail pipe. It was just something I'd wanted for a really long time and didn't want to share. Much like Presley. But given the choice between my car and my girlfriend, it wasn't even a competition.

"Is this a trick question?" she asked, lifting herself out of the swing and walking toward the car. "Or do you have a concussion I don't know about?"

To prove my point, I threw it into neutral, pulled up the emergency brake and opened the driver's side door. "And if I had a concussion, are you *not* going to take advantage of it?" I leaned back against the door, folding my arms across my chest as I smirked.

She closed the gap between the car and swing, putting her hands either side of me as she leaned in. "Then you better let me in before you come to your senses."

Our lips met, my body pushed against the car while we made out, in what was probably the hottest threesome I could ever think up. And that kiss, it wasn't vulnerable. It was hot and needy for a different reason.

Pulling back before anything got too out of control, I moved to the side, taking her with me and opening the driver's side door. She looked like a kid on Christmas, scrunching her fists in excitement as she looked inside.

"You know how to work a clutch, right?" I laughed nervously, showing her the pedals. It was a little late in the game to be asking, but I was serious about not wanting to lose my transmission.

Her eyes rolled, sliding into the driver's seat and adjusting it. "Please, I learned to drive in my dad's car. You know the man will probably be the last person on earth to give up a stick shift. Now stop stalling and get in or I'll leave you here."

She wasn't kidding either, attempting to close the door while my body was still blocking it. It was the first glimpse of the old Presley I'd seen in days, the smile on her face radiating pure happiness.

Worried I might screw it up by mentioning it, I did what the lady told me to do and got into the passenger seat. It was a long ass walk back to Midtown and I didn't want to have to call Tibbs and ask for a ride home. I'd never hear the end of it. One, because I let his sister drive my car instead of him, and two, because she stole said car.

I'd barely fastened my belt when she let off the brake, taking off like a bat out of hell. She quickly transitioned from first to second, taking the stick like a natural as she flirted with the speed limit.

"You know we're still in the suburbs, Pres, and not a NASCAR circuit." I glanced over, knowing it would piss her off.

"Shut up, Leighton." She laughed, making her way through the gears. "Don't be such a pussy."

"Oh, I'm being a pussy?" I laughed, loving that smile and knowing I had something to do with putting it there. "Let's see who's a pussy once you get on the 495 and you can really open her up. And if you're not red lining, you're not doing it right."

Taking my taunt in the spirit it was intended, she took the entrance ramp, her grin widening as she tightened her grip on the wheel. The speed limit was fifty-five on the LIE, which was what you travelled at if you wanted to get some other car's grill right up your ass. Everyone else did seventy to seventy-five, which suited us just fine considering Elena could do a hundred and not even work up a sweat.

Once we were on the interstate, there was no stopping her. Presley using every single one of those 526 horses to get herself out in front of traffic and get Elena purring. It was making me hard, both of my girls on fire as we left Long Island in the rear view and headed toward Manhattan.

The air was electric, Presley laughing as she switched lanes so she wouldn't have to slow down. Everything about her was infectious, the light that had been missing from her eyes making a reappearance.

She didn't slow down until we got to the tunnel, easing off the accelerator as we hit a wall of brake lights. And even though I'd been worried, there was no backward slide as we made our way onto the island.

It must have been on her mind too, her eyes cutting from the road and over to me and giving me a big smile. "Thanks," she said, bringing Elena down to a crawl as we hit East 37th.

"For what?" I shrugged, thinking the gratitude was a bit much just for letting her drive my car.

"For everything. For being here, sticking around, and not pushing me. I feel like I'm so much drama right now, and honestly, given the choice, I'm not sure I'd stick around."

It was hard to hear but her words were honest, and that was the only thing I expected from her. She could be messy or dramatic, and fly off the handle as much as she wanted. Some people were worth sticking around for, and what we'd been through wasn't even close to my limit.

I reached over, covering the hand that was cradling the gearshift. "None of those are things you're ever going to have to thank me for. I'm here because I want to be with you, and even on your worst day, I'd still count myself as lucky."

And that was it right there.

I was lucky.

Even though shit wasn't perfect, I'd take a slice of imperfection with Presley than a guarantee of smooth sailing with someone else. There wasn't a doubt in my mind that she was the woman I was going to marry, and if she wanted, have a couple of kids with.

Yeah, lucky was an understatement.

Chapter 25

Presley

I HAD A lot of anger.

Confusion, hurt, and guilt as well, but anger was by far the worst. And most of all, I was angry at myself. Angry I couldn't snap out of it. Angry I couldn't stop replaying the possibilities in my head—of Hayden being hurt or something worse happening—and angry that I should've known better.

And I didn't wake up one day and suddenly the anger was gone. There were days I was better at handling it—along with all the other emotions—and then something would just set me off and I'd snap. Like my mother suggesting I move back home.

I understood why, and intellectually I knew storming off was an overreaction. But I couldn't make myself stop. It was like the part of me that had always been rational had taken a vacation, and what I was left with was a ticking timebomb I never knew when it was going to explode.

Jared had been amazing. Asking me to drive his car home had meant more than I could ever put into words. Apart from the obvious, where it was just a fun thing to do, and letting me drive Elena before Tibbs. *I was going to totally rub salt in that wound.* But it made me feel like he was *literally* putting me in the driver's seat. He wasn't trying to fix me or solve my problems, sitting beside me as I got there on my own.

There was no talk about me going back to see my parents and apologizing. Or even telling me that they were only doing it because they loved me. He didn't talk about it at all, instead just holding me and telling me it was okay.

That *I* was okay.

And it made me feel valid.

Even though part of me felt weak for even needing that external validation, I realized that he was just giving me what I couldn't give myself at the moment. It wasn't a competition, and no one was keeping score.

After my initial night off, I went back to work. I had a modified schedule, delegating where I could and trusting the people around me. Bennett and Rae stepped up in a huge way, making my reduced hours barely noticeable to the other staff. And like Jared, they didn't coddle, letting me find my way through it with the best cheer squad in history.

Therapy helped too, talking things out allowed me some perspective I hadn't seen before. It was refreshing, feeling that maybe I wasn't totally crazy and that letting go of some of my thoughts wasn't a defeat.

I still hadn't really spoken to Hayden, feeling it was something I just needed to do. We shared a connection even though we barely knew each other. It had started with that conversation at the bar, and then solidified by being terrorized by the same man. Sure, we'd seen each other and had polite exchanges, but it wasn't even close to what I needed to say to her. Not that there really had been the time.

Mack and Hayden got married quickly.

There was barely an engagement, the chief proposing to her at the hospital and then a speedy service at the City Clerk's office as soon as she was out of bandages. It was followed by a casual reception at the pizza place not far from the stationhouse, which was amazing except for when Mack's ex-wife turned up. Melinda was sprouting crazy like usual and Hayden had totally handled it in stride, shutting her down with a grace that had been so under appreciated.

Which only made my decision easier.

"Boss." Bennett rapped at my door before letting himself in. "Hayden's here."

It was early, the club still not open, and Mack and Jared were both on duty. I'd wanted the opportunity to talk to her alone, asking her to meet me at the club early in the afternoon.

"Show her in, B." I shuffled the papers at my desk, standing while I waited.

I'll admit, I was a little nervous. There was no way to know if a trip back to *Diablo* might accidentally trigger her post traumatic stress, or if she'd just been too polite to stand me up. And that wasn't even taking into account what I was going to ask, which on paper looked a little unorthodox.

Hayden smiled as she strode in, her new wedding rings shining almost as bright as her smile. "Hey, Presley, how are you?" Her arms opened, offering me a hug I wasn't sure I deserved as I welcomed her into my office.

"Thanks so much for coming, Hayden. I'll admit, I didn't think about it until later that it might be hard for you to be here. And I want you to know that if at any time you're uncomfortable, we can leave and go somewhere else." It really had been an oversight, my invitation feeling more than just a little insensitive.

She pulled away, still wearing her grin as she took a seat. "I'm not uncomfortable. I liked being here, and before seeing Lewis in the parking lot, I'd been having a good time."

Usually I went and sat behind my desk. It was a power move, the separation it afforded me giving me the upper hand as I strolled back, sat in my chair and assumed the position of authority. Which was a total mind fuck because sitting behind a desk didn't give you any more power than if you didn't. It was purely perception. But I didn't do that with Hayden, taking a seat beside her instead. "I know you're probably wondering why I've asked you here, and while I try to be more patient these days, I'd rather cut to the chase."

She turned her head, looking at me with interest. "O-kay," she laughed. "What was it you wanted to talk to me about?"

I took a breath, letting the air slowly expel from my lips. "I blamed myself for what happened to you. I felt that you were only here because I asked you to be, and if you'd waited for Mack at the station, you'd have never gotten shot."

Her head shook, opening her mouth despite my raised hand trying to stop her. "I could argue it was my fault. I was out in the parking lot, Presley. If I'd stayed in the club, Lewis wouldn't have had the opportunity. Or we can blame the walls, their inability to allow a signal to travel through them making it so I *had* to step out. Hell, we can even blame the mafia or whoever it was that he owed that money to. If they hadn't been threatening his life, he wouldn't have been so desperate. But do you know the only person I blame?" she asked, only continuing when I shook my head, "Lewis. He's the one who decided to hurt us. He made his choices, and he could have walked away at any time."

"I know," I nodded, "it might have taken me a little longer than you to get to the same conclusion, but I know he is the only one that needs to be blamed. I'm in therapy in case you're wondering. Extrapolating my thoughts with assistance is new to me, I'm more of a DIY kind of girl."

She laughed, covering her mouth with her hand. "I'm sorry, I didn't mean to laugh. But I love that you're so matter of fact about it. And I agree, it shouldn't be something to be ashamed of. I've been seeing someone myself, whatever helps, right?"

"Right, thank God mine doesn't make me rake sand or talk about my childhood," I chuckled. "And if I'd had to lay on someone's couch and re-imagine my birth, I'd probably still be rolling my eyes. I mean, I can appreciate being woo-woo and all, but come on."

"Well I'm glad we're on the same page." Hayden reached out and touched my hand. "And the club seems to be doing well. Mack said you barely took any time off, you must be exhausted."

"Yeah, so remember how I said two minutes ago that I was impatient? Well, other than talking about Lewis and making sure you were okay, I had another reason for asking you here." I smiled, unable to draw it out anymore.

Hayden dipped her chin, her brow scrunching in confusion. "And that would be . . ."

"A job offer, I want you to come work for me. Mack told me you left Target, so I think it's the perfect time for you to join the team at *Diablo*."

She laughed, assuming I was joking. "Me, in a club? You know how old I am, right? And that I have no qualifications other than some hospitality experience years ago. I really appreciate the offer, Presley—"

"So appreciate it and accept it." I dismissed her rejection, refusing to accept it. "You'll be running my inventory and taking over my compliance portfolios. I can train you on the software, and you can take some college classes online. I'm going to be opening a second site, and I can't be in two places at once. I'm going to need someone I trust, someone willing to work hard and isn't scared about a little uncertainty. And we both know you're wasting your potential in retail, Hayden. I'd be an idiot to let you go get another job like that. For purely selfish reasons, of course."

She eyed me with suspicion. "Purely selfish reasons, huh? You think I'm going to believe that?"

"If you think that I wouldn't benefit from this deal, then you aren't as smart as I gave you credit for. Think about it, I can hire and train you specifically for the role I need without having to break existing bad habits you got from another EA job. I also get someone I trust, which at this point is almost more important than anything else."

Hayden was about to shake her head when she stopped. "I'm going to be upfront with you, Presley. Mack and I were going to try and start a family. It would be irresponsible for me to accept a new job and then leave you high and dry later."

"So, have a baby, have ten. You'll be working days, no nights and other than some of my staff, the bar will be empty. We'll set you up with an office that has room for a porta cot and some other baby stuff as well as a desk, and you can bring the little goofball in with you. I can even set you up remotely, half the stuff can be done offsite anyway. Which means when you get close to delivery and after you've had the baby, you can still keep working if you want to. I'm not saying you have to, because I can only imagine how intense it would be to push out a human, but if you did, you wouldn't have to make the choice. We'd work it out. And not to brag, but I'm a really good boss."

I'd been overselling it and I knew it. To anyone it was a good deal even if I'd only put in half the effort. But part of it was being brave enough to show my vulnerability, even if I'd never do it in business with anyone else.

"Do you always get what you want?" she asked, her eyebrow lifting.

"Yes," I answered without apology. "I have to work my ass off for it, but once my mind is set, then it's already mine. That's not to say I don't fail sometimes or have disappointments, the self-doubt is new though, and to be honest, I'm not a fan." I laughed, shrugging. "But surprisingly, it didn't change who I am. You know you can be a badass and still have a bad day, who knew?" I leaned forward, nodding in surprise. "And I'm working on the patience thing too, more so with myself than anyone else."

It was more honest than I usually was, but I didn't regret it. Apart from the bond we shared of my psycho ex, there was something about her that I just liked. Maybe because I could see that fight in her too, and I wanted to be around it.

"So you might as well agree, Hayden. I'm not known to back down."

I felt like I was back in Jared's Mustang, my hands locked around the steering wheel and my foot planted on the gas.

The smile edged wider on her lips, and I knew she wasn't going to turn me down. "Okay, I'm in. But I still want to take those college classes as well. If I'm going to do this, I don't want to half-ass the effort."

"I'd expect nothing less."

We hugged again, sealing the deal, and it occurred to me we hadn't even discussed important things like income and benefits. I guess that told me that she trusted me too, which made me feel even better.

I handed her a contract I had already prepared and told her to go home, read it and bring it back when she was ready to start. I had a hunch it wouldn't be long, expecting to see her in the next week.

"So, you going to sneak to the firehouse and go fuck your hot boyfriend before we open?" Raelle waltzed in, not bothering to knock since Hayden had left the door open. "Because if we're taking a poll, that's where my vote will go."

I rolled my eyes. "I am *not* going to go have sex at the firehouse. I don't want our first time to be a quickie in public."

Shit.

Of all the things I'd meant to share, that hadn't been one. I blamed all the extra talking I'd done in therapy, my lock a little looser on my emotions than it used to be.

Raelle narrowed her eyes, pointing a finger accusingly. "What do you mean your first time? You've had sex before. Jesus, you had sex in this office, and God knows where else. I'm surprised we haven't had a visit from the Health Department."

"It's been a while, okay. No big deal. We're just going through a little dry spell."

What I hadn't told Rae was that I'd previously used sex as a coping strategy, a distraction. Which initially I thought was a good plan until I realized how that must feel for Jared. And in case I had any doubts, my therapist recommended that I didn't have sex, dealing with things in other ways and abstaining for a while. The woman was crazy, had she not seen how hot my boyfriend was? How the hell was I supposed to keep my hands off that? But me and my big mouth had casually mentioned it to Jared, and suddenly we weren't having sex.

It was a challenge, the imposed embargo making me want it even more. Jared didn't cave, digging deep with his willpower and not backing down. Not even when I gave him a lap dance, almost getting myself off with the bulge in his pants. Instead he kissed me, told me how hot I was making him and went and jerked off in the shower.

"A dry spell, what are we talking? A few days? A week?" Raelle asked, ignoring the boundaries most people had.

I cringed, clearing my throat as I announced, "a month."

"A month? You haven't had sex in a month?" she shouted. You know, in case Hank at the bar needed to hear about the sexual habits of his boss.

"Keep your voice down," I hushed, grabbing her arm and giving it a squeeze. "I shouldn't even be talking about this with you."

Deciding not to tempt fate any further, I moved to the door and closed it. Not sure it mattered much anymore, the damage had already been done. "And lots of couples take a break. Not everyone is screwing like fucking rabbits all the time."

Raelle scoffed, taking a step back as she screwed up her face in disgust. "Well, the smart ones are. And I can say this because you know I love you and it comes from in here." She tapped her heart. "But the two of you are both hot. Like if there was a porno and you were both starring in it, it would be a bestseller for sure. I just don't know how it's possible."

"Okay, okay, we are not talking about this." I waved my hands, before pointing to the door. "We both have work to do, and I'm finalizing the second site for *Diablo* tomorrow. Go look busy."

She sighed dramatically, shaking her head and whispering, "a month," under her breath like it was a dirty word. And worse, I couldn't disagree, my hormones at levels that couldn't be healthy.

"Uhhhhhhhhhh!" I had my own moment of drama, feeling the subtle throb between my legs whenever I thought about it for longer than a second. "This is such bullshit."

But like I'd told Hayden, I always got what I wanted.

And regardless what anyone thought, I was going to get laid.

Chapter 26

Jared

’D TRIED TO be quiet when I’d entered Presley’s apartment. It was eight a.m. and we’d both been working, Presley already asleep in her bed.

So I followed the usual routine, stripping down to my boxer briefs and slipping into the bed beside her. I liked holding her, loving how she instinctively curled into me whenever I was there and slept with her body on mine.

It had been a while since we’d had sex, her therapist suggesting we take a break while she worked stuff out, and I was willing to do whatever it took. Not to say it was easy, my balls drawing up tight and my dick getting hard with just the slightest encouragement, but I wasn’t going to cave.

Nope.

Not me.

Sure, I’d jerked off so many times I was at risk of developing RSI, but other than my new steady relationship with my hand, it wasn’t anything I couldn’t handle.

Hell, there wasn’t a lot I wouldn’t do for her, my heart feeling so full it was a wonder it still fit inside my chest.

I'd barely gotten under the covers when she let out a sigh. It was low and sexy, and sent a vibration right to my shaft. She did that a lot in her sleep, the little whimpers and moans making me offer more prayers to the Virgin Mary than I had in my entire lifetime.

Ignoring my hard-on, I circled my arms around her and shuffled in close. It was only when my hand rested on her hip that I realized what she was wearing. It was that pink slinky thing she'd worn the first day I'd come over. It was soft and clung to her every curve, advertising everything underneath that was just out of my grasp. I was convinced it had been spun in the pits of hell by the Devil, the demonic cloth torturing me some more as she moved against me.

Jesus. Christ

No, really, Jesus. Because praying to the other saints and angels hadn't fucking helped, and I was doing my goddamn best. So, if someone upstairs wanted to throw me a lifeline, I'd sure appreciate it, because I was *really* close to losing all fucking sensation in my legs.

My hips rolled without permission, shaking my head as I tried to stop.

Too late, my dick pressed against her ass, letting me know I was on my own.

"Fuck's sake," I cursed under my breath, thanking *whoever* was listening that I still had my underwear on. It was probably the only thing stopping me from fucking the fabric like a deviant, the feel of it in my hands making my eyes water.

I needed to jerk off.

It was either that or dry hump her ass until I came in my boxer briefs, so jerking off was definitely the better plan.

Giving her hips one last squeeze, I rolled to my back so I could slide out of the bed without waking her. But the second I moved, she rolled over too, the barely-there straps falling off her shoulders and exposing one of her tits. She pressed it against me, her nipple hardening as it made contact with my skin.

Really?

I looked up at the ceiling and flipped it off, any hope of heavenly help being torched as her hand came to rest on my waistband. I couldn't even think straight, trying to recite the batting order of the Yankees in an effort to get a handle on the situation.

"Mmmmmmmm," Presley breathed out, her eyes still closed as she tilted her head up and kissed my neck.

I wasn't going to make it.

My skin itched, my hands flexing and releasing while my nerves jangled like a junkie desperate to score. And the second her lips moved to mine, I knew it was over.

Fuck. It.

If I was going to burn in hell, I might as well enjoy it.

My tongue slid into her mouth, a breathy moan vibrating up her throat as one of my hands landed on her ass. My fingers played with the fabric, pushing it up her back so I could touch her bare skin as she arched into me.

"Presley, please tell me you're awake," I begged, dancing on that blurred line of consent as I continued to kiss her, unable to stop.

"Yes," she groaned into my mouth, moving farther onto my chest as her fingers threaded through my hair. "I'm awake and desperate for you, please tell me you want me too."

Tell her I wanted her? I wasn't sure I could remember my middle name, my ability to talk lost as she ground against my leg. So with words not being an option, I decided it was best to show her, hauling her on top of me and letting her ride my hard-on.

"Does that feel like I want you," I panted against her mouth, bucking up from under her as her hips circled. "Or do you still need me to tell you?"

The strap from the other side had dropped, both of her perfect tits swaying as she moved. I leaned forward, those pretty pink peaks too fucking delicious not to taste as I sucked on one and then the other.

"Jared," her pelvis pushed down, the thin fabric of her panties getting wet. "I want you. I want you so badly."

And fuck medical advice. If my baby wanted me, then I wasn't going to tell her no.

My fingers reached for her ass, yanking at her panties until I heard them tear. She yelped, my hand slapping her skin the minute it was bare, making her lift just enough so I could pull her destroyed panties all the way off.

Doubling down on the opportunity, I pushed my boxer briefs off my hips, letting my dick spring free. She didn't waste time going back to what she wanted, lining herself up on my length and continuing her teasing glide.

Maybe we could just do that, I mean, technically it wasn't sex, right? The gray area one I was happy to exploit as she made me feel fucking awesome while getting herself off.

Her hands pressed against my chest, holding herself upright as she worked us both over. It had been too long, everything feeling waaaaaaay too good as I focused on making sure she came before I did.

"I want to fuck you," she breathed, her voice reed thin as she continued to move. "I want you deep inside of me when I come."

So much for the gray fucking area.

"Okay." I nodded like an idiot, agreeing to whatever she wanted regardless of the consequences. It couldn't be helped, both of us too far gone to resist, slaves to our hormones like two savages.

I'd barely got my hand around my dick, ready to guide it in, when she sunk down, taking my whole length in one deep slide. It was intense, both of us groaning as we stopped moving, my heartbeat ringing in my ears. "No condom," I gritted out, trying like hell to be responsible while my balls were telling me to shut the fuck up.

"Pill. I'm on it. Always take it. Please don't stop."

Her broken sentences were just as sexy as the rest of her, and she was doing a stellar job at pleading her case. Who needed a condom, we sure as hell didn't, especially not when it felt that good.

"I won't stop," I promised, fairly sure I'd lost the capacity around five minutes ago. "I need to feel you come, Presley."

It had only been a month, but it felt like a year, my mouth needing hers as we started to move.

With every one of my up thrusts, she pushed down, both of us finding a rhythm that was both hard and fast, getting me in deep.

It was a mess of tangled hands. Hers on me like she couldn't get enough, and mine touching her everywhere, like I was discovering her for the first time. She was beautiful, every inch of her more perfect than I remembered, and I could barely believe she was mine.

So.

Goddamn.

Lucky.

"Ahhh," she cried out, tensing as I pushed in. "I'm so close."

She wasn't the only one, not knowing how much longer I was going to last as my thumb dropped to her clit.

I'd barely touched her, the pad of my thumb slightly grazing her sensitive skin as she pulsed around my shaft. And that pretty much did me in, sending me over the edge and chasing her as I came too, exploding with a shout.

I said her name over and over again, feeling like my soul had left my body as my hands circled her waist. I was still moving, unable to stop until I teased the last shudder from her.

"Come here." I pulled her down to me, kissing her hard as she pressed against my chest. "I know we broke the rules, but I can't find the motivation to care. I love you."

She laughed, and it was the most amazing noise I'd heard in a long time, warming me from the inside out. "Which rule are you worried about? Unprotected sex or just sex in general? Because I'd say we had multiple violations."

"I'm not worried about any of it. I've had all the regrets I'm going to have and none of them involve you."

Our eyes locked, her gaze softening as she leaned gently against my shoulder. "I love you, come shower with me."

I knew the significance of what she was asking, having told me that previously it had been a no-go zone for other men. I'd been the only one, and while our first shower hadn't gone so well, I was hopeful for the future. "You know, I'm never going to ask anything more from you than you're ready to give me, Presley. I'll wait, for however long it takes. But if you offer me something, I'm not ever turning it down."

Her eyes lit up with excitement, pressing her lips softly against my neck. "Good, then come shower with me. And then, we'll work out the rest as we go."

"You said that to me once before, you know," I reminded her, wondering how much of an idiot I'd been for fighting her from the start. "You said it wouldn't get serious. We'd stay friends."

Her shoulder lifted gently as she chuckled. "Guess I lied. We were never just friends. But I promise, it will be the first and the last one I ever tell you. You forgive me?"

"You're right, Presley." I kissed her. "We were never just friends."

Epilogue

Jared

THERE WAS LITERALLY a handful of miles between *Diablo* and *Vault* aka *Diablo* 2.0. But in Manhattan, it made all the difference.

The meatpacking district was a different kind of animal, the cliental ready to spend their hard-earned green on the next shiny thing. It was stockbrokers, models, and people who wanted to be seen. They traveled in packs, documented everything, and were more interested in getting in where others couldn't, than having a good time.

It had taken Presley exactly eight months to open, when everyone had told her it was almost impossible. Between building permits, the interior fit out and the liquor license, it was cutting it close for sure. But Presley Tibbs never backed away from a challenge, especially one where the odds were stacked against her.

"Wow, it looks like a bank vault." Evans's eyes widened, seeing the inside for the first time. "How the hell did she get all this shit fabricated in such a short amount of time?"

"My sister's a genius, Rookie." Tibbs handed him a beer. "Which is why she'd never have dated you." Tibbs winked at me.

"Dude, I haven't been the rookie in six months. I thought we were done with that shit when we got Rizzo," Evans protested, not sharp enough to know the more he complained the more Tibbs was going to give him.

Tibbs eyed him hard, pointing his long neck at him. "Well, Rizzo isn't here, and we outrank you. Anyway, you should count yourself lucky you even got an invite. You know how hard it is to score one for tonight? If it weren't for us, your ass would be on the sidewalk with all those other losers waiting to get in."

He was right about that. Opening night for a new club in the Meatpacking district was like a fire sale on iPhones, everyone wanted in on it. Add in *Diablo's* reputation and that Scott Collins and his posse were special guests, and you had a line down the block that could fill the place ten times over.

"Where is the genius?" North asked, clapping my shoulder. "Ava's teething and Quinn has an early shoot in the morning. I need to go charm my little girl to sleep."

"She's with David Cheng, her business partner. He flew in yesterday from Hong Kong." I pointed to Presley at the far end of the club. She was wearing that gold dress that drove me crazy and a diamond ring I'd slipped on her finger earlier in the day that was an extra special accessory.

We hadn't announced it yet, not wanting it to overshadow the opening, but we weren't denying it either. Raelle had spotted it right away, *Vault's* bar manager screaming and pointing to it the minute we'd walked in. Tibbs knew I was going to ask, my intention to marry his sister, something I hadn't bothered to hide.

I'd had the ring for a month, looking for the right time to ask. Considering we were already living together, I assumed the answer was going to be yes. But even a cocky asshole knew there was always a small possibility of a no. Maybe she wasn't ready for it or maybe she didn't want the piece of paper. But I wasn't going to let that stop me, deciding I'd waited long enough and finally got down on one knee in her bathroom that morning. It felt like the right place for it, and I was more than ready to have her wear my ring.

The yes had come without a second of hesitation, making the opening night of *Vault* one we were never going to forget. That and I couldn't wait to have sex with my fiancée in her new office, but we'd do that after David left.

Fiancée. Man, I loved saying that word. The only one I liked better was *wife*, but it was going to be a year before I could say that. Presley had a tough twelve months ahead of her, managing two clubs wasn't for the faint hearted, but I didn't doubt she'd rock it. But waiting also meant that when we finally did take the walk down the aisle, we'd be able to take a honeymoon too. It had to be somewhere hot and near a beach, requiring the least amount of clothes possible. Other than that, I didn't care, with no intention to sightsee, other than the inside of our hotel room.

"Anyone hear from Chief?" Evans asked. "Is he stopping by?"

North laughed, shaking his head. "Evans, Hayden is due any day now, he isn't going anywhere. And you guys thought I was bad when Quinn was pregnant, Mack takes that shit to a whole new level."

Other than Presley's new club opening, there had been some other changes as well. Mack got Hayden pregnant almost immediately, the idea North could be dethroned as Mack's favorite kid, a very real possibility. And I moved into Presley's fancy loft, leaving Tibbs in need of a new roommate. Evans was itching to take my old room, but Tibbs was holding out. I didn't know if it was to piss him off or because he'd gotten used to living alone, but either way it was entertaining to watch.

"Hey, is everyone having a good time?" My future wife—okay so maybe I was already saying it—sidled up next to me. "Make sure you try some of Scott's wine, he donated thirty cases of it."

"Thirty cases?" I raised an eyebrow. "A little excessive, don't you think? One might think he is trying to charm you."

"He's already tried and failed, Leighton. No need to get territorial." She grinned, rubbing a hand down my chest.

Of all the problems in my world, Scott Collins wasn't one of them, but I'd be a fucking moron to think he wouldn't try.

Presley was the whole package, and any man would give their right arm to have her. I still don't know how any of her ex-boyfriends could've walked away. All of them fucking idiots, and I was eternally grateful for their stupidity.

But of all the dumbasses, there was only one I truly hated, the dickstain who was still serving time for attempted murder, aggravated assault, kidnapping, and a few other crimes. He literally had more charges against him than braincells, his future including a jumpsuit and cell bars. And if he ever got out, there'd be a welcome party waiting for him that would have him begging to go back in.

"So," Presley yanked on my arm, lowering her voice, "you want to go see my office? I have a pretty impressive desk."

She was killing me, her eyes doing all the suggestions her mouth didn't need to with an ironclad guarantee I'd follow her right off the edge of that cliff.

I coughed, clearing my throat as I whispered back, "I thought we were waiting until David left. And unless he has a twin, he's still sitting at the bar talking to Raelle."

"C'mon, Leighton. Don't be such a pus—" She didn't get a chance to finish, my hand around her waist, already making excuses for our hasty exit.

"Sorry, guys, we'll be back in a bit. A VIP needs Presley's attention and I'm a fan." The words tossed over my shoulder as I almost carried her toward her office.

She laughed, closing the door behind us. "Wow, who knew calling you a pussy would get you so riled up. Sucks to be you, now I know your weakness, I can exploit it anytime I want."

"You're my weakness, Presley, not being called a pussy." I lifted her, setting her on her fancy new desk and settling between her legs. "But if you wanted to prove a point, I'm not going to stop you."

"What if the point that I really want to prove is that I'm going to love you forever." She wrapped her arms around my neck, brushing her lips against mine.

"That's one you're never going to have to worry about." I kissed her back, without a doubt in my mind.

"Oh yeah?" she asked, a wicked grin pulling at her mouth. "Swear on your mother."

I laughed, shaking my head. "Never going to let me forget that, are you?"

Her tongue darted across her pouty red lips. "Not a chance."

THE END

To keep up-to-date with all T Gephart's news, appearances, and releases, please subscribe to her mailing list (http://eepurl.com/bws5Av).

Also please consider leaving a review on your retailer of choice. They help the author and future readers and we're all eternally grateful.

Acknowledgements

Thank you so much to my biggest supporters who have been overlooking my crazy for so many years, "thanks" seem inadequate. Gep, Jenna, Liam and Woodley. You're the dream team, and I love you guys so much.

Thanks to Kelly Elliott who has talked me off the ledge more times than should be allowed. Girlfriend, we need pie and a road trip, but until then you have my eternal gratitude and love.

Thanks so much to my extended family and friends who I adore more than words. I love you guys, thanks for your support, acceptance and unconditional love. We need to hang out more.

Thanks to the amazing Gayle Williams who is one of the most selfless people I know. You believe in me even when I don't, and together we're stronger for each of us. I'm glad you ignored my resting bitch face and saw past the "business" me. You will always have a place in my heart. Thanks so much for keeping the T Gephart train running too, I know I'm not the easiest person to keep on the tracks.

Thanks Kimberly, Aimee, and Caroline and everyone at Brower Literary and Management. Love you all and hope to see you again when this madness ends.

Thanks to Nichole Strauss from Insight Editing who not only works super hard on my edits but is incredibly understanding of my "fluid" timelines when I'm having a breakdown. This one was hard, thanks so much.

Massive thanks to MK whose extra eyes give me so much more than just a beta read. You are a rare gem and I adore you.

Thanks so much to Elaine York from Allusion Graphics LLC, Publishing and Book Formatting. You make my pages look amazing and I love working with you.

Of course, it wouldn't be the same without a Hang Le cover! Not only is your graphic design AMAING, but you are without a doubt one of the most brilliant people I know. You are one in a million, and I'm blessed for your friendship.

Thank you to my eagle-eyed proofreader Rebecca from Rebecca Fairest Reviews Editing Services. Our first book together, hurray! Am excited about the many more to come!

Special thanks to my author friends who not only support my habit for fiction but have come to be some of my dearest friends. Love you guys, thanks for standing beside me on the battlefield. Also, I will always ask for proof of life when you go quiet until you tell me to back off. *Sings Whitney* And I will always love youuuuuuuuuu.

A MILLION THANKS, love and adoration for all the bloggers, reviewers, bookstagrammers, group admins and promoters who read, promote, review, and share my work. I will never take any of it for granted and am so thankful for all your LOVE.

Thank you, Liz, MJ, and Jillian at 1001 Dark Nights.

THANK YOU TO THE T GEPHART REVIEW CREW AND ENTOURAGE. It's a small group but we're a friendly bunch, and I love being in there with you! Thanks for making it such a positive place and for digging my personal brand of crazy.

And lastly, as always, thank YOU. To the person who is reading this boo,k who picked me out of the sea of so many other. I appreciate you and thank you for letting me entertain you for a little while.

About the Author

T Gephart is a *USA Today* and International bestselling author from Melbourne, Australia.

With an approach to life that is somewhat unconventional, she prefers to fly by the seat of her pants rather than adhere to some rigid roadmap. Her lack of "plan" has resulted in a rather interesting and eclectic resume, which reads more like the fiction she writes than an actual employment history. She'd tell you all about it, but the statute of limitations hasn't expired yet. But all those crazy twists and turns have led her to a career she loves—writing romantic comedy.

When she isn't filling pages with sassy and sexy characters with attitude, she's living her own reality show in the 'burbs of Melbourne with her American husband, two teenage children, and her fur child—Woodley.

She loves adventure, to laugh, travel, and strives to live her life to the fullest.

Connect with T

tgephart.com
Facebook (https://www.facebook.com/tgephartauthor)
Goodreads
Twitter (https://twitter.com/tinagephart)

Books by this Author
The Lexi Series
Lexi
A Twist of Fate
Twisted Views: Fate's Companion
A Leap of Faith
A Time for Hope

The Power Station Series
High Strung
Crash Ride
Back Stage

The Black Addiction Series
Slide
Sticks
Stand